SUMMER AND SMOKE

CORALEE JUNE

To Mr. June. You drive me absofuckinglutely crazy.
Thanks for letting me warm my tundra-toes on your legs when
I'm cold at night, and for being a damn good father. Thank you
for waiting out those three long years in the friend zone.
Thanks for pausing your video games to pretend to be interested
in the various plot points I'm dissecting. Thanks for taking the
trash out. Thanks for fighting for us. Thanks for always finding
the remote when I lose it. And most of all, thanks for getting my
humor and not making me words the sappy shit. That's just
not us.

PROLOGUE

Nix

THE COFFEE SHOP had an eclectic vibe. It was a small café in lower Manhattan. Rigid businessmen fumbled down the sidewalk, clutching their coats tightly against their bodies to ward off the mid-November chill. They all looked stressed. The world was wound up tight today, you could practically feel it in the air. My lifestyle might not make sense to many, but I liked being my own boss—and everyone else's. I didn't have to answer to anyone or anything. Stress was just a side-effect of the expectations we allowed others to put on us, which was why answering to Summer's long lost boyfriend was making my palm twitch. That handsome mobster was a hard ass, and I'd like nothing more than to *loosen him up*.

I made a mental note to bring Summer here once all the smoke cleared. She loved finding quaint corners of the world almost as much as she loved coffee. There had been times between hacking jobs where we didn't have two nickels to rub together, but I always made sure my best friend had her drug of choice—caffeine.

I wasn't much of a coffee drinker, but I needed the energy boost. I swirled the spoon in my cup, scraping it against the edges while staring out the window. I'd always wanted to live in New York. Baltimore was fun, but there was an entirely different energy here. You were never alone. I loved the vibe. The tension.

Moretti's fancy burner phone vibrated in my pocket, and I slid it out of my tight denim jeans to check the alert. On the screen was video footage of Paul Bright leaving his town-home in DC. Shit. I needed to tell Moretti. Summer's dad didn't so much as take a shit without my knowing; my new boss had insisted on it. Moretti was one seriously sexy pain in my ass. I wasn't exactly sure how I became his surveillance lackey, but I'd spent the last five days watching Paul Bright's every move. It was driving me crazy. A man who'd murdered dozens, if not more, was just on the other side of my screen, waiting to be brought to justice.

Gavriel used my love for Summer to manipulate me, signing me up for the jobs I didn't want while dangling her happiness over my head. It didn't help that her emotions had been teetering on that precarious edge of hysteria lately. Summer was suffering, and I loved her enough to suffer right along with her.

I almost dialed Moretti's number to let him know that Paul Bright was on the move, but I was immediately distracted by a thin, bleached blond woman walking through the front doors of the café. Clarice Bright was tall but pale. Her caked on makeup and hair extensions might have appeared beautiful to the untrained eye, but I saw her for who she was. Her carefully constructed image couldn't hide the fact that she looked absolutely miserable. Delivering my clients their ultimate fantasies had trained me to see beneath the facade. Maybe behind that fake bravado was a woman that loved my best friend, but whatever fire was once within her had long since burned out.

"Clarice?" I called out while standing and gesturing to the wooden chair beside me. Even though I was meeting with a woman I didn't respect, I was chivalrous after all. Blame it on my Southern roots and my beauty pageant obsessed mother. Above all else, Phoenix Bailey was a goddamn gentleman.

Clarice simply nodded then sat down. Her pursed lips were pinched as she glared at me, and I could read each loathing emotion rolling off of her. Upon closer inspection, I noticed that her red lipstick was slightly smeared in the left corner of her mouth, and her false eyelashes didn't stick fully to her eyelid. She was wearing a dark gray pantsuit. The gaps between each button on her white cotton shirt were gaping at me, revealing a lace bra underneath.

"Can I order you anything?" I asked with a half-hearted smile.

"Blackmail is a federal offense, you know," she replied with a frown. Oh, so she wanted to dive right in? Perfect. I hated to waste time.

"So is murder," I replied, cocking my head to the side. I threw her one of those judgemental stares I knew would make her squirm. I kept my manipulative meanness holstered like a weapon, only to be used in desperate times. Damn, I loved a good bitch fight though.

Clarice didn't flinch at my retort. She didn't bat an eye or even let out a huff of air. Summer's mother was numb to the life she led, and it both pissed me off and scared me. There were moments when Summer acted unaffected, and I wondered if she inherited that trait from her parents.

"Well, I'm glad we can skip the pleasantries. There are a

few things we need to discuss. I'm sure you understand what's at stake?"

"How do you know my daughter?" she asked, her frown deepening as she assessed my bronze skin, pale pink button up shirt and glasses. I'd recognized her almost instant unfavorable opinion of me. She wasn't the first to make assumptions about who I was, and she wouldn't be the last. Clarice Bright didn't approve, and I didn't give two fucks. I stopped requiring validation ages ago.

"She's my soulmate. My better half. My best friend...and the only reason I'm wasting my valuable time to warn *you*." My voice was laced with venom. "I don't think you deserve the warning I'm about to give you, but your daughter is a better person than I am." Summer had a heart of gold. It was her weakness.

Clarice gave me another once over, an unimpressed scowl perched upon her face. She then leaned forward before saying, "Get on with it then. Paul thinks I'm at the spa for the weekend, but he has eyes everywhere, and I need to get moving."

I didn't waste time. I was just as eager as she was to get this over with. "We know about your husband. We know the part you played. How you sent your daughter off alone to defend herself. We know that you're a coward." I didn't lower my voice. I felt no need to hide the truth. Although I danced around the semantics, I made sure to keep my voice even so that the innocent people enjoying their breakfast near us could hear. She looked around with anxious uncertainty, clicking her nails on the table to emphasize her discomfort. She was worried. Good.

"I found your daughter in an alley a couple winters ago," I then said. This wasn't part of the plan. I wasn't supposed to divulge details of Summer's life. Clarice didn't deserve the knowledge, but there was something that had been bugging me since learning about her mother's role in all of this. "I just happened to take a different route on my way home. It was a shortcut. I was running late for my favorite TV show," I said.

Do you think the universe fights for people to be together? I've always thought the world was organized. People didn't just meet for no reason. Sometimes, things seemed too perfect to be an accident. I was meant to meet Summer in that alley that night.

I settled into my seat, shifting and resting my arm on a nearby chair while breathing in the aroma of coffee. "She was passed out. Half starved, lips blue. It wasn't my first time to stumble upon a homeless person. But something about her drew me in. I can't explain it. It was fate, I think. I called an ambulance and held the hand of a stranger all through the night, staring at her haunted face while wondering what brought this beautiful woman to the brink of starvation and hypothermia."

For a flash, Clarice's features softened, like she was caught off guard by the sentimental yet brutal honesty. I wondered if she cared about my best friend—her daughter. "How does it feel to know that a total stranger took better care of your child than you?" I asked, my voice cruel and unyielding. "You're pathetic. You're nothing. No one. I'm giving you a chance to run because, for some fucked up reason, Summer still cares about you. But our girl's got herself some powerful friends, now. Friends that want to see your husband dead."

Clarice gasped and grabbed her chest. As she shifted her eyes back and forth, I took in her fearful expression. But after a moment of terror, her frown slipped into a smile. "You really think they can kill him?" she whispered, her tone low, as if she was too afraid to hope.

My eyebrows shot up in surprise. Did she *want* us to kill him?

"Yeah," I replied.

"Will everyone know?"

"That's the plan. We have evidence," I lied. The asshole was good at covering his tracks. Almost *too* good. I was the best fucking hacker there was. Or at least, that's what I told myself. Santobello must've been dumping a shit ton of money into making sure Paul Bright's recreational activities kept under wraps.

"I see."

I sat back in my chair, crossing my arms over my chest and once again wondering how this woman raised Summer. Where was her brightness? Where was her strength? Did Summer inherit anything from her?

"Can you do me a favor?" she asked while gathering her purse and clutching it to her chest. "Can you just tell Callum I'm sorry? I would have never told them if..." She shook her head then looked out the tinted window towards the busy street. I recognized the faraway look in her eyes. It was something Summer did regularly. She was thinking. Planning.

A waitress walked up to our booth and tapped her pen against her pad. "Can I get you two anything?" she asked while dragging her green eyes up and down my body, and I made a mental note to give her my card before leaving. The tall waitress with plush lips and legs for days looked like someone that would enjoy *my* kind of fun.

Mrs. Bright coughed, bringing my attention back to her. Her lips were once again fixed in that thin line of judgement. "Take care of Summer, will you?" she asked before standing.

I nodded. I'd always take care of Summer. There was something innate about our friendship that demanded it.

The waitress hovered, intruding on our moment. "Go back behind the counter. I'll order when I'm ready," I commanded, borrowing the stern voice I reserved for the bedroom. While I was here, I might as well make the most of it. The brunette waitress's chest flushed. Oh yes, she'd be a perfect candidate for a night in my bed.

I went to address Mrs. Bright once more, but she had already gone, slipping out the door while I was distracted by the waitress. She stood on the busy street without a second glance. I watched her from the café window as she paused on the sidewalk for a moment, staring up at the sky as a light drizzle of rain started to fall. Her blond hair got wet but she didn't care. It was then that I truly saw the resemblance between her and Summer. Carefree hope pulsed through her body as she stood there, not caring what anyone thought, about me, or this fucked up situation her husband created.

She then spun around and paced back towards the café until she was standing in front of the window by my table. She stared at me, eyes blank and emotionless. Taking a moment to peer at me through the tinted glass, she reached into her purse to pull out a tube of lipstick. Puckering her lips, she dragged the chalky makeup along her pout then slipped the gold tube back inside her bulky purse. A sense of dread saturated my soul. She began digging again. Sifting through her bag, she kept her eyes on me until her hands connected with what she was looking for. Clarice Bright then pulled out a black revolver.

I shot up from my seat. Around me, patrons screamed in terror. Men shuffled out of their chairs, not sure whether they should stop her or hide. I didn't even have time to leave the table. Couldn't even choke out a plea for her to stop. She placed it against her temple and threw me a peaceful smile, one that held all the secrets of her sad little existence. With eyes clamped shut, she barreled through the threshold of eternity. Blood splattered against the window, and more screams broke out around me.

I stared in awe and disgust. She killed herself. She actually *killed* herself. I couldn't breathe, couldn't think. Gore covered the window, and the sounds of the frantic restaurant went silent because all I could hear was the pounding of blood in my ears.

Clarice Bright was finally free.

1

MY MOTHER'S funeral was on a Saturday. Men and women in suits crowded around my father, offering condolences and sad smiles of compassion. My father wore grief like a mask. He'd perfected the forced expression of someone who wanted to look tortured but also strong. His grey, emotionless eyes would go glassy with unshed tears as he accepted pats on the back and brief hugs.

It made me sick.

I never imagined that I'd be forced to watch her funeral from the safety of Gavriel's living room in New York. Her death had caused quite a stir. Paparazzi were hounding my father, questioning him about her *very* public suicide. He blamed the doctors. Her grief. Her undiagnosed depression.

Me.

His very candid press release still haunted me. "My wife never recovered from our daughter's disappearance. I just hope that she finally found the peace she'd been looking for."

I was wearing a stained tank top and some sweatpants, watching a recording of her funeral once more. It was late.

After four days of rewatching it, I could recite the preacher's sermon by heart.

"Clarice Bright was a beacon in this world. Her achievements and volunteer work too extensive to list. The world lost a good woman."

I was stuck somewhere between hating her and grieving her. There was something profound about the way people picked out her good qualities to cover up the ugly inside. The media wanted to paint her as a victim of prescription pills and depression. Her friends and acquaintances described her as a saint. My father spoke of her unending devotion. They claimed this too-harsh world was too much for her too-good soul.

But me? When I wasn't blaming myself, I was blaming him. For the first time in my life, I didn't let my father's insane views of right and wrong twist me up into something I wasn't. Paul Bright drove her to this. My mother was always too obsessed with her image, and the thought of our family's dirtiest secrets coming to light destroyed her—not me.

"Sweets. You can't keep watching this," Nix said while sliding onto the black leather couch next to me. I quickly turned off the TV, feeling guilty that he'd caught me watching it again.

While I was busy blaming my father, Nix blamed himself. He didn't have to tell me that he was questioning if he was too harsh or if he pushed too far. I saw it in the way he looked at me.

"How was your night?" I asked with a guilty smile. I knew I had to at least pretend to have my shit together for Nix, he'd call me out on it otherwise.

"It was fine. I met a lovely new couple that wanted to get to know me...*intimately*." He waggled his eyebrows for emphasis. "But when I tried bringing them home, the guard didn't allow them admittance. He said it was a security risk."

I winced, feeling guilty for the millionth time that I'd dragged Nix into this crazy world that had become my life. "It's okay, you can make it up to me if you'd like," Nix said in a husky tone, and I rolled my eyes, already knowing where this was leading.

"Oh really? How could I possibly do that?" I gave him a coy smile, playing along.

"Well, you could start by stripping out of these clothes," he said while trailing his hand up my arm. He slid his index finger under the strap of my tank top and pulled it down over my shoulder.

"I want you hot and wet, Summer. I want you bent over, with that tight ass of yours in the air, lathering up your sweet little body for me in the shower," Nix hummed into my ear before smiling against my neck, a barely contained chuckle bouncing in his chest. "Because you fucking stink. When was the last time you showered? Or even left this damn building for that matter?"

I playfully shoved at Nix and stood up. As I stretched, he rolled his eyes at my messy appearance before picking up the remote control to the TV and pocketing it. He was worried about me. They all were. "Fine, I'll go shower," I said.

Nix stood up and wrapped his arms around me, stroking my matted, greasy hair and whispering in my ear. "You, my queen, are pure Sunshine. Badass girlfriend to an infuriatingly annoying mob boss. You've survived much worse, Sweets. Start acting like it."

My damn best friend and his bossy compassionate ways were going to make me do something stupid—like cry. Again. And I was really done with crying. I was done with feeling sorry for myself and for my family.

"Would you like a bubble bath or shower?" he asked while grabbing my hand to lead me to the bathroom. Once down the hall and at the door, we went inside, and I started disrobing. Nix bent over to pick up my clothes, holding the sweaty fabric a safe distance from his nose before tossing them in a laundry basket.

"Bubbles. Always bubbles," I replied in a high pitched, dignified accent. Nix turned on the water in Gavriel's claw-foot tub, dropping lavender oil and soap in the steamy water. We'd done this many times before back in our old apartment. He'd run me a bath and wash my hair, scrubbing and massaging my scalp until the bubbles were long gone.

"You think Gav will be home tonight?" I asked while settling into the hot bath. My skin burned with just enough discomfort to make it pleasant.

"I'm not sure. I saw him put some brass knuckles in his pocket before leaving. If I had to guess, I'd say that he won't be back until morning."

I started shaving my legs as Phoenix pumped shampoo in his hands, lathering it up in his palm before scrubbing my hair. Two days after my mom died, Gavriel sent Blaise on a bounty hunt, and he'd just finally came back. They were both currently interrogating a man I wasn't allowed to know the name of. "Your boyfriend is scary...in a tragically hot kind of way," Nix said while continuing to massage my scalp. I closed my eyes and leaned back, moaning a bit as his nails slid along my skin. "If he weren't so goddamn annoying, I'd have a crush on the bastard too."

A laugh escaped my lips, and it was the first true smile I'd worn in days. It felt like an invisible burden was lifted from my shoulders.

"I don't know, Nix. I think maybe you *like* being bossed around. Are you worried you've lost your touch?" I asked with a hint of playfulness that felt freeing.

Phoenix pulled my hair back, forcing me to look up into

his beautiful eyes. "You think I've lost my touch, Sweets?" he growled. "I can assure you, I've still got it."

Nix started tickling me mercilessly. I squirmed in the tub, laughing as I slipped along the porcelain and soap. "Oh God, please stop," I choked out with sputters of laughter as splashes of water spilled over the edges. Happy tears trailed down my face, and I squirmed to get away, not really having anywhere to go. In a last ditch effort, I wrapped my arms around his waist and pulled him into the tub with me with a resounding splash. We both laughed as he slipped around, trying to get up. Each time he fell, I laughed more, until genuine tears of amusement were streaming down my face.

Giving up, Nix settled, fully clothed, on the other side of the tub. "You're a hot mess," he said, as I settled deeper beneath the water, placing my feet on each side of him.

"So are you." A lingering giggle escaped my lips.

We sat in comfortable silence for a while before Nix spoke again. "You're gonna be okay, Summer. I promise it. I wouldn't be your best friend if I didn't take care of you."

I knew he would. They all would. We just had to go through hell and back first.

Ryker was going to kill me.

Each time he wrapped his toned arms around my body and flung me onto the foam mat, I wanted to drag my nails along his muscular back and sink my teeth into his bottom lip.

Gavriel came home at five that morning, insisting that I

start self-defence lessons with Ryker. He'd looked dark and tortured when he walked through the door. Three hours later, he had a gym rented out near his penthouse in the Upper East Side so Ryker and I could practice alone.

Ryker had a fight tonight at an underground club somewhere in the city. He'd followed us to New York while we figured things out, but he still needed to maintain his reputation in the scene. It was supposedly a small fight with an eager opponent from the Bronx, looking to prove himself. Gavriel forbid me from attending, mumbling something about my "sensitive state" before ordering me not to bring it up again.

Regardless of his extensive fight day ritual, Ryker was determined to start my training. Since the night I revealed why I ran, he had been itching for a way to feel useful and work out some of his rage. While we practiced, my bodyguard, Joe, sat outside and smoked a cigarette. I guess he was tired of watching Ryker kick my ass, and I couldn't blame him.

"Are you even *trying* to get away?" Ryker asked with a frown. I was hoping that today would be playful, or at the very least enjoyable. But instead, it became just another avenue for Ryker to lash out his guilt at me. It was like a whip, striking any chance he got.

"Nope. I like having you toss me around, Ry Baby." I had started calling him that once I learned it drove him crazy. He liked to be known as the fierce yet wise silent one, but I knew better. He wanted to shout out all his declarations of love and pain at me, he just didn't know it yet.

"Stop calling me that," he pleaded before advancing towards me once more. I turned around as his tall frame collided with mine, pressing the curve of my ass into him. He wrapped his arms around me, criss-crossing his forearms between my breasts. God, he felt so good. I took advantage of our position and began grinding my ass against his erection. He was just as turned on as I was.

"Is that what you're gonna do when someone attacks you?" he asked, his voice smoky and warm. "Are you gonna dry hump your opponent?"

"If they look like you, then yes," I replied without shame. If he wasn't holding me down, I would have shrugged. I was tired of his moody behavior. Since the revealing of my secret and then my mother's death, the Bullets had become one giant clusterfuck of guilt, fear, and anger.

"Not funny."

Ryker let go of me, and I spun around to greet his green-eyed stare. I knew that it wasn't fair of me to expect them to swallow the truth of my disappearance overnight. I had five years to cope—or run—from my shitty past. I'd been surviving since Summer Bright died. But I had hoped that they would handle the news better. Couldn't we go back to normal? Or at least back to the frantic fucking-to-feel-something from when I'd first returned?

Last night with Nix ignited a fire within me. I couldn't keep clinging to my depression. It wasn't doing me any favors. I had to fight. Wrapping my hands around Ryker's back, I leaped up, circling my thighs around his waist. "Is this right, Ry Baby?" I asked in a sultry tone. My breathing was shallow as I grinded against his tented athletic shorts, whimpering when heat shot through me like tendrils of passion.

Ryker dropped to his knees and pinned me beneath him, keeping my legs wrapped firmly around his waist. He held my hands over my head as I bucked on the foam mat. I half-heartedly twisted my body to get free, but he didn't budge. "To win a fight, you have to know your opponent's weaknesses," he urged, gasping for air as he kept me pinned. Instead of struggling to free myself, I leaned up to kiss his salty lips, moaning when he immediately responded to my taste. Our kiss was like a fight, and I'd happily let him win. He released my hands to slip beneath my tight sports bra, pushing the tight fabric up to roll my nipple between his thumb and finger. I dropped my legs from around his waist. When I finally broke the merciless kiss with a satisfied smirk, he paused to ask, "What was that?"

"*I'm* your weakness, Ry Baby."

He sat up on his knees, dumbfounded by my words, as if it hadn't occurred to him that he even *had* a weakness. I took advantage of his confusion, and Ryker watched me as I scrambled to the other side of the foam mat and crouched down in the ready position Joe taught me earlier. Knees bent, arms raised to block a punch. I didn't adjust my bra though. Letting my heavy globes fall, I wanted his hungry eyes on me. "Yeah," he began, matching my stance and lifting his fists to block his face. "You are."

Ryker was all or nothing. He plunged headfirst into the depth of his feelings, owning each of them. Once he decided you were worth his time, there was no going back. I just wished he'd love himself.

With a considerable amount of effort, and looking far less sexy than I would have liked, I stripped out of my tight sports bra and circled Ryker once more, enjoying the way his hooded eyes took in my pebbled, pink nipples. It was a risk. We only had the gym for another fifteen minutes. Pretty soon the owners would walk in. Just the idea that we could be caught had me feeling giddy.

The air was thick with lust and the smell of his sweat. A fluorescent light above us flickered, giving the room a dark mood. Despite it all, Ryker still made me feel desired, and that fact alone had me tingling all over with an anticipation so heavy that even my pulse felt labored. Ryker gave me a knowing smirk. What was it about him that made me want to risk being seen?

"You know what you're doing," he growled before advancing on me once more. I side-stepped him, but he was too quick. Using his left leg, he wrapped it around my hips, locking me between his thighs before bringing me back down to the mat with a thud. My head bounced against the ground with a small slap. I moaned, half from lust, half from pain. *God*, I wanted him to fuck me right here, right now.

But Ryker was stubborn. He was punishing himself for what he didn't know, holding back from what he wanted because he thought he didn't deserve it. It wasn't just Ryker fighting his instinct to fuck me senseless. The rest of the guys didn't know how to proceed either. My hair was fanned out around me, my cheek against the mat. "Are you going to do something about that erection digging into my side, or are you going to continue feeling sorry for yourself?" I asked.

When we first reunited, there was so much pain, anger, and need to feel close that our bodies practically collided on instinct. I knew the guys were punishing themselves, and I was sick of it. "You're pushing me, Sunshine," he moaned into my sweaty neck, trailing his tongue up and down my skin.

"Good," I whimpered back. I twisted until we were facing one another, and I stole another kiss. Ryker let out a groan of frustration as he rocked back and forth, pressing his cock into that sweet spot of oblivion just outside my thin yoga pants, when I lifted a leg up and rested it on his hip. I was giving Ryker access to that delicious friction I craved, and he was taking full advantage of it.

"Stop acting like you don't deserve this," I said between kisses. "Stop punishing yourself. Don't let *him* take that from us too."

At the mention of *him*, Ryker went icy, his heart suddenly so cold that despite the heat from our workout, I had to shiver from the chill of his mood switch. All hot and heavy playfulness was completely gone. After a moment, Ryker pulled away and tossed me my sports bra. "Get dressed, our reserved time is almost up, and I need to get ready for tonight."

I pouted. "You're so wrapped up in the fact that you hurt me, that you're hurting me again," I choked out before threading my legs through the ropes boxing us in.

"Sunshine," Ryker called after me. But I didn't stop. I put on my bra as quickly as I could then met Joe on the busy street outside.

"Take me home, Joe," I pleaded with tears making a slow processional down my face as the door to the gym shut behind me. I knew that Ryker wouldn't follow after me. He didn't think he had a right to. In typical Joe fashion, the sight of my emotional face made him cringe. I wondered if he was debating on running away from me. The man was practically *repelled* by feelings.

"For fuck's sake, wipe the stress from your eyes, kid. People are going to think I hurt you or something," he said while looking around.

Men in suits walked by, and I slipped Blaise's hoodie over me, pausing to inhale and smile at the comforting scent of cinnamon. "Calm down," I joked with a sniffle. "I swear tears aren't contagious. Want me to buy you an ice cream? Are you feeling a bit hangry?"

I'll admit, Joe had become an unlikely pseudo-uncle figure in my life. He hated me, but I knew that beneath his permanent scowl was a man that just was repressed by his need to be macho. When he thought I wasn't looking, he'd call his wife to keep her updated on his whereabouts, giggling into the phone like a schoolgirl with a crush. He wouldn't tell me her name or any information about their relationship, but I knew the man was absolutely pussy whipped.

"Haven't you ever seen your wife cry?" I asked. "Women do it sometimes. It's normal."

He grunted in response and threw me a murderous glare, as if just the thought of his wife being unhappy had sent him spiraling. I held up my hands in surrender with a grin, "Okay, okay, I won't bring her up again. I know you go all macho protective where she's involved."

I was determined to meet Mrs. Joe. When I was feeling particularly pathetic, I liked to pretend that Mr. and Mrs. Joe would adopt me. I imagined a future where we ate authentic Italian spaghetti in their apartment on Sunday nights. I just wanted to belong to a family, was that so bad?

We made our way to Gavriel's apartment, and my new phone pinged in the pocket of my hoodie. It was from Ryker.

"I'm sorry."

Simple, to the point. Typical Ry Baby. I wanted to respond but knew that he wasn't much of a texter or even a talker. Ryker bottled up his feelings and fucked or fought them out. He had a fight tonight, so I'd just let him take out his anger on whatever poor motherfucker was up against him.

When the Bullets barged back into my life, it was too much all at once. It was like someone ripped the bandaid off an unhealed wound. I was bleeding. I was vulnerable. But now that all my secrets were out in the open, I felt like I could finally go back to using the carefully constructed coping mechanism I'd mastered these last five years:

On tough days, I'd deflect with humor.

On harder days, I'd keep so busy that my body physically couldn't process the trauma.

And on those days where I could barely get out of bed,

I'd sleep. I'd take that tiny pill of oblivion and pass out until my dreams bled into reality and I forgot everything.

Was it healthy? Maybe not. But it worked for five years. Exhausting twelve-hour shifts at shitty jobs, sarcasm, and pills were what helped me survive. I didn't need the men I loved ripping apart every piece of my brokenness just to examine the pain. Sometimes, when shit hits the fan, you have to fake it until you make it. I just wished they would go back to pretending they hated me. I'd rather focus on that than the demons I was running from.

I stared up at Gavriel's building. It was huge. Towering. Intimidating. I sighed. I wasn't ready to go back to my pretty prison. My leaving allowances had been few and far between, and I wasn't sure if it was because they were scared Santobello would find me or that I'd run away again.

"Do we have to go back?" I asked. I knew Joe was feeling just as stir crazy as I was. With any luck, he'd let me walk the block a couple more times before we went upstairs.

"We do have fifteen more minutes..." he said with a huff.

"Perfect. Just enough time to walk the block another time. And if we're late, I'll just take my top off and Gavriel will forget he's pissed at me."

Joe made choking noises like he was going to throw up, and I laughed at the bright blush on his puffy cheeks. I shot a quick text to Nix, letting him know my plan, and he immediately responded.

"Come back late. I love to see your man all worked up."

Pocketing the phone with a smile, Joe and I then walked. We didn't talk; we didn't really have to. It was nice to just see New York outside of Gavriel's tower. From down here, I could see the energy of the city. People were happy. Angry. Full of life.

We stopped at a coffee shop, and I ordered my usual: black coffee with a splash of hazelnut syrup and two sugars.

"We should probably head back," Joe said while glancing at his watch. He shifted back and forth on his feet, looking around uncomfortably while a slight blush covered his cheeks. "You think, uh, your distraction tactic will work?" he asked, refusing to make eye contact.

I burst out in a fit of sarcastic laughter. "Yeah, Joe. I think it will."

2

GAVRIEL'S PENTHOUSE in New York was everything I'd expected it to be. Lavish and exclusive. The bellman looked like a tattooed, retired pro fighter. The decor was modern with a memorable view. It was gritty and extravagant—like Gav. I expected nothing less from my excessive Bullet leader but also didn't like staying here. His home was cold and lacked personality. And with security teams constantly coming and going, I felt like there was no privacy. Two weeks here, and I'd had enough.

"I'm dying for some pizza," I groaned to myself. Joe was standing nearby, close enough to hear me but far enough to ensure I didn't get any funny ideas about a friendship. Luckily, I kept the freezer fully stocked with vanilla ice cream. He may hate me, but he loved his sweets. I wasn't above bribery.

Telling the guys about my father lifted a heavy burden off my shoulders. It was like I'd finally taken a breath, my lungs could reach their full capacity, and my senses weren't on high alert. But telling them had its consequences too. Gavriel took his controlling protectiveness to an entirely different level. Not only did I have a Joe-sized shadow, he'd nearly tripled security.

I could handle the protectiveness. In fact, I enjoyed it. I was the only one responsible for my survival for so long that it was nice trusting him to make sure I stayed safe. Some might feel suffocated by that sort of attentiveness, but I found it freeing. I didn't have to look over my shoulder as often.

But with that, Gavriel started treating me like a fragile doll. His kisses were tentative and soft. I felt like a piece of cracked glass he was trying not to shatter further. I wasn't sure if he felt guilty for causing my last panic attack, or if he didn't believe that I was strong enough to handle his brand of passion. Either way, the tender approach was driving me mad.

"Which one of them are you thinking about now?" Nix asked while settling beside me on the couch. It faced the south window, giving me a perfect view of the city skyline. Lights twinkled in the distance as I shifted beneath a chunky, woven blanket. "Gavriel," I answered honestly.

Nix was amused by my curious relationships. "That man is going to be the death of me," he scowled while looking off towards the man in question. In the sophisticated open concept kitchen, Gavriel was speaking with one of his business associates. He'd been working like a madman, constantly scheming ways to bring down Santobello and my father.

"He can be..." I drifted off. There was longing in my voice. I craved the kind of control Gavriel offered. The care. I wanted him to take away the burdens of my past. Take the fault for our unique relationships so I could just enjoy without fear or regret.

"Commanding. Rude. Annoying. Demanding," Nix answered for me. He set his cup of tea on a nearby coffee table before lying down in my lap. I smiled down at my best friend while scratching his scalp with my long nails. We'd done this many times back in our old apartment. The scenery might have changed, but he hadn't. I could always rely on feeling comfortable and safe with Nix.

Joe rolled his eyes and coughed loudly, not so subtly reminding me that the football game was on. He might not be allowed to watch TV on the job, but if I so happened to turn on the game, it was allowed. I changed the station on the TV playing in the background to the Giants game, hoping that he'd stop looking at me like I pissed in his Cheerios. Watching me must be boring, but it shouldn't be torturous.

"Can we please leave the apartment sometime soon?" Nix asked. Aside from my brief outing today at the gym, I hadn't gone anywhere since my mother's suicide.

"Sunshine, come here for a moment," Gavriel growled while eyeing Nix in my lap. They'd been butting heads at every turn. Nix smiled, taking a full minute to twist and stretch in my lap before sitting up. He made sure to throw my stressed Bullet leader a big, satisfied smile and a purr before squeezing my knee. "I'm gonna go check the surveillance feed, Sweets."

I nodded. The guys insisted that Nix set up camp on the opposite side of the penthouse from my room. They wanted to avoid me stumbling across the image of my father. I was annoyed by their tactics. Maybe that's why I had become so obsessed with watching the funeral footage. I wanted to prove I could. There was a huge difference between feeling protected and feeling babied. My little panic attack in California had them thinking I was weak, and I needed to amend that.

I stood and made my way to the large, modern kitchen where Gavriel was. He stood next to a towering, double-door, stainless steel refrigerator. Muscular arms crossed over his chest, his black tattoos were proudly on display. His dark hair was ruffled, probably from him constantly running his hands through it. Joe followed and stood off to the side, his usual scowl firmly set.

"Yeah?" I asked, looking up at him through my thick lashes while shuffling my feet.

"We're taking a trip," he said. His voice had that sexy gravely tone I loved, but I knew it was from lack of sleep. He was more determined than ever. Santobello was blocking his weapons imports at every turn.

"Who are we running from?" I asked.

Joe snorted but quickly looked to the floor when Gavriel gave him a menacing glare. "Gavriel Moretti doesn't run from *nobody*," he growled at me. I sighed. There was something incredibly sexy yet annoying about the way he slipped into the third person. I guess it was a mob boss thing.

"You've been spending *way* too much time watching old mobster movies, Gav," I teased to dispel some of the tension, but Gavriel didn't seem to take the bait.

"We're going to Chesterbrook."

"No." My response was immediate and sure. There was no way in hell I'd go back to that place. Chesterbrook held too many memories for me. Too much pain and sadness.

"Callum wants to see the cabin, Love," he said, uncertainty in his tone. Ah, Callum. When we came to New York, he begged to be granted a month to pin something on my father. He was determined to do things the right way, navigate the justice system, and get Paul Bright punished accordingly. The only reason Gavriel was amusing him was because he wanted to catch Santobello—and because I'd begged him to. He knew that I needed time to cope, and he couldn't take on Santobello with brute force. He was far too protected. My father would die by Gavriel's hand, but Santobello would die in a jail cell—that is, if Nix could lock down his location again. The slimy bastard was escaping at every turn.

"I can't go back there," I said. Just the thought of seeing the cabin again had my pulse rising. The cabin represented everything I feared in this world. I knew I could handle it, but that didn't necessarily mean that I wanted to rush head-first into my past. Sometimes being strong meant knowing when to avoid the things that made you weak. Eighty percent of being courageous was about being self-aware. You had to know your weaknesses to develop your strengths.

"I'm not heartless, Love. I'm not going to make you see it. Your directions weren't enough. We're struggling to find the property, and right now, Callum is convinced the key to incriminating your father is there. I'm really trying to respect your wishes about this. I'm giving him an opportunity to do things his way at *your* request," Gav said. My heart hurt to think about Callum. He'd been in Chesterbrook since I got to New York. He was determined, but I worried that once he was away, he'd change his mind about the Bullets. About me.

For the millionth time, my mind drifted back to The Rose. Would Callum have picked me if Gavriel weren't forcing him? A hand on my chin brought my thoughts back to the present. I could see my doubt reflected in Gavriel's expression. "Get out," Gavriel barked to Joe and the other bodyguards. Bulky men in suits filed out of the kitchen, but Gav kept his black-eyed stare on me. He placed his hands on my hips then lifted me up to sit on the granite countertop behind me.

"Do you trust me?" he asked. I nodded, knowing Gavriel's need for my complete submission had little to do with me. He controlled me to feel worthy. The more I trusted him, the more he felt *deserving* of my trust.

"I won't make you go back there and relive what that fucker put you through. But I'm going to challenge you to take back some of your power. I'm going to make you uncomfortable, yeah, but I'm also going to make you better."

"Why now? What happened that's made you so scared? Don't think I didn't notice how shaken up you were this morning. And what's with the fighting lessons?"

"I'm not scared," he barked out immediately. He then didn't say anything for a moment, calming his breath while unclasping and refastening the watch on his wrist.

"The man we brought in had some interesting things to say. Santobello's reach and influence is much broader than I expected. I'm going to keep you safe, but I'm also no fool. I know when to act, and now? We need to act, Love."

I sighed. I'd been running for so long, it was all I'd ever known. After spending five years away from Chesterbrook, how could I go back? "I need Blaise and Ryker there too," I whispered. I couldn't face the demons of my past without them. Even though Ryker and I had an argument today, I knew I couldn't face my past alone.

"I already called them," Gavriel replied, shuffling forward so that he was standing between my legs. "Ryker is flying there separately after his fight."

"I can't go inside the cabin," I whispered. "I'm not going in there."

Gavriel leaned forward and kissed me on the lips. His touch was soft and tentative. It was the first time any of them had initiated any sort of physical affection since the night I told them everything, but it wasn't what I wanted. I wanted Gavriel's all-consuming passion, not this fear of breaking me.

I lightly nipped his bottom lip, encouraging him to take

our kiss deeper. I craved his destruction and control. I needed to let go. The only way I'd make it through whatever lie ahead of us was with them by my side. His groans made a satisfied spark of arousal travel up and down my spine, but still, he didn't push further.

"Damn, Moretti, you look like you're kissing a wet noodle. I thought you said he was great in the sack, Sweets. He looks scared to break you." Nix's teasing voice washed over my arousal, and I pulled away, praying to whatever God was listening above that Gavriel didn't pull the pistol from his holster and shoot my best friend.

Gavriel went impossibly rigid but didn't spin around to face Nix. I looked over Gav's shoulder to see my handsome friend chomping on an apple and leaning against the fridge. My eyes fluttered back to Gav. I didn't know what to expect. Nix was good at pushing his buttons. Surprisingly, Gav didn't berate Nix. Fire bloomed within his dark eyes, and he crashed his lips to mine.

Gav's hands wrapped around my back, yanking me forward to the edge of the countertops so that my core pressed tightly against his erection. He bit my lip as I thrust my hands through his hair, pulling at his locks and smiling against his lips. God, I missed this.

Gavriel moved his hands up and pulled my oversized sweater off my shoulder then traveled down my neck to pepper kisses along my skin. I looked at the ceiling, reveling in the sensation of his lips. I then tilted my head down when I felt eyes on me. Nix stared at us, his expression heated but amused. That sneaky bastard knew *exactly* what he was doing. Gavriel didn't stop worshipping each inch of my collarbone and neck as Nix smiled.

"You're welcome," he mouthed before spinning around and walking back down the hallway.

Gavriel took his hand and gripped the waistband of my

yoga pants, dipping his fingers inside as I let out a breathy moan. I was just about to shift off the counter and let him take me on the floor of the kitchen when his phone started going off.

"Fuck," he barked, tearing himself away from me with a scowl. He yanked his phone out of his pocket, chest heaving from the intensity we felt. "What?" he answered while staring at me. I went to adjust my sweater, but his hand snaked out and clasped around my wrist, stopping me from covering up. He stared with hooded eyes at the plush pillows of my cleavage as he listened to the person on the other end of the line.

"Seriously?" he asked while rolling his eyes and letting me go. "Fine." I raised my eyebrows, looking questioningly at Gav. "I have to go check on something at the docks. But Blaise is on his way up."

"Is everything okay?" I'd missed Blaise while he was out looking for whoever Gavriel sent him to find. I was happy to have him back, but Gavriel's murderous expression had me worried.

"The less you know, probably the better. I'm just going on a walk, Love."

My mouth dropped open in shock as Gav leaned in to nip at my swollen lip once more, pulling back as the front door opened. Blaise strolled towards us, his boots clacking against the marble floor of Gavriel's penthouse.

"Sunshine!" he yelped while jumping to a jog. Gav moved out of the way just in time for Blaise to pick me up and spin me around in his signature greeting. Slowly, ever so slowly, he slid me down his muscular body, pulling me against every last hard inch of him.

"I missed you," I whispered, my lips brushing against the ridge of his ear. He smelled like pizza. "Why do you smell so yummy?" I pulled away with a grin.

"Because I stopped for a slice at Prince Street Pizza. Remind me to take you there sometime." He smiled, and I briefly kissed his lips once more.

"I'll have to get some pineapple pizza when we get back from...Chesterbrook." My voice stuttered on the last word, and my throat closed up as if on instinct. Looking to Blaise, I knew he recognized the terror on my face, but he didn't comment on it—thankfully.

"I refuse to stand by while you ruin the best pizza in all of New York."

"You're such a pizza snob," I said with a smile, rolling my eyes before looking over at Gavriel who was putting on a suit jacket.

"You coming back tonight?" Blaise asked him. It didn't escape me that they didn't greet one another. Was Blaise his friend right now or an employee? I felt like I couldn't keep up with their ever-changing dynamic.

"Don't wait up," Gav finally replied before giving me a steel look full of protective adoration before meeting Joe in the hallway. I hadn't even noticed my broody bodyguard standing there but still called after him.

"Be safe, Joe!" I yelled, giggling when he shook his head as I smiled. Joe had been talking on the phone, and lowered it to respond to me.

"One pineapple pizza is on its way, Miss Bright."

Damn, I loved that man. Next step was convincing him to let me call him Uncle Joe. I smiled widely, knowing that if I ran up to hug him, he would cringe in discomfort. So instead, I saved him the embarrassment and nodded while saying, "Thank you."

"So what should we do?" I asked before leaning back against the counter and biting my lip.

"I was thinking we break into Gav's wine stash. Maybe watch some trashy television?" Blaise offered with a shrug while walking over towards a bar cart in the living room. The open concept penthouse made him visible from my spot in the kitchen.

"You don't want to talk about Chesterbrook?" I asked.

Blaise uncorked a bottle of wine and wrapped his perfect lips around it before taking a gulp of the red that was probably worth more than the bounty he'd just delivered. He pulled it away with a frown, and I laughed when he wrinkled his nose at the taste. "Rich people wine is shit," he groaned before plopping down on the couch and patting the seat beside him.

I made my way over to him as he spoke. "Do *you* want to talk about Chesterbrook?" he asked. I thought about it for a moment. All I'd ever done since California was talk about Chesterbrook. I'd been forced to go over every detail I could remember. Recount my father's words, his actions. My mom's admission. If I was being honest, Chesterbrook was the last thing I wanted to be thinking about.

"No," I finally replied.

"So why don't we just have a night where we don't have to think about it? Is Nix here? He can join us."

"Already ahead of you, lover boy," Nix said while putting popcorn in the microwave and slamming the door shut. I grinned. Nix and Blaise had developed a truce of sorts. I think mostly because Nix had a crush on him.

Nix settled beside me and leaned against my shoulder while Blaise held my hand, and I smiled, feeling happy and thankful for this peaceful moment. I knew this would be short-lived. I knew that, eventually, I'd have to "reclaim my power" as Gavriel put it. I'd have to go back to the beginning. I'd have to face the place I'd been running from.

3

BLAISE
Eight Years Ago

CHESTERBROOK WASN'T ALL that bad. My new foster mom was flighty and reminded me a bit of Ma. They both had that high pitched laugh and a variety of addictions. The only difference between them was that Mrs. Jameson was wealthy and intelligent enough to hide her bad habits.

When I arrived last week, I wasn't expecting the gated neighborhood with massive houses lining the streets. I'd been so used to trailer parks and shitty apartments that I wasn't prepared for my social worker, Mrs. Smith, to drop me off at a fucking mansion. Maybe the rest of the world thought it would be cool to end up on the wealthy side of the tracks, but I knew better. Bigger houses just meant they held bigger secrets.

The school was fine, I guess. All I had to do was smile and crack a few jokes, and by lunch, I was at the top of the social ladder. Some people fought with their fists, I preferred to fight with influence.

From what I gathered, my foster brother, Gavriel, preferred to be mysterious. He had that broody expression chicks loved. Unlike him, I liked to establish my place in the world with charm. He simply demanded it. I learned to command a room from Ma. She was pretty. She knew how to use her looks and charisma to get what she wanted.

Gavriel was an asshole.

When I moved into one of the spare bedrooms, he barely glanced my direction. It was like he didn't find me worthy of noticing. He just roamed our big, empty foster house and the crowded halls of Chesterbrook High like he owned the place. It kind of pissed me off. He didn't trust me —yet. But I didn't blame him.

When the last bell rang, dismissing us from class for the day, I collected my bag and winked at some chick that gave me her number earlier. What was her name again? Blaire? Becca? She practically swooned when I smiled her way. I knew that I'd have those pretty little lips wrapped around my dick by the end of the month.

Outside, I made my way over to Gavriel, expecting his signature pissed off expression. There was a difference between charming a crowd and making friends. One was necessary for survival and the other was useless. Most foster homes had a revolving door of fucked up kids, all just trying to survive until they're eighteen. I didn't necessarily want his friendship, I wanted his approval. Everyone liked Blaise Bennett.

And I mean *everyone*.

It was the one thing I could count on when I moved from town to town. I was adaptable. Likeable. So why the fuck couldn't I get this guy to at least crack a fucking smile?

I was expecting to see Gavriel's annoyed scowl, but

instead, he was grinning ear to ear while talking to a girl with long black hair. She didn't look remarkable from behind. Baggy clothes covered her thin frame, and her backpack was stuffed to the brim with books. An overachiever, probably.

It wasn't her that got my attention. No, it was the ridiculous grin on his face as they chatted. Since arriving in this shitty town, not once had I seen him so happy. Deciding that she must be someone worth knowing, I headed towards them.

"Hey, Gav, gonna catch the bus?" I said in my chipper voice. I knew that it pissed him off to see me so happy. Maybe that's why he hated me. They both turned my direction, and I had to catch my breath.

Yeah, okay. She was pretty. And by "pretty," I meant pretty fucking gorgeous.

Hazel eyes, bright and unassuming. Perfect, plush lips that just ached to be kissed. No wonder Gav had a fucking smile. I'd be blissed out too if I had her undivided attention —which I planned to have very, very soon.

"I'm gonna walk Sunshine home, actually," he growled at me, like a dog pissing on a patch of grass. So he was territorial? Even better. I loved a little friendly competition.

"It *is* a beautiful day for a walk," I replied while throwing this Sunshine gal a wink and making her blush a perfect shade of pink. "I like your name, by the way. I'm Blaise." I shot out my hand to shake hers, and she grabbed it tenderly. I made sure to hold tightly and brush my fingers along her wrist as she pulled back. As expected, she shivered. I'd pulled that move a hundred times, but watching her reaction made me want to touch her again.

Hook. Line. and Sinker.

"Gavriel's the only one that calls me Sunshine," she said with an adorable giggle that made me want to wrap her up in a hug. It wasn't forced or one of those cheesy laughs girls that wanted attention threw at guys' feet. It was genuine nervous laughter.

"How'd you get that nickname?" I asked, earning another territorial growl from Gavriel. He kept his gaze between us, eyeing me with concern.

At my question, she burst out into more laughter, going so far as to wipe a tear from the corner of her left eye. I liked the sound of it a little *too* much. I wanted to hear more of it. "When we first met, I insulted him. So he started calling me a 'little fucking ray of sunshine,' " she answered, eyeing Gavriel and elbowing him in the ribs. He rolled his eyes, but that smile was still there. I was too busy trying not to moan at the way her mouth looked as she said "fucking."

Gorgeous *and* sassy? Count me in. I opened my mouth to ask what insult she threw Gav's way, but was interrupted by the asshole himself. "Let's go, Sunshine. You've gotta get home soon, right?"

She turned back to Gavriel and brightened at his voice. "Yeah, we better get going. Thanks again for walking me. Can't stand the bus," she said, her voice softer now. It didn't escape me how her eyes zeroed in on the sidewalk at her feet. What put that sad look on her face?

"Well, I'll join you. I'm new here. Could always use some more friends, you know," I added with a wink.

It was about a forty-five minute walk back to our street. When I learned that Sunshine—or Summer—lived next door to the Jamesons' house, I started imagining what it would be like to crawl through her bedroom window. I flirted relentlessly with her, cracking jokes while Gavriel's scowl seemed to become permanently etched on his face.

"So what do you do for fun? I've been here a week, and it feels like there's nothing to do in this fucking town."

She tucked her dark hair behind her ear, as if wondering

how to respond, and I waited patiently for her answer. She was shy—there was no denying that—but not in the conventional way. She still walked like someone that could take on the world if pushed to. She engaged in the conversation, and I recognized the fire beneath her cautious stare and the steel in her step. Her expressions were clear and undeniable. I'd always been good at reading a room, reading people. I could predict a person's actions long before they acted them out. But there was something almost transparent about the way she responded to Gavriel and me. "I don't really do much," she said with a shrug. "My extracurriculars keep me pretty busy."

"What extracurriculars are you involved in?" I asked. Please say cheerleading. I would give my left nut to see her in one of those tight little uniforms, prancing about.

"Uh, debate, ballet, chess club, track, and student council," she listed off, going so far as to tick off each hobby on her fingers, as if she was forgetting one. "I was in tennis but not anymore. Oh! And math club, but I hate it there."

My earlier assumptions were right. She was a chronic overachiever.

"Wow. So when do you have time for fun?" I asked, although what I really wanted to know was if she had time for dates.

"My walks home with Gavriel have been pretty fun," she said with a shy shrug. He looked at her from the corner of his eye but kept walking, neither confirming nor denying that he enjoyed his time with her too. Damn, he needed some lessons on wooing a woman.

We turned down the road towards our street, and I found myself feeling not quite ready to say goodbye. At the end of the street, a group of who I assumed to be our classmates were laughing loudly and shoving one another. One of them, a taller guy with lanky limbs, swatted a girl on the ass while chuckling. She gave him a scowl before stalking off, adjusting her too-short shorts as she walked. Beside me, Summer went rigid and slowed her steps. Did one of these assholes mess with her?

My eyes drifted to Gavriel. He was scowling, but for the first time since meeting him, it wasn't directed towards me. No, that anger was reserved for the asshole loitering down the street. I assumed that he came to the same conclusion as me: this asshole was the reason Summer didn't like the bus.

We exchanged a glance then, one solidifying look that only those who'd been in foster care understood. It was the recognition that shit was about to go down, and even if I hadn't gotten the chance to know Gav, I knew that our shitty childhoods had bonded us. He'd have my back, and we'd have hers.

"Come on, Sunshine," I said with a smile, placing my hand on her lower back and pressing her forward. I'd also decided in that split moment that I wouldn't let Gavriel hoard the perfect nickname. In that moment, she needed to be strong. So I not so subtly reminded her that she was an unconventional ray of sunshine and sass.

We made our way towards the group, Gavriel and me puffing out our chests like the barbarians we were. They'd started congregating right in front of what I'd assumed was her house. Probably an intentional decision. I saw the intimidation tactic for what it was.

"Look! It's little Miss Perfect," the tallest called out as we walked closer. Was that supposed to be an insult? Or did he, too, realize that she was fucking perfect and completely too good for him? That nickname suited her well, and it didn't set right with me that he was tossing around the truth like it was something to be ashamed of. "You gonna tell your Daddy I'm harassing you again?" he asked, ignoring Gavriel and me as he stalked closer to her. Out of the corner of my eye, I noticed that she'd grabbed the strap of her backpack tighter, as if preparing to run.

Oh hell no.

I'd seen guys like this. Ma had a line of them outside our front door for more years than I could remember. It's mostly why I've been in and out of the system. "Back the fuck off," Gavriel said, his voice low. I liked his style. Straight to the point.

"Oh, you got a bodyguard now?" the guy asked, laughing over his shoulder at his group of friends. The people around him smiled broadly, enjoying the show down. I didn't consider myself much of a fighter, I was a lover. But I could scrap with the best of them. And guessing by the steam coming off Gavriel, he was more than ready to teach this guy a lesson. Hell, he looked ready to take on the world.

"Lionel, m-my father said if you bother me again, he'll get a restraining order," she said. Although stuttering, I was proud of her for standing up for herself. We would need to work on that delivery though.

"Daddy does everything, right?" He sneered at her, and I flexed my muscles. I took a step forward, but a police cruiser descended the street, making me pause. Beside me, Sunshine let out a curse as the group dispersed.

"I'll see you later, Gavriel," she said while squeezing his hand, and a spike of jealousy swirled in my gut. "Thanks for walking me. It was nice to meet you, Blaise." Her bright smile had me wanting to ask her to come over to the Jamesons'.

"Hey, Dad," she said while stepping away before I could respond. Damn, I usually had it together. Normally, I would have brushed her hair behind her ear, or some other flirty shit that would make her putty in my hands. A man wearing a uniform stepped out of the cruiser with a frown on his face. He looked right at us, and I knew immediately that he'd never be a fan of me. Some people couldn't be charmed. Some people just thought they knew everything. I could practically feel the superiority complex rolling off of him in waves.

This dad could be a problem.

I watched as they went inside, and I turned to head back to the Jamesons' when Gavriel placed a palm on my chest. "She's off limits, Bennett." I smiled then. So Gavriel had a crush. Cute.

"I'm just making some friends!" I said, throwing up my hands in mock surrender. "Some really fucking gorgeous friends with lips I'd like to see around my co—"

The punch came out of nowhere. And for the love of Sunshine, it hurt. My cheek hit the pavement, scraping my skin. I rolled over on my back while massaging my jaw line. Cheap shot, motherfucker.

I squinted, trying to block the sun from my vision until his silhouette blocked the bright rays from view. He leaned over, staring at me while massaging his fist. "Stay away from Sunshine."

Fucker.

I couldn't really sleep that night. My room at the Jamesons' was by far the best of all my foster homes. Probably the best I've had of anything. The bed was plush. They had a maid that kept things clean. I could even rub one out in the privacy of my own room. So why the hell was I lying here in bed, awake, and thinking about a girl I just met?

My door opened and in strolled Gavriel wearing all black and looking evil. "Get up."

Color me curious. "Why?"

"You wanna be in Sunshine's life?"

"Come on, I just met the chick. You're being a little extreme, don't you think?" I feigned indifference. One thing I learned during my stints with foster care—don't get attached. And if you do? Don't let anyone know. The things you want tend to not last, and what *does* last can be used against you.

"Look, you can stop dicking around and help me kick that prick's ass, or you can sit here. Either way, I'm out."

Gavriel turned around, leaving me alone in this bedroom. This house was nice. Did I really want to go start a fight and risk it? But the temptation to learn more about my foster brother as well as see Sunshine again was too great. Mrs. Jameson said she'd be out late, and Mr. Jameson was fast asleep. They probably wouldn't notice if we'd left.

Fuck it.

I made my way downstairs and outside, where Gavriel was leaning against a tree. He stared down at the ground with a tiny smirk, and it kinda pissed me off that he waited for me. Pretentious much? I looked up at the next door neighbors' house. The light was on in one of the upstairs bedrooms, and a thin shadow walked by the window, disappearing before I could see if it was her.

"Come on," Gavriel said, drawing my attention back to him. "Lionel and his friends like to get drunk at the bridge. Let's go."

"What's the bridge?" I asked, following after him as he traveled down the road. The crickets outside were chirping, and the air was thick with humidity.

"It's a hangout where shitty humans like to visit. I personally don't understand the appeal, but apparently it's where he is."

The moon was full as we descended Woodbury Lane. Gavriel was wound up tight, twitching and pacing towards this so-called "bridge" like a rabid animal. "So how long have you had the hots for Sunshine?" I asked while following him down a park trail. A faint smell of pot hit my nose, and I smiled when I realized that even if tonight was a bust, maybe I could bum a little fun off of someone.

"I met her when I moved here," he answered. "She's just a friend."

"When did you move here?" I asked.

"About eight months ago."

We continued to walk, but I didn't know what more to talk about. The dude had some serious demons; I didn't expect to have show and tell. I didn't expect much of anything. Expectations were just another thing we foster kids learned not to have. "Well, I'm from Texas, originally," I said, filling the silence. "Ma liked to dance for cash. She also liked men with drinking problems. She liked them more than me, apparently, because everytime she got a new boyfriend, I landed back in the system. That's how I got here, actually. Because last week, one of them shot her."

Gavriel looked at me from the corner of his eye, and I knew that he was unsure of what to say. I'd always been an oversharer. Honesty was in my blood, that's what Ma used to say. People always felt pressured to share back though. But not Gavriel. He kept is mouth firmly shut. "I'll admit, Chesterbrook might be the nicest place I've ever lived in. The houses are nice. Mr. and Mrs. Jameson seem okay. Not too shabby."

"It's alright," Gavriel said. In the distance, shouts and loud laughter could be heard. Gavriel left the paved trail to crouch behind a large oak tree, and I followed suit. For all my talk of observing people, I still hadn't quite figured him out. Of course there was talk. I'd learned on my first day that he was the son of a mob boss. His little Bullet Boy fairy tale had me rolling my eyes, but the chicks liked it.

He had that mysterious, scary asshole persona. Within my first hour at the Jamesons', he made it clear that he cared about one person and one person only—him. So why was he sneaking out in the middle of the night to teach a bully a lesson? I think this Sunshine chick was under his skin. If I wanted to learn his secrets, I'd have to get to know her.

Not that I was complaining. I'd like to get rid of the smirk on that asshole Lionel's face. Long after Sunshine disappeared into her house, I'd found myself wondering about that dynamic. Was Lionel the reason she didn't ride the bus? Or did she just enjoy walking with Gavriel?

I needed to get a car. A sexy car.

"Do you know how to fight?" Gavriel asked. I scoffed. Every foster kid in existence knew how to fight. I let him get a cheap shot off me earlier, but I could defend myself. I didn't like it, but I could throw down in a pinch. I think seeing men punch my mom all my life made me a bit of a pussy. But I wasn't dumb. Violence was all about motive.

"Yeah."

"You sure? You didn't even try to block me earlier," he replied. I heard the amusement in his voice. And even though the only thing illuminating the woods was moonlight, I knew he was smiling within the dark shadows.

"I *let* you hit me. I just was helping your sensitive ego," I replied with a smirk.

Gavriel shook his head then peered over the bushes. I shifted to get a better look, rustling the leaves and making him sigh at my noisiness. "Could you stop?" he whispered.

"They're too drunk to notice," I replied, ignoring his angry tone. I almost wished we'd brought Sunshine. At least with her around, he pretended to be a polite member of society.

"Three of them. You ready?" he asked.

"After you," I said in a cocky tone while tossing him a smile.

When we emerged from the bushes like motherfucking badasses, they didn't even flinch, ruining our entrance.

Where was their sense of theater? "Hey, guys? Is this where all the people who peak in high school hang out?" I called out with a smirk. Gavriel once again let out a huff.

"You're the new bastard kid the Jamesons took in, right?" Lionel asked while standing up. He had been leaning over the bridge overlooking a river, dropping empty bottles of beer over the edge.

"Littering is bad for the environment," I said with a small smile. I couldn't help it, I liked to rev people up a bit. Lionel gave me a pointed stare before tossing another bottle over the edge.

"Oops."

"What did you do to Summer Bright?" Gavriel asked, stealing my thunder. "She hasn't taken the bus in three weeks."

Lionel laughed then, his crooked teeth shining in the moonlight. Behind him, his friends stumbled forward. One was short with a round stomach, puffy cheeks and blue eyes. The other was built like a truck with a glazed-over expression. They looked high as hell.

There were pros and cons to fighting a drunk. Their reaction times were slow, so they couldn't dodge your attacks as well. But they also were numbed to the pain. Your kicks and punches didn't do much.

"I was just messing with her. She overreacted." I watched as Gavriel slowly made his way down a rocky path towards the bridge. Broken glass crunched beneath his feet as I breathed in the herbal smell of their weed. "She doesn't like to be touched. Her prick of a father called the school. Asshat. I bet he doesn't give two shits about his daughter. He was more concerned that it would make him look bad. Can't protect the town if you can't protect your own."

Interesting. So the dad wasn't overprotective? Just image

conscious. Maybe my chances of spending time with Sunshine were salvageable after all.

"Well, *he* might not care, but I sure as fuck do. You'll stay away from her. And you're gonna start walking home from now on so she can ride the bus." Gav eased his way closer to Lionel, and I followed after him.

"Or what?" Lionel replied, his stupid lips curling.

Thankfully, Gavriel ended the ridiculous banter with a punch to the face. It knocked him flat on his ass. The idiot didn't even use his hands to break his fall. Fuck, was that what I looked like when he punched me earlier? I seriously needed to start working out.

The muscular guy took a swing at Gavriel, so I went up to intercept his punch. I grabbed his arm, pulling back before it could connect with the back of Gavriel's head. "You fight like a pussy," I said with a grin, releasing his arm as the short and pudgy friend helped up Lionel.

Once he was firmly on his feet, the real fight started. Lionel swung at Gavriel and missed, but his short, stubby friend didn't. He was so short that he barely met Gavriel's chest, and his first hit was even lower. *Ouch.*

I leaned forward and grabbed him by the hair before thrusting my knee in his face. The crunch of bone made me cringe. "Damn, man, I bet that's broken," I said while taking a step back. Lionel kicked Gavriel in the stomach, so I stormed forward and punched the lanky asshole in the jaw.

But unlike Gavriel's hit, he barely faltered. *That's it, I'm going to work out more.*

The punch he returned was expected; the alcohol had slowed his system, but it didn't make it any less painful. I'd definitely have a black eye in the morning. The guy *not* bent over crying on the floor and holding his broken nose picked up a bottle. I watched in slow motion as he hit it against the metal bridge, shards going everywhere. The biggest piece remained firmly clasped in his hand.

I assumed that he intended to stab me with it, but he was too late. Gav had zero fear. He was upright and sprinting towards him before I could even contemplate running. When his hands connected with the guy's chest, it sent him over the edge of the bridge and to the river below.

We both spun around to stare at Lionel, who was staring at us in shock. "You fuckers are weird," he said with a grunt. Gavriel started running past me and lunged at him again. I watched alongside the guy with the broken nose. Gavriel was powerful. Each swing packed a punch, and Lionel was bloodied and bruised within a minute.

"Stay away from Sunshine," he growled while pinning Lionel down on the ground and holding him at the neck.

"Who?" the pathetic fuck choked out.

"Summer Bright," I called after him just as Gavriel delivered the final blow, knocking Lionel out. I wiped my hands on my jeans and turned to look at the chubby guy with blood pouring out of his nose.

"Dude, you should probably get that looked at," I said with a wince. If he didn't get it set, it would look fucked up for life. And with a mug like his, he didn't need anything else hurting his already poor excuse for a face.

"Yeah, I'll go tomorrow. Good hit, Moretti," he choked out as Gavriel stalked closer. Was this guy serious? Don't compliment the guy you just junk punched. Rookie mistake. Gavriel was still flooded with adrenaline. Every bone in his body rigid with a tension that made him look lethal.

The guy beside me trembled, his teary eyes widening as he watched Gavriel walk across the bridge towards us. "You," Gav said while pointing at him, "you tell everyone that'll listen. If you mess with Sunshine, you mess with the Bullets."

He swallowed. "Wh-who are the Bullets?"

"Us."

My brows shot up. So we had a name now? Cool, cool. If he started talking treehouses and code words though, we might need to discuss things.

The kid scurried away as fast as he could—which wasn't very fast considering he was high as fuck and had a complete lack of coordination. He stumbled over a rock and slipped in mud, clawing at the dirt to escape us. I took a moment to look over the bridge. Glass shank guy had swum over to the banks and was lying in the mud, his chest heaving as he caught his breath. "So, the Bullets, huh? Does this mean we're friends now?" I asked. Gavriel looked at me with a large frown. A drop of blood collected in the corner of his mouth, and he wiped it with the back of his hand before answering me.

"I guess so."

4

SUNSHINE
Present day

WHEN I WAS A YOUNG GIRL, my father signed me up for tennis. I hated the sport. He'd make me go to the country club for practice, and Mom would dress me up like a Barbie. My coach never hurt me, but everytime he helped with my form or adjusted my grip, I felt his eyes linger on my body a little longer than I would've liked. Practice was every other day, and after three months of being terrible at the sport and hating my coach, I told my father that I wanted to quit. To this day, I still remember his response.

"The Brights don't quit, Summer," he sneered. "Grab your practice gear. We're going to work on your form."

For six hours, my father made me swing my racket, gradually getting angrier as I missed the sailing tennis balls through the air. The club was closed for renovations, but who could deny the Chief of Police? I remember wishing someone would come practice beside us so my father would slip back into his pleasant image. My arms shook with exhaustion as I swung again and again. "You're an embarrassment," he screamed until tears were freely pouring down my cheeks. I knew he didn't like me showing weakness. Tears were an imperfection.

It wasn't until my legs were wobbling that he finally relented. "Fine. Let me show you." Taking my racket from me, my father strolled up beside me and demonstrated the proper form. "Stand closer, Summer. I want you to see how to hold it."

I remember moving beside him and shaking with fear as my father readied his stance and swung. He was all power and force, slicing through the air with precision. The tennis racket connected with my gut, and I fell backward onto the court.

I couldn't scream. The air was knocked out of me. All I could do was stare up at the Chesterbrook clouds as a black haze clouded the corners of my vision. After fifteen seconds of wordless agony, my father leaned over and stared at me with his signature frown of disapproval. It wasn't until I was gasping for air again that he finally spoke.

"Brights don't quit."

Being back in Chesterbrook was like a hit to the gut, delivered by Paul Bright himself.

"What are you thinking about?" Blaise asked. We were standing on the tarmac at Chesterbrook's small private airport and waiting for Gavriel's limo to arrive.

"Tennis," I answered with half honesty. My father made me play for five more years after that. I was never any good, but I never gave up. It wasn't until my mom commented that my arms were looking too muscular for a young girl that he let me focus on other activities.

Blaise gave me an amused smile at my answer. "Tennis, huh? Didn't you used to play?" he asked. "I never got to see you in one of those short tennis skirts."

I laughed to hide the darkness swirling in my chest, the phantom pain of being here was just too much to handle. "I did. I was terrible at it."

"I doubt that," he replied. We were leaning against a brick wall in the shade while Gavriel paced and yelled into his phone about the delay of the driver. "From what I remember, you were good at everything."

I could see how Blaise could feel that way. I was groomed from a young age to look and act like I was perfect. "I hated it. The day my parents let me quit, I was so happy that I cried." I remember running to Gavriel and jumping into his reluctant arms to give him a hug that day. I also remember his small but confident smile and how he held my hand on the walk home from school. In fact, if I remembered correctly, that was just a few weeks before Blaise arrived in Chesterbrook.

"So what made you think of it now?" he asked. I wanted to lie to him, but Blaise deserved better than that. Besides, he knew me too well.

"This place brings up bad memories, Blaise." Why does everyone fear the journey? That's the easy part. I've always feared coming home.

He opened his mouth to respond but paused when my phone started ringing. I answered it, grateful for the distraction. "Hey, Nix," I said while forcing myself to smile. Nix was another one of those perceptive ones. He could sniff out a gloomy mood even over the phone.

"How you doing, Sweets?" he asked.

"Not too bad."

"Liar," he growled. "I hate that I have to stay behind, but you'll be back in two days, right?"

"Yes, two days and we can go back to being locked up in Gavriel's ivory tower," I joked. Phoenix stayed behind to keep tabs on my father. I think Gavriel just wanted some distance, and Nix appreciated the break from my moody mob boss. I knew that if I had asked him to go with me, he would have, but this was something I needed to do with my guys.

"I'll see you soon," I choked out, missing him.

"Love you," he cooed before hanging up.

"Love you too."

In the distance, a limo made its way up the road and towards us. The cool, crisp air made my lips chap as I curled my jacket around myself. I pushed myself off the brick wall before heading towards Joe and a stoic-looking Gavriel. The flight here was exhausting. I couldn't keep up with how many phone calls and decisions Gav made during the short two-hour trip.

"Tell him to have my money deposited by midnight."

"I don't negotiate with insignificant people."

"You're all talk, my shipment better be ready by tomorrow, or you'll end up like Santobello's son."

It was a tricky time. People were questioning Gavriel's influence and power. Santobello was cutting off his trade routes at every turn. When he wasn't trying to bring down my father, Gavriel was attempting to re-establish himself as a powerful crime boss.

Behind the limo was another car with dark, tinted

windows. Once it parked, Callum got out of the driver side door and jogged towards me.

"I missed you," he said with a genuine smile as he wrapped me into a hug. I'd been worried that he would be weird around me since the night at The Rose, but if he was uncomfortable around Gavriel, he didn't show it. I think, if anything, my revelation was enough to put all other awkwardness on hold.

Nuzzling into his chest, I replied, "I missed you too." Three weeks without Callum was hard, but I loved him enough to commit to his need for justice. He still had hope that the world was organized and that sick people would have to answer for what they've done. I didn't want to ruin his views with the truth—Paul Bright had to die, and it would most likely be Gavriel that killed him.

A loud cough behind us made me roll my eyes. Joe was standing by the limo door with his arms crossed over his chest. Gavriel was possessive to a fault, so I'm sure to outsiders, it was strange seeing Gavriel okay with the affection I showed others. "We have to go," he grumbled.

Gavriel held his hand out to me, motioning for me to sit beside him. "Ryker is at the lake house waiting for us," he said.

Callum kept his arms tightly around my waist and looked at Gavriel with his determined stare. "I wanted to take Summer —I mean Sunshine—somewhere first," he said. I felt a little heartbroken at the way he stumbled over my name. In so many ways, it represented his conflicted feelings about being a Bullet.

"Oh really?" Gavriel asked while getting out of the limo once more. He made his way over to us with a slow and steady walk, confidence practically oozing out of him. The standoff between Callum and Gavriel made my throat go dry. I'd hoped that there would be no awkwardness, but there was a massive power struggle between them, and I knew in my gut that Gavriel would win.

"I wanted to take her to where her mother was buried since she didn't get to go to the funeral. I know we weren't big fans of her, but I think Summer needs the closure."

I squeezed my eyes shut, feeling warm appreciation swell up and bubble within my chest. Callum was so thoughtful and kind. "Is that something you want to do?" Gavriel asked me. I didn't miss how he ignored Callum. Gavriel was all about making me feel in control and making sure I stepped up and asked for what I wanted. I knew that if I couldn't handle seeing my mother's grave, he'd take the blame. He was more than okay with telling the rest of the world to fuck off where I was concerned.

But I didn't want to be weak. Maybe this was what I needed to move on. I never got to tell my mother how much of a disappointment she was, or how angry I was at her. I never got to truly forgive her. I ran and pretended that time stopped back here in Chesterbrook. I didn't know the woman that killed herself. Maybe it was time to go and introduce myself.

"I-I'd like to go," I whispered as Blaise got out of the limo and strolled towards us. I prepared myself for his brutal honesty.

"Are you sure, Sunshine?" Blaise asked. "If it's too soon, we can make a special trip out here when you're ready. You don't have to face all your demons at once. In fact, I'd prefer if you didn't."

My shoulders slumped, and I took in a deep breath while looking at the three of them. "I can do this. I need to do this. We will catch up with you in a little bit." I grabbed Callum's hand and pulled him towards the other car without saying goodbye. I held steadfast to my resolve to be strong, knowing that if I didn't go now, I probably never would. When I settled into the front seat, the back passenger door opened, and Joe shifted his bulky frame into the compact car.

"Can't go anywhere without my shadow, huh?" I asked as Callum cursed under his breath.

"I can handle this," he said while flashing Joe a cruel glare in the rearview mirror.

I didn't turn around to look at him, I knew that Joe would give his unamused shrug and ignore us. He didn't get a choice. Gavriel controlled him as much as he controlled the rest of us.

I held Callum's hand as he drove the long way to the cemetery. Although the local airport was just a couple miles from the cemetery, Callum made sure to take the backroads around town, avoiding the street I grew up on. Outside, everything looked the same. A few new subdivisions had gone up, and large homes seemed to tower over the street. Various high-end cars drove past, and I tried to remember if Chesterbrook had always seemed full of pretentious people or if my perceptions had changed.

I guess becoming poor made me more aware of the vicious cycle. The rich just got richer—and most of them lived here. "She's buried by my parents," Callum finally said. He turned left on a paved road and kept going down the drive towards the cemetery. Tall oak trees created a canopy of dying leaves overhead, and a gust of wind made them float to the paved road like blood-red drops of autumn.

"They were good friends. I'm sure she would have liked that," I replied while leaning my forehead against the cold glass pane.

"Knowing what she did...it makes me not want to have her anywhere near them," Callum growled with a frown.

"It's a little late for that. I mean, I'm sure Gav knows a guy that could dig her up, but even though I hate the woman, I don't necessarily want her swimming with the fishes," I joked in my best Brooklyn accent, pushing past the nervousness I felt with sarcasm.

In the backseat, Joe let out a short laugh but slammed his mouth shut before another sound could escape his mouth. He loved my jokes, I knew it.

"I went to the funeral," Callum then said.

I already knew this. I had to watch from Gavriel's living room as he shook my father's hand. It was a grim necessity. We couldn't let my father know that Callum was on to him. He'd been a family friend for so long that it would have looked weird if he hadn't shown up.

"Yeah?" I asked.

"I could have killed him right there. And if I were Gavriel, maybe I would have. I imagined a thousand different scenarios of how to end his life. It scared me how much anger I felt."

I nodded, absorbing his words. I knew exactly what he meant. I'd spent the last five years imagining ways to kill my father. It scared me because it made me wonder if my need for revenge made me like him. The only difference was that my need for bloodshed was fueled by hatred, and his was because of his twisted mind.

The cemetery had pristine, manicured lawns and polished tombstones dating back to the seventeenth century. My father once told me that he could trace his lineage all the way back to the Mayflower here. It seemed fitting that my mother would be buried in the elite grave-yard of town—not that it mattered. She was dead now. Status and money were for the living.

Parking the car, I sat still while Callum rushed out and went to open the passenger side door. I felt silly wearing worn jeans and a bulky jacket. This was the funeral I never got to attend, and I was vastly underdressed. Mom would be furious.

"I'll stay in the car and keep an eye out," Joe said, and I barely held back a smile. Leave it to Joe to avoid any sort of situation that involved feelings. Not even Gavriel could force him to follow me to my mother's grave for a quick cry.

"Sure you don't want to hand me tissues as I sob?" I asked him. I just couldn't help it, I loved goading the guy. Callum shook his head and placed his palm at my lower back, guiding me away before Joe could respond.

"You really like messing with that guy, don't you?" he asked with a laugh. The bright sounds of his chuckle felt out of place here. And as if realizing so, Callum's laugh died off, leaving us to walk in silence.

I knew exactly where his parents were buried. I still remembered the day they died. Callum was away at college, and Mom got the phone call. We were on our way to my ballet lesson. I never knew exactly what my dad said on the other end of the line. She seemed shocked by his words. She had to pull over her car because she was so emotional.

"What's wrong, Mom?"

I still remember the way her voice shook. "Mr. and Mrs. Mercer are dead."

Callum grabbed my hand as we walked, bringing me out of my memories. Even though he would be strong for me today, I knew that he needed to borrow a bit of my strength too. Coming here was hard for him.

"I should have brought some flowers to put on Mom's grave. She loved roses. Dad would bring her home a bouquet all the time," he whispered as we approached the side-by-side tombstones. "Shit. I'm making this about me and..."

Someone weaker than I might have felt envy that he had such a picture-perfect childhood. But I loved him too much to feel anything but thankful that he was gifted with parents worthy of grief. Whenever I thought of my own mother, all I felt was shame.

I couldn't miss her. I couldn't physically force myself to miss the woman that gave me life. I tried to compile a list of redeeming qualities about her but came up short. I wasn't mourning my mother, not really. I was mourning myself. I was mourning the fact that no matter how hard I tried, I couldn't feel something for someone I was supposed to love.

I directed my attention to the matching tombstones on the ground in front of us. Mr. and Mrs. Mercer were well-loved in the community. And not just because of what they wanted the world to see. They were genuinely good people.

I didn't look to the left, where I knew my mother's grave was. I took a moment to appreciate Callum's parents, to send up a little thanks that they raised such a strong man. "Your mom made the best cookies," I said out of nowhere. I was a terrible cook. My mother liked to think that she made gourmet dishes, but she often just bought pre-made items from the store and carefully arranged them on her silver platters.

But Mrs. Mercer? She could bake and cook better than anything. We would go to her house on Thanksgiving. I remembered my mother's frown as my father compared their dishes. My mom loved Mrs. Mercer, but she didn't like the effortlessness about her perfection. Goodness naturally flowed throughout her. She was what my mother strived to be, and she didn't even have to work for it.

"I would kill for one of her chocolate chip pumpkin cookies," Callum said, and my mouth watered just thinking about them. "Thanksgiving is just a few days away, and I would give anything to have one of her famous dinners."

I nodded my head, feeling the same way. Last year was the first Thanksgiving I'd celebrated since I ran away. Nix and I were helpless in the kitchen, so we saved every dime we had for an entire month so that we could eat at a steakhouse on the nicer side of town. I dressed up in my most elegant dress, which admittedly, was tattered and worn. We strolled through the front doors like we owned the place, and even though it was my favorite Thanksgiving to date, I still missed Mrs. Mercer's famous dinners.

"If you still have her old recipe books, I could try to make it for you?" I cringed, knowing that my efforts would be futile. If anything, I would probably ruin the good memory he had of his mother's cooking.

Callum must have sensed the unease on my face because he then laughed. "That's okay, Baby. I'd rather remember hers. Besides, what if you inherited your mother's cooking abilities?" He joked while elbowing me in the side.

I let out a half-hearted laugh, trying my best to keep upbeat despite the grim mention of my mother. I knew that just two feet to the left and six feet down was a pretty little coffin filled with her ugly remains. "You're the one that always showed up for family dinner," I replied. "I wasn't sure if you were brave or starving."

Callum lifted his hand and brushed his thumb along my bottom lip. "Neither. I stomached her bad food so I could see you." *Damn Callum. Just when I thought I couldn't fall for him any farther, he went and said shit like that.*

I directed my eyes to Mr. Mercer's tombstone and smiled when I saw the quote engraved deeply within the solid rock. No matter how many times I came here, it still made me chuckle.

"Go away. I'm asleep."

Callum cracked a small smile, and I thought back on all the silly jokes Mr. Mercer used to play. For someone involved with keeping the peace, he sure did play a lot of jokes. He thrived on laughter, making sure to lighten the load of anyone near him.

"I never realized how lame my father's humor was until I read his will and found out I had to put that on his tombstone," Callum said. "Gotta love the dad jokes."

We stood there for a moment in silence, both of us reminiscing over the various memories we had of his family. I enjoyed thinking back on them with fondness. Although Callum and I had a five year age difference, we had known each other throughout our childhood, going to the same events and parties with our parents. I mourned his parents alongside him after their death.

When it was time to face my own mother's mortality, I took a moment to close my eyes and find comfort in that dark part of my mind that believed she died five years ago. The moment she sent me away to live on my own, to fight this world without her guidance, was the day I accepted that the mother I wanted was no more. My father twisted her into a dark and sad little imitation of life. I knew that closure was necessary, but I also knew that seeing her grave wouldn't break me, because I broke a long time ago.

I opened my eyes and turned to look upon the tombstone marking where my mother was. The dirt surrounding it was still fresh as if it were just filled. There was nothing unique about her headstone. It was large, casting a shadow over the Mercers' plots.

"Loving Wife and Mother," I said, quoting her tombstone. "How original."

I let out a dark chuckle, and once again, Callum placed his palm at the base of my back. He guided me closer as if forcing me to come to terms with what I was looking at. "It's a pretty little spot," Callum said. Just behind her grave was a large tree. In the summertime, it would shade her plot. My mother did always like to hide in the shadows.

"Am I supposed to say something? Do something?" I asked Callum while turning to face him. I wanted to reminisce, maybe even talk to her. But I didn't know what to say. I didn't know how to act.

"You can do whatever feels right," Callum answered. He started rubbing little circles along my spine, and I leaned closer as the breeze picked up. There was a cold front coming through, spearheading a storm. I felt the oncoming chill deep in my bones.

"Nothing feels right, Callum." My answer was probably the most honest I'd been about my feelings since learning of her death. Sometimes, there was power in admitting what you didn't know.

"I hated you forever," I said, directing my attention to the rock that was supposed to somehow metaphorically represent the woman that left me to fend for myself. "Am I supposed to grieve you? Am I supposed to feel sorry for you? Am I supposed to cry at your grave and mourn the woman that ruined my life? You abandoned me. You picked *him*."

Although I told myself I wouldn't cry, tears began streaming from my eyes like bullets from a gun. There was no holding the force of them back. "Why did you pick him? Why were you such a coward?" All the things I wanted to know but never would find out were spewing from my lips. I stomped on the ground to accentuate my frustration. "And you know what the worst part about all of this is, Mom?" I asked before dropping to my knees at her grave. "I still miss you, and I hate myself for it."

After kneeling there for what felt like an eternity, I felt a hand on the back of my neck. I stood up and wiped the stress from my face. Staring at the ground, I averted my eyes from her plot until my gaze locked onto another tombstone directly beside her.

"What is this?" I asked before taking a step closer.

Callum cursed before grabbing my elbow as if to direct me away. "Summer, I forgot. Come on, let's go."

I ripped my arm out of his hold and stared at the tombstone that said my name. "Summer Bright."

I moved forward and touched the groove of the rock where my birthdate was carved. "What is this, Callum?" It was surreal, seeing my name there. It felt like, once more, the tennis racket was connecting with my gut. It didn't feel like I was really here.

"When you went missing, your parents decided to have a small ceremony. Your mother claimed that it would help her cope."

I rolled my eyes with the sniffle. "More like she wanted an excuse for all the attention to be on her," I growled. I could almost see it now. My mom probably wore a flattering dress, all black and all eyes on her. She probably carefully applied her makeup and dabbed at the corners of her eyes to look like she was crying.

"This is so fucked up," I said. I wanted to kick the tombstone over, I wanted to prove that I was alive. I survived, dammit. I didn't like that this thing, this piece of rock and concrete, was trying to take away all that I'd work so hard for.

"Did you attend?" I asked. I needed to know.

"I didn't want to. I knew you were alive, Summer. Nothing added up, and I just felt it in my gut that you weren't dead. But I was also grieving when you left. If you don't like that your parents did this, fine. I understand. But it gave me comfort, if it makes you feel any better."

"But I'm alive," I said, mostly trying to convince myself. When you've been close to death, it made you question your own existence. My breathing grew more rapid as I pinched my skin, as if trying to feel the pain so that it would further validate my point. I was here, wasn't I?

Two hands clamped down on my shoulders, and I looked up at Callum's blond hair and blue eyes. He was frowning, obviously doubting himself for bringing me here. "Of course you're alive, Baby. I feel you right here. You feel me?" He grabbed my hand and placed it on his chest. For a moment, I closed my eyes and counted the beats of his heart.

"I'm alive, Callum. Don't let anyone take that from me," I whispered.

Overhead, more clouds began to roll through. They were a dark and ominous gray, but the high-powered winds were nothing compared to the fury inside of me. I needed to do something. I needed to feel alive at this moment. I wasn't just some cheap funeral or scapegoat to further my father's agenda and my mother's need to be in the public eye.

Callum grabbed my hand and turned as if to head back up and over the hill to where Joe was parked on the other side. No one could see us here, which was why I made the rash decision to yank him back towards me and pull him in for a kiss.

I didn't think about where we were or the fat raindrops plopping down on my flushed skin. I didn't feel the icy chill in the air or the way the mud beneath my feet seemed to sink with each step.

All I felt was the press of his lips against mine and the clashing of our teeth as we clawed our way closer to one another. His fingers threaded through my hair, and I pressed harder against him. "Baby, you're here," he whispered against my lips. Thunder crashed in the distance, and I wondered if we were always meant to collide this way. I wondered if our love was always meant to be fostered from suffering. This kiss wasn't pleasant, nor was it intended to make us feel better. This was the dance of two lonely people fighting to feel.

"Feel me," I moaned. "Tell me I'm real."

We met during the calm before the storm. It was easy to form our bond within the safe innocence of my childhood. But now we were lightning and thunder. We were crashing floods and destruction.

Callum guided me beneath the nearby tree and laid me down beneath the barren limbs. There were no leaves to protect us from the storm, but I welcomed the cold icy rain as the earth and fallen leaves crushed beneath my back. I was on sensory overload, and the bitter pain of the weather was bringing the pleasure of his kisses to new heights.

He was quick to rip off my boots and slide down my jeans; I shivered as the cool, wet air hit me, but Callum's hot body was on me again before I could settle in the icy feeling. Lifting my leg up, he propped my calf on his shoulder as I leaned up to kiss him once more. Nipping at his bottom lip, he slid inside of me with a single thrust. "You're here. You're alive," he said.

We were both huffing, our breath making clouds of fog between us as he moved deep within me. I liked that it was uncomfortable and that nothing about this was perfect or right or meaningful. I loved that Callum and I came together somewhere between the screaming sky and the dead.

I cried out with each thrust, "God, yes." Callum was being a selfish lover, taking and claiming all that had been denied him.

"I like you shaky, naked, and beneath me," Callum growled. I closed my eyes to accept each punishing thrust, but he wasn't having any of that.

"Look at me," he said with a sigh. "See me."

I didn't orgasm. There was no loving coaxing of our

bodies. We didn't find comfort or even resolution. I let him pound me raw and use me up until he was screaming my name louder than the thunder around us. It wasn't until I saw his tears mixing in with the rain that I *truly* saw Callum.

Today wasn't about my closure. It was about his.

MY CLOTHES CLUNG to my body during the drive to the lake house Gavriel rented for a couple of days. I clenched my teeth while forcing the shivers away. My hair had mud and leaves tangled in each strand, and there was a deep-set chill in my bones I couldn't get rid of.

Callum looked worse than I did. I'd never seen him so messy. My clean-cut guy was covered with dirt, and his eyes were red from the salty tears he'd released. We weren't speaking, partly because we didn't know what to say and partly because Joe was still in the back seat looking horrified.

"Mr. Moretti is going to kill me," Joe finally said while massaging his temples. I was thankful for the break in silence.

"I won't let him hurt you, Joe. You're the only one of his guards that I actually like," I replied while flipping down the mirror and staring at my reflection. The red lipstick I'd put on this morning before my flight was smeared along my chin and streaks of mascara-lined my cheeks. I didn't have that post-sex glow everyone always talked about. I looked like I'd just been through a war. And maybe in some ways, I had.

"That's not reassuring," he grumbled in response. "You look like you just got the shit beat out of you."

I reached for Callum's hand, but he pulled it away from me before I could grab it. It felt like there were miles of distance between us now, and I wasn't sure what I thought about that. I thought that sex with Callum would have brought us closer. I had hoped that it would solidify the intense emotional bond between us, but instead, it seemed to crumble whatever weak foundation we'd barely established. Callum must have seen the confused expression on my face, because after glancing at Joe in the rearview mirror, he let out a sigh and spoke.

"I didn't want *it* to happen like that. Right now, I feel like the shittiest human on the planet, and I can't even look at you without hating myself, let alone touch you. I just...I need a minute, okay? It has nothing to do with you."

"I have no regrets about what just happened, Callum," I whispered honestly. It might not have been perfect, but it was real.

"But I do. I'm not Gavriel. I don't *do* that. All those years of waiting and I just..." Callum punched the steering wheel, and I heard a grumble from Joe in the backseat. "Just give me a minute, okay?"

I tried not to feel hurt by his need for space. Callum needed time to process everything. It's just how he was. I couldn't count the number of times he would disappear to handle things. Anytime he was overstimulated emotionally, you could find him hiding from the world and sitting in silence. It was how he coped.

I craved some sort of validation though. Regret was a powerful emotion, and I didn't want to be one of the things he thought about late at night. I didn't want to be something he questioned or considered a mistake. I'm not one who needed hours of cuddling after sex. I was more than capable of cleaning myself up, getting dressed, and leaving before they woke up.

But with Callum, it was different. What just happened was so rushed, so emotional, that I felt like I needed something—anything—to feel like he didn't hate me.

When we pulled up to the lake house, I wasn't surprised to see the three-story log house with huge windows looking out over the lake. We were secluded from everyone else, but still about ten miles from where the Jamesons' old boathouse used to be. The rain was still pouring down, creating ripples on the water and crashing waves. Leaves were picked up and blown around with each gust of wind. It was beautiful but haunting.

"Wow," I said in awe.

"Just once, I wish he'd pick a smaller house," Joe grumbled. "Look how many points of entry there are." He gestured towards the house in frustration as Callum parked.

Joe got out of the car, fighting the wind and rain as he ran up towards the front door. "You okay?" I asked Callum as he turned off the car and reached for the door handle.

"Are you?" he asked.

"Yeah?" I replied though it sounded more like a question than an answer. Callum leaned back in his seat before turning his head to look at me.

"I'm sorry that happened like that...all I can think of right now is how much you probably hate me."

I leaned forward and kissed him tenderly on the mouth, not caring how his lips didn't respond to mine or how he tasted like rain and mud. Callum had a lot of ideas about how the world was supposed to work. He thought love was this pretty little thing to treasure. He restricted himself to what he thought romance and affection were supposed to be. But that's not how it worked. Love was just this potent emotion that burst from the seams. It hurt, it moved, it healed. Callum needed healing, and there was nothing we could do to stop what had just happened. We were inevitable, he and I.

"I don't hate you. I loved what just happened. I'll love when it happens again. I'll love when you plan it out and when it's spontaneous. I'll love when it's gentle and slow, or rough and punishing. All I care about is that it's with you."

I didn't give Callum the opportunity to respond, because I knew he didn't necessarily understand what I was talking about. It would take a while for him to let go of his stringent code of conduct, and I was willing to wait and show him every dirty little piece of his soul and how it fit perfectly with mine.

Inside the house, Ryker was lounging on a leather couch. The lake house had an open concept layout. The kitchen was a bit outdated but still impressively large and well stocked, with a double stove and granite countertops. I didn't see Blaise or Gavriel, so I assumed that they were working on something. Callum kissed my cheek then disappeared down a dark hallway.

"Were you mud wrestling?" Ry asked before standing up from the couch with a wince. His cheek was bruised, and his left eye was swollen. I noted a couple stitches on his jaw and was thankful for not watching his fight the night before. He moved like he was sore, but still managed to make his way over to me to wrap me up in a hug.

I shivered in his embrace, and he pulled away to stare at me more. The last time we'd spoken was still replaying in my mind, but I didn't want to focus on that; I wanted a hot shower and some comfort.

As if reading my mind, he said, "Let's get you all cleaned up."

My room had the best view. I was sure the guys planned it that way. I took a moment to stare outside, breathing on the window pane and letting the glass fog up. Branches looked like they were going to snap from the wind.

The attached bathroom had a free-standing tub with white tile and a walk-in shower. Windows lined the shower wall, showing off the beautiful view, but they were tinted so no one could see us bathe.

Ryker turned on the water for the double showerhead, and hot steam started to fill the room. I made quick work of getting out of my wet clothes as Ry watched in fascination.

"I'm kind of pissed but also intrigued by all the marks on your body, Sunshine," Ryker said while removing his own clothes.

I gasped when I saw a collection of dark bruises along his ribs and stomach. Gavriel said he had won last night, but I guess it was a close match. Would I ever get used to his fighter lifestyle?

"I could say the same for you, Ry Baby." Ryker looked down at himself then trailed his hands along his defined washboard abs before smirking at me.

"I think you got yours in a much more interesting way than I got mine," was his response.

Shaking my head and biting my lip, I stepped in the shower and let the burning hot water thaw the chill in my muscles. Ryker followed close behind and stood under the second stream of water coming out from the shower head on the other side.

We watched each other for what felt like forever, never breaking eye contact as the water beat down on our backs. "You wanna talk about it?" Ryker finally asked.

Instead of answering, I turned around and grabbed the shampoo from the ledge near me. After pumping some in my hand, I began lathering my hair. Looking down, I watched the mud in my hair wash down the drain.

"Now I'm *very* intrigued," Ryker said while stepping forward. I felt fingers on my back running lines up and down. "You've got scratches all along your back. It looks hot as fuck."

"It's the bruises you can't see that you should be worried about," I said, instantly regretting my words. I was still raw about today. Seeing my grave had made me livid. I didn't honestly know what to say to Ryker. Callum's and my first time was nothing like what I'd expected. It was angry. He claimed me then fled. And although I accepted each part of my complicated relationships with all four of them, I didn't necessarily want to go into detail with Ryker about the most intense sex I'd ever had.

I felt Ryker go still at my back. Turning around, I took in the multiple bruises on him. "You look..." I began as the hot water continued to beat down on me, chasing away the shiver, "terrible."

Ryker's lip quirked up just a millimeter, but I saw the amusement he was trying to hide. "That's not necessarily what any man wants to hear when he's naked in front of a woman," he replied.

I rolled my eyes and wrapped my arms around him. I still wasn't sure how to act. I kept messing things up. "Have you been crying?" he asked me before kissing my temple.

"Did you know my parents have a gravestone for me?" I asked. I wasn't sure why, out of everything that had happened there, I was still clinging to that. It was like my father was standing there triumphantly, and I was just the ghost of the girl that died in that basement.

Ryker stopped hugging me to pull away and stare at my expression. "What?" he asked incredulously, and I saw the rage on his face despite the swelling and bruises. "That's fucked up," he finally choked out.

I bit my lip and looked down at the floor of the shower, knowing that I couldn't look him in the eye as I said what I needed to say. "I don't know why it affects me as much as it does. In the grand scheme of things, it's not the worst that he's done. If anything, I'm being a little ridiculous. What kind of person focuses on that when their mother died a couple weeks ago?"

Ryker began massaging my arms. A small moan escaped my lips as he rubbed little circles along the muscle. "I think it's normal," he said. Ryker gently guided me to spin back around and began massaging my back. "Back when I lived with my dad, I would find myself staring in the mirror after one of our...fights." Ryker's voice didn't waver as he spoke about his father, but I knew better. He was strong in all things, but talking about his dad still bothered him.

"I used to count the bruises. I would stare at the dark, discolored spots along my stomach and rib cage. I would press on them, pour peroxide on the cuts, and enjoy how it burned," he said. His voice was even as he dipped his fingers to my lower back and rubbed the knots of tension there. "I liked the visible proof of my survival. I liked to feel the ache. The soreness. Sometimes, we just have to prove to ourselves that we're still here. So you're not going to hear any judgment from me, Sunshine."

I rolled my neck as the water streamed down my breasts. The walk-in shower was full of steam now, and my chill from earlier had melted entirely into desire for Ryker.

"I survived," I said, mostly to myself. I still couldn't figure out why I was so determined to prove that. For five years, I didn't care if the rest of the world knew whether or not I was alive or dead, but being back with the Bullets and seeing that no one knew how much of a victim I was, genuinely disturbed me.

For so long, I'd been running from my past, convinced that nothing could stop my father. And now that I was starting to have hope for justice, I was angry. I was mad that my story had been twisted into something that put my father and mother in a positive light. People felt sorry for them. People loved them through my disappearance, but no one loved me. No one except Nix, that is.

I had no idea that by finally opening the floodgates of my truth and telling the Bullets what had happened, I'd want to tell the rest of the world too. It wasn't enough just to kill my father. "What if I want other people to see my bruises?" I asked. "What if I want the world to see the evidence of what he's done?"

Ryker stopped massaging my back and spun me around to face him. His lip was cut from his fight the night before, but I still found myself wanting to kiss him. "I'll do whatever you want, Sunshine," he said. His voice was husky but tender. "If you want the world to know, I'll shout it out for you. And if you want this to be quiet revenge, I'll do that too."

I leaned in and kissed Ryker on the neck, silently thanking him for being so understanding and saying all the things I needed to hear. I turned back around to face the tiled wall, pressing my back into his chest. He reached over me and removed the handheld showerhead from its perch and began running the water over my back, washing away the soap suds. He had me so turned on that I couldn't think or talk. All I wanted was to feel his body against mine.

I let out a little whimper as he massaged my breasts with one hand and directed the spray of the water at my stomach. "I want to fuck you from behind right now. I want to dig my teeth into the skin of your shoulders and back."

I squirmed and arched my back, pressing closer, and he wrapped his free arm around my middle, securing me tightly against him. "But I think lately the world has been taking a lot from you. So I'm going to give that wet pussy of yours some relief."

"So you're done punishing yourself and holding back?" I asked.

"If you can face your demons and come here, then I sure as fuck can get over my shit and make this easier on you." I felt his lips on the back of my neck as he aimed the shower-head lower, directing it between my thighs at my clit. Fuck. Yes. Ryker kept me steady as my legs shook. He led a trail of kisses along the scratches on my back. It stung where he touched me, but I didn't care.

"Feels too intense," I cried out as my sensitive nub seemed to protest. I felt too much, too soon. I was past the point of going back, but Ryker was determined to slam me against my threshold of pleasure.

"I'm going to kiss you in all the places you ache, Sunshine," Ryker said in a husky voice as he continued to lick and suck every single scratch and bruise that hurt. It wasn't just my body he was comforting, it was my soul. He held me still, coaxing each little thing I was frustrated about with his words. He was demanding that I deal.

"God, it's so intense," I said through gritted teeth. Ryker might want to make this about me, but he was determined to do it on his terms. There was nothing about Ryker that wasn't punishing. Even his bliss came with stipulations. Ryker wasn't like the others. He was selfish but self-assured. He was accepting but determined to make his mark on my soul. He was determined to be unforgettable. I was thankful for this moment because it forced him to stop treating me like the broken girl he once knew, and more like the woman I'd become.

"I'm so close," I said in an airy tone while focusing on my breathing. I'd never been one to announce an orgasm, but I wanted Ryker to know. He was enjoying hearing my cries of intensity.

"You're going to come so hot for me, Sunshine," he growled into my ear. The unrelenting tension building up in my body was too intense, too carnal. And as if summoned by his words, I shattered in his arms, crying out as he kept the water pressure held on me, making it feel so good, my body literally couldn't handle anymore.

It wasn't until I went limp that he pulled back, and I sank in relief. Every bone in my body was loose, it was like I'd spent hours stretching. I'd relaxed in the purest way. Ryker forced all the tension in my mind and body to explode within me, leaving me empty but satisfied. I tried to protest, eyeing the bruises on his ribs and stomach, but Ryker still picked me up to cradle me anyways. "My Sunshine. So perfect," he murmured before carrying me out of the shower.

6

CALLUM MUST HAVE LEFT while we were in the shower, because he was nowhere to be found when we finally emerged from the bathroom. Ryker made sure to make me come two more times before I nearly blacked out. He was relentless, tentative, and everything I needed after my intense morning with Callum. We then snuggled on the couch in silence, not bothering to turn on the TV. We merely watched the rain pour down outside while enjoying the comfort of one another.

Gavriel and Blaise arrived an hour later carrying paper sacks with the logo for Virginia's Diner on the front. The moment I saw them, I shot out of Ryker's arms and ran to grab the food from their hands. "Oh my gosh! I haven't had this in ages!" I squealed, all too happy to enjoy the mediocre food of my favorite diner.

Blaise looked at me then chuckled. "You're more excited about the food than seeing me. I'm not sure how I feel about that," he said in a teasing tone. There was something off about his voice though. Like he was forcing himself to sound lighthearted. I gave him a swift kiss on the cheek before settling onto a stool at the kitchen island and unloading the contents of the bags. Gavriel moved to the sink to wash his hands.

"Food will always be my first love, Blaise. I thought you knew this?" I chuckled while shifting on the wobbly bar stool. "Where were you guys?" I asked while biting back another squeal at the sight of my favorite dessert: pumpkin pie with homemade whipped cream on top. I dived in, not waiting for their response. It wasn't until my mouth was sufficiently stuffed that I looked up from my plate to stare at my men. I was expecting some quip about how much food I'd managed to consume in mere seconds, but instead, all that greeted me was nervous concern.

"What's going on?" I asked, sitting back in my chair and crossing my arms over my chest. I was wearing one of Ryker's shirts that smelled like his cologne, and my hair was a mess of untamed waves.

"We have to go back to New York. The cabin search is canceled for now," Gavriel answered before shutting off the water. He slowly made his way towards the mess of carry out then went rifling through one of the bags. When he pulled out a salad, I all but rolled my eyes. Gavriel was a health nut.

"Why? Catch another lead?" I asked.

Gavriel ran a hand through his hair and brushed his lip with his thumb. He was wearing dark denim and a black shirt. If I weren't so excited about the food, I would have found *him* delicious. "Nix called," was his answer.

"...and?" I prodded. I didn't like where this conversation was going, and I started to wonder if this food was supposed to soften the blow of some bad news. It was something the guys regularly did when we were younger. Prom night, I came down with the flu and couldn't attend. They couldn't come over because Mom and Dad were home, but we got an anonymous delivery of soup that night.

"Paul Bright got on a plane at noon and arrived here a little over an hour ago. We don't know why he's here, but we do know we need to get you away from him."

I swallowed, my mouth suddenly feeling very dry. This was a pivotal moment. I could succumb to the flashbacks that assaulted me anytime I saw my father, or I could prove to my men that I was strong—that I could handle it. "So? Why do we have to leave?" I asked, making sure to keep my voice even and composed.

"Because I don't want that rat bastard anywhere near you," Ryker growled.

I played with my fork, scraping it against the plastic container of food while processing what was happening. I was concerned, yes, but more so, I was curious. Did he know we were onto him? "I need to call Callum and let him know," I began before shifting to get off my stool. Even though things had been weird for us after the cemetery, I still thought he ought to know.

"He is already aware," Gavriel said in a clipped tone, seemingly displeased.

"What do you mean he's 'aware?'" I asked.

"He knew Callum was here and invited him to dinner. He's got something up his sleeve," Blaise explained.

"All the more reason to leave," Ryker added.

I didn't like knowing that Callum was enjoying a civilized dinner with a serial killer, but there wasn't much that we could do. Until we made our move, Callum had a part to play—we all did. And my part was to be invisible.

"I want to find the cabin. What if we go now? While Callum has him occupied?" I stood up, stretching while refusing to meet their gazes.

"I'll be honest," Blaise finally spoke. He moved around the kitchen island to stand by me. Grasping my elbow, he gave me a brief look of solidarity before continuing. "I'd been considering that. But it's dark and stormy, I think we should stick with our original plan and go in the morning. What could he possibly do?"

"The whole point of us going is so Callum could find some evidence to pin on Bright, and even that was a moot point. I don't even think there's anything there. Men like him and Santobello don't leave behind messes or clues." Gavriel pushed his plate aside then began rolling up his sleeves. "I wish you'd both abandon his need to do this his way."

"I promised him a month. I want to do that for him. And as for the cabin? I want to go for me," I said. "Sometimes, I doubted myself that it was real. Let's go and figure out what we can. Even if we find nothing, at least we could..." I didn't continue the last words. I couldn't say that I wanted to find *myself*. Blaise squeezed me once more as if knowing what I was too cowardly to say. I felt so disconnected lately, unsure of what I was doing or who I was.

"I think it's fucking stupid," Ryker finally said. "You need more time to...cope. I didn't really support this to begin with, and I sure as hell don't support it now." I knew that there was no point in arguing with Ryker. He wasn't the sort to let up. Instead, I looked to Gav. Ultimately, he'd be the one to decide.

"Okay, Gav," I said while letting out a slow exhale. "Tell me what to do." He licked his lips, a slight smile marring his severe frown. Every time I displayed a level of trust, that cocky teen from our youth would reappear, rewarding me with a smile for trusting him. He stared at me, analyzing my expression, taking in the calm way I relinquished control. If he thought I could handle it, I could. If he didn't, then I couldn't. It wasn't necessarily that I was one way or the other. It was his faith in me that made all the difference. We were symbiotic in that way. I trusted him, he believed in me.

"If we go, will you stay by my side at all times?" Thunder crashed outside, echoing his point.

"Yes, sir," I replied, no hint of teasing in my tone. This was an exercise of trust, and I was more than willing to play.

"Will you tell me if you feel uncomfortable or feel a panic attack coming on?"

"Yes, sir."

Ryker began pacing back and forth. "You can't be serious," he growled.

"Let's get this over with. I think this would be good for all of us. It's time for Sunshine to prove how much she can handle. And maybe if we find nothing, Callum will stop clinging to the idea that we can do this his way."

I let out a breath I didn't even know I was holding. What did it say about me that I was willing to go to the scene of the trauma? Everything I did made me wonder if I was like him. Maybe this could prove once and for all that Paul Bright didn't mold me in his image. I broke the mold long ago. "We'll stick to the plan and go in the morning. But the moment we're done, we're out of here," Gavriel added.

Ryker and Gavriel argued for a bit longer as I got dressed for bed.

"Ms. Bright, come here," Joe said from the corner of the room. He was eyeing Gavriel and Ryker with annoyance but stopped staring when I got there.

"Did you eat anything?" he asked. I turned to look longingly at the abandoned food on the table then shook my head. After learning that Callum was with my dad, nothing sounded good.

"Did you?" I asked.

He rolled his eyes at my question as if the idea of me fussing over him were preposterous. "Here," he said while handing me a revolver in a hip holster. "Tell me you know how to use it."

The truth was, I didn't. I slept with a knife when I lived on the streets, but I avoided buying a gun. It wasn't that the weapon scared me, it was that I didn't like how much power it gave the person wielding it. Paul Bright's blood ran through my veins, and I didn't trust myself with that sort of authority. Authority was what twisted him into what he'd become, and it would be what ruined me.

"Nope."

Joe let out a huff of exasperation. "How did you survive for so long? Any street rat with a lick of sense can handle a gun." He took it back then started digging in the pockets of his jacket, pulling out a small but sharp knife.

"You know what to do with this?" he asked in a mocking tone. Even though he was being sarcastic, I detected a hint of warm affection hidden behind the annoyance.

"I don't need a weapon, Joe. I wouldn't be able to..."

His eyes softened for a split second before slipping back into hardness. "When I got back from my third tour, I slept with a gun. I had nothing to fear, but there was something comforting about feeling the cool metal beneath my pillow. I've noticed how you cope. You get hyper-focused on your surroundings. When we get there, you put this knife in your hand."

He placed the handle in my palm as if to further his point. "Count the grooves in the handle. Rub your thumb along its edges. Place the cool blade against your thigh and put all your attention on how it feels."

I felt my neck break out in a sweat at his words. "Focus on the thing that'll save you instead of what can kill you, *capiche*?"

It was the most Joe had ever said to me and was probably one of the most profound life lessons I'd ever heard.

"Can I adopt you as my Godfather?" I asked in response, lightening the mood. Joe tended to flee when emotions were involved, so I wanted to reward his thoughtful advice with an easy answer, even though I was feeling a bit more attached. I had enough daddy issues to last a lifetime, but Joe was someone I once again found myself wishing would adopt me.

"No," he said, deadpan, before stalking towards the front door.

I stared at everyone as they discussed the plans for tomorrow until Blaise gestured for me to follow him to bed. I lingered, staring at the room with uncertainty as I ran my thumb along the ridges in the knife's handle. One. Two. Three. Breathe in, breathe out.

"Let's go to bed, Sunshine," he called out to me.

"Be right there."

7

DESPITE BLAISE'S comforting arms wrapped around me all night in our cozy room as it rained, I strained to listen for Callum's arrival. I couldn't think straight, knowing that he was having dinner with my father. I was angry that after our time in the cemetery, he went to him instead of comforting me, even though I knew why he had to. It wasn't until four in the morning that I heard footsteps down the hallway from my room. I got out of bed and tripped over Blaise's boots on the floor to catch who was outside.

I opened my bedroom door just in time to see a blond head of hair disappear into the bedroom across the hall. I wished that I could have spoken to Callum, asked how he was doing, and seen for myself if he was okay, but I kept my mouth shut. I hated how uncertain things were between us. How could one day change so much? When I got back to bed, Blaise nuzzled into my neck, breathing me in as I tried to calm my racing heart. I was teetering somewhere between feeling pride at my ability to conquer my fears and this sick sense of dread. Everything felt off. Like we were teetering on the edge of disaster, and there was nothing to do but tip the scales.

"You okay?" Blaise asked, his voice warm as he spoke against my skin. His lips were chapped and rough against me, making me shiver.

"I'm worried about Callum."

Blaise pulled away, shifting to hover half of his body over me while stroking my lips with his thumb. Our legs were a tangled mess of limbs. "My little Sunshine, always so worried about everyone else. You're the one about to face some pretty fucked up memories. Let Callum worry about himself."

I opened my mouth to protest. "I just..."

"You know I'll tell you how it is, right?" Blaise asked before kissing my forehead. "I've got chronic honesty. Doctors say there's no cure," he said with a smirk that made me want to kiss him. I nodded. "Even when we were kids, you'd spend all of your time focusing on us so you could ignore the shit bothering you. I'm not going to let you make yourself sick worrying about us because it's easier than worrying about yourself."

I pursed my lips, wanting to disagree with him, but he was right. The Bullets crashed into my life when I was at the height of unhappiness at home. I focused on them, learned about them, and internalized their struggles because it was easier than processing my own. Even now, I was more concerned with how they were responding to this crazy situation than how I was coping.

"Five years ago, I was okay with you pouring all your attention on us. I was a selfish fuck and wanted to take whatever pieces of you I could. But I've grown up some since then, and I love you enough not to let you use me—us —anymore."

"But what if I *want* to use you?" I asked with a small

smile, knowing that it was easier to be coy than respond to his declaration. I'd never considered him or the others as selfish, but maybe he was right? Perhaps it was time for me to focus on myself.

"You look absolutely kissable right now. How about one last distraction, for old time's sake," he purred before lowering to kiss my lips. Moaning into his mouth, I immediately responded to his kiss, matching pressure for pleasure with my movements. When he pulled away, I found myself pouting. "Promise me you'll take some time for self-care?" Blaise asked. It was infuriatingly sweet how well he knew me—how well he knew what I needed.

"I promise," I replied before grabbing his sleep shirt and pulling him back to me. We didn't sleep much after that. We mostly spent the morning kissing each other and talking about the things I wanted to do but have been too scared to vocalize. Blaise mentioned me going back to school, and I kissed him to ignore the sadness I felt. Right now, going to college and trying to pick up where I left off felt inauthentic to the girl I'd become. I didn't know what I wanted, I just knew I wanted them.

As I got dressed, I made sure to put the knife Joe gave me in the back pocket of my black pants. The tall rubber boots I wore would be perfect for wading through the mud. The rain lasted long through the night, and I bet we'd be in the thick of it today. Blaise met Ryker outside, gathering shovels and supplies should we need to break into the house.

In the kitchen, Gavriel was making breakfast, and I smiled at how domesticated my big, bad mob boss looked, leaning over the stove and flipping pancakes. It was a sight I wanted to wake up to daily. "Smells good," I said, my voice weary with lack of sleep. My lips were swollen from all the kissing Blaise and I did. We were like two teenagers, grinding against one another and exploring the boundaries of foreplay. I'm sure my skin was still flushed, and the pony-tail I'd put my hair up in did little to hide how flustered I felt.

When Gavriel looked at me with his exploratory gaze, I refrained from rolling my eyes. He was taking in each aspect of my appearance and cataloging it in his crazy, overprotective brain. "You look like you got no sleep," he said before giving Blaise a scolding stare.

"I was worried about Callum, is he up yet?" I asked while spinning around to look down the hall, wincing once I realized that I was doing precisely what Blaise told me not to. I couldn't change a lifetime of concern in one night.

"He should be out soon. Is everything okay between you two?" Gavriel didn't skirt around the hard questions, he just bulldozed through my defenses and hit my memories with a punch.

Ah, the man I knew was back.

"We fucked at the cemetery yesterday," I said in a nonchalant tone, but I knew that he'd hear the slight way my voice wavered.

"Oh really?" Gavriel asked while setting down the spatula he was holding to brace himself against the kitchen island. He wasn't wearing his usual suit and button down shirt. Sweatpants hung low on his body, and the black shirt he wore was tight enough to show off every carefully crafted crevice on his body.

"Really."

Ever since our reunion, there was this unspoken understanding that they were okay with sharing me, and since revealing the trauma from my past, no one seemed willing to broach the subject once more. For now, we were just...surviving.

However, Callum seemed to be on the outside of that agreement. Gavriel initiated him as a Bullet against his will, but was he truly one of them? Would they share me at all, let alone with him?

I saw my uncertainty reflected in Gavriel's eyes. There was a war going on in his dark gaze. Gavriel dived into his need to take care of those he loved. He claimed and led with an iron fist, clinging to his control because it was the only thing in this world that was certain. "I told you I'd give you all the things you're too afraid to ask for," Gavriel said before straightening and picking up his spatula.

"I'll take care of you, Love. But with that comes removing the things you're too scared to lose. I'm going to give him—and you—time to navigate this. But at the end of the day, I'll do what's best for you. I'll *always* do what's best for you."

I swallowed as Gavriel turned around and resumed pouring batter into the frying pan with an easygoing posture, as if he hadn't just taken my heart out and stomped on it. I knew that Gavriel would do what was best for me. Giving him that sort of control over my life had its consequences. But it still hurt, and the idea of not having Callum anymore left me feeling gutted. Could Callum let go of his guilt and truly accept the darker parts of himself? The parts of himself that wanted me more than he wanted normalcy?

With his back to me, Gavriel then called over his shoulder, "You hear that, Officer Mercer?"

I spun around to face Callum, nervous about how much he'd heard. His hair was wet like he'd just gotten out of the shower, and he was clutching a jacket to his chest, squeezing the material like it had personally offended him.

"Loud and clear," he growled out before settling at the kitchen island beside me.

There was an entire summer I lived at the library. I bathed in the bathroom sink, napped on one of the couches in their reading lounge. It was my home, my safe haven. The public library was like a homeless shelter full of books. Since I was spending a lot of time there, I spent every waking moment reading. I studied trauma first. I wanted to understand what my mind was going through; I tried to hack my way out of a painful situation and get back to being a healthy, functioning human being.

I'd read once that when a person experiences severe trauma, sometimes the brain warped your memories. It twisted your perceptions into a pretty little box that was more manageable.

That scared me almost as much as my father did.

I didn't want to forget. I didn't want my brain to compartmentalize my experience into smaller, easier to chew bites. I forced myself to get better and swallow the bitter pill that was my experience, because the alternative was forgetting what my father was capable of.

But now, sitting in the SUV Gavriel rented for the weekend while driving up the main highway near the lake, I doubted myself, wondering if I made it all up. What if my brain had tricked me into believing that I got away? There was a gravesite with my name on it. Maybe this was all an elaborate joke.

"I swear it was here," I choked out. My eyes were starting to water as we drove. My fingers shook as I clutched my knees. The road I'd taken to escape the cabin was gone. "It was just right here, I know it."

By now, I was mostly talking to myself, willing my brain to remember everything that had happened five years ago. I didn't look around the car, knowing that looks of sympathy and annoyance would greet me. My chest grew tight as Gavriel pulled yet another U-turn on the road. Muddy tracks covered the pavement, and I focused on breathing in and out.

"Sunshine, if you want, we can go back and rest for a while. We don't have to..." Blaise offered.

"Stop the car," I pleaded while knotting my sweater in my lap. My fingers were cold, and when I stepped out of the too-suffocating car, I let out a short scream of frustration, my cries sharp and crisp in the chilly air. It was real, wasn't it? My perceptions of what was real and what wasn't were starting to get warped. My mind and my memories were betraying me.

I wrapped my arms around myself while staring at the sky. To my left, memories of my phone call to my mother flashed in my mind's eye. Right there, next to that sign welcoming everyone to Chesterbrook was where I parked and cried for her to save me. Right there was where she denied me, where she picked her fear of Paul Bright over me.

"It was right here," I whispered, mostly to myself. Ryker had his arms crossed over his chest as he stared at me while Joe kept an eye on the road. Gavriel and Callum stayed behind in the car. From here, I could see that they were arguing about something, despite the tinted windows. Gavriel had grabbed the collar of Callum's shirt and yanked him closer to look Gav in the eye. I took a step to intervene, but a gentle hand on my shoulder stopped me. Blaise.

"Remember what I said...worry about yourself today,

Sunshine," he whispered. I wanted to curse him and stomp forward anyways, using anything to get my mind off the fact that the drive leading to the cabin had disappeared. But just before I could, Callum got out of the passenger seat and made his way towards me, a determined look on his face.

"Summ-Sunshine. Baby. Look at me," he said before pulling me in for a hug. "Close your eyes," he instructed. I didn't really care what we were doing, the fact that he was finally holding me meant that things were getting better, right? Even if Gavriel was forcing him to do this, I didn't care. I greedily took his comfort.

"Think about where you were. Think about the smells. The scenery."

I dropped back into that forgotten part of my brain, the part that hid away the sordid details. It was unseasonably humid that day. It smelled like fresh dirt. Dad's car smelled like cigarettes and rust. The leaves were green. The road was...rocky.

I opened my eyes and pulled away from his hug to go inspect a small clearing in the trees that looked oddly placed in the woods. Looking around at the men staring at me, I then walked over to the clearing and bent over, inspecting the mud.

I heard a car door slam behind me, but instead of turning to look, I began digging. Dirt seeped under my nails, and I sunk to my knees, the cold, wet earth making my denim pants wet. I probably looked like a mad woman, playing in the mud, searching for the road to hell. I kept digging through the mud until my fingers hit rock. Shoving all the dirt aside, I smiled when I saw the white gravel beneath.

"Good job, Baby," Callum said as I let out a sigh of relief. This was real. I was real. Sometime during my digging, he had moved to stand over me. My protector. I turned to look at Callum and itched to hug him once more, but he shied away.

Guess he was only okay with comforting me when it suited him.

"I'm not trying to avoid a hug. You're covered in mud," he said as if reading my mind. I looked down at my jeans and legs then laughed.

Ryker traveled further up the muddy trail and crouched down a little ways away. "There are tracks here," he called out over his shoulder, and we all followed him.

Sure enough, distinct tire markings were deep in the mud here. They were fresh too. Sometime last night, someone with large tires drove through then somehow covered up their tracks near the main road.

"Do you think whoever it was is still there?" I asked in a shaky voice. My father was in town. If he were here, then things would come to a head much sooner than we'd initially thought. Ryker stood, dusting his hands off on his thighs before exchanging a predatory look with Gavriel. His determined expression was haunting beneath his bruised skin, which showed just how familiar with pain he was.

Cracking his knuckles, he finally answered me. "We'll sure as fuck find out."

8

I COULDN'T FORCE myself to feel anything as I walked through the woods. I tried, I really did. I wanted to feel fear, at least. It would show that I was alive. Maybe even curiosity? I could work with curiosity. I tried to conjure regret. Remorse. Grief. But since seeing the proof of the road, all I could feel was numbness. My pesky mind was doing that protective shield thing again, anticipating emotions too strong for me to handle. I was thankful for it, really. Because at least this meant I could prove to The Bullets that I could handle this.

I was in self-preservation mode and wrapped up in a destructive blanket. I was a shell, going through the motions and preparing for the inevitable fall, the crash and burn that I just knew was on the horizon. Why did I let Gavriel convince me to do this? How could I claim my power when there was none left to claim?

The muddy ground made my boots sink deep in the earth with each step, almost like even the woods didn't want me to continue. The whispering trees knew something I didn't, begging me to stay back. My intuition was telling me

—screaming at me—to turn around and let go of the past. Did anything good ever come from digging up forgotten history? Each struggling step had me gasping for air.

I felt a hand on mine as I struggled to lift my boot through a particularly muddy section. The calloused palm guided me through the slippery terrain, pulling me upright. It was Ryker, strong despite his soreness and bruises, helping me through. Callum was on my left, wading through the mud with about as much ease as I was. Where I sank through each staggering step, he persevered through, determined to get to the end of this road.

"What did you and my father talk about last night?" I asked, breaking the silence with Ryker's grip still firmly on my elbow. I knew the hard questions would make me feel something again, but I didn't care. I was curious. I was grasping at straws.

Callum sucked in a deep breath, and I noticed Gavriel giving him a warning stare from over his shoulder, as if daring him to say something that would make me spiral. We should have never come here.

"First, he talked about politics. Then he talked about...your mom. I think he was trying to gauge if I blamed him? He seemed manic." Callum's voice was distant as he thought back on the night before. Something was off about his tone. "But it was when I was leaving that things got...weird. He asked if I was going to the cemetery and told me to tell you hello..."

I stopped walking, my heart like a hammer in my chest. Gavriel let out a curse then spun around to glare at Callum, his hand resting on the gun in his holster. "I'm not going to sugar coat this for her," Callum said to him, spit flying from his lips. There was no bite to his tone, only hopeless resignation.

"He knows I'm here," I whispered as Ryker pulled me

closer to him, as if to shield my body with his own. Slowly, tiny nudges of emotion made themselves known but never fully broke the surface. Terror. Sadness. Anxiousness. I took a moment to lean into Ryker, stealing a bit of his strength for myself. And my mind, being the powerful thing it was, shut each emotion down as I straightened my spine.

"Good," I finally said before trudging forward, even more determined to get to the cabin. "He should be scared. He's getting reckless, showing his hand."

Gavriel cocked his head to the side, squinting in disbelief at me as a raven flew past. The sounds of his caw and wings slicing through the chilly air were haunting. My labored breath made a steady fog fill the space around me as I heaved. The mud soaked through the knees of my pants, making me shiver as we continued our trek. I started to take in my surroundings, the barren branches, the distance between us and the car. The mud would be a problem if I had to run, but I could roll in a pinch...

"You okay?" Ryker asked as I remembered Joe's words last night.

With a steadying breath, I answered him, "Yeah." Instead of obsessing over the forest, I pulled the knife from my pocket and started to touch the edge of the blade, running my thumb across it and smiling as I counted the notches in the handle.

One. I was safe. We had a team of people.

Two. I was in charge of my emotions, I was the master of my own brain.

Three. This cabin had no power over me.

"I don't recognize you when you look like that," Ryker whispered as we walked. I'd almost forgotten that he was still clutching my elbow.

"What do you mean?"

"I've seen it a couple of times now. You go to this place of determination unlike anything I've ever seen before."

I became self-conscious of my expression, wondering if there was a look in my eyes or a frown on my face. "I don't feel any different," I replied honestly.

Ryker stopped, pulling me with him as the rest of the group continued. "Sometimes, I think there are two versions of you, each fighting for dominance. When you get determined like that, I get to see the woman you were when you went on the run."

"Do you like her better, Ry?" I asked. My voice was soft and for some unknown reason, I feared his answer.

"I love all of you, Sunshine. It makes me feel less guilty, seeing you so strong. But then it makes me scared too. Like whenever you slip into that role, I lose the girl I knew. I also hate myself a bit for wanting you to be dependent on me. Gavriel wants to see you strong so he won't worry about breaking you, but I wanna see you weak so you never have a reason to leave."

I focused on a tree beside us, zeroing in on the bark and each groove in the rough trunk as I considered his words. "Well, I guess it's a good thing I have all of you then. Because there will be times I'll want Gav to break me, as well as times I want you to build me up." I looked ahead of us where the rest of the group, excluding Joe, had kept going. "Blaise is my safe place to land, my constant comfort."

"What about Callum?" Ryker asked. There wasn't jealousy in his tone, only curiosity. How did I get so lucky to have men that weren't bleeding with dissatisfaction over who my heart loved? Would they ever stop being okay with this dynamic?

"He's different. I'm still learning his place, if I'm being honest. I think, with how much I need the three of you, he's the only one that truly needs me back. It's kind of freeing." I turned to look at Callum in the distance, slipping on a muddy patch as he marched forward.

Ryker nodded his head thoughtfully before looking off after them too. "I think you're right, Sunshine. And something tells me he's going to need you a lot here pretty soon."

It wasn't until we saw a clearing in the woods that my breathing started to pick up, my coping mechanisms working overtime to wade through the familiar surroundings. Joe bent over, looking at the tire tracks in the mud and furrowing his brow when he saw that they turned off to the left and disappeared.

"Whoever was here isn't anymore," he said, mostly to himself. I peeled my eyes looking around the empty lot with disdain. It was supposed to be here, but all I could see was the leveled ground and fresh dirt covering the plot where my father's cabin was supposed to be.

"Fuck," Gavriel said while inching forward. I leaned to the left to peer around Joe's bulky frame, Ryker keeping his hold steady on me as I looked. There, in the middle of the plot where I'm sure the basement would have been located, was a teal box with a white bow on top. It was small, only about the size of my fist, but it looked too clean, too perfect to be a coincidence.

"Gav, don't touch it," I called out. Ryker tucked me into his side, wincing when I touched his bruised ribs but keeping his face stern and ready to act. I recognized the color, it was one of Mom's favorite shades of teal.

Gavriel didn't care; he stormed forward through the open lot with anger rolling off of him in waves. I cringed as he bent down to pick up the box, and Blaise moved to my vacant side, entwining his fingers with mine before whispering in my ear, "You're so strong, Sunshine. I'm in awe of you."

Blaise, always so sweet.

I couldn't see if Gavriel had opened the box yet, and Callum made his way over to him, joining in on the curiosity of the situation. "It was real," I whispered to myself while viewing the empty lot. "I swear it was here."

I knew that the house had been torn down. The area where no trees grew and the gravel road were evidence enough of that. But it was like I had to vocalize the truth of its existence. Paul Bright was good at playing mind games, tricking you into questioning reality then molding it to fit his perfect and prim world. The cabin was here, once, even if I couldn't see it. I could sense the evil that had happened here. I could feel the ghosts of his victims traveling over my skin, dragging the knives of my survival over my chest. The ghosts were mad that I got away when they couldn't. This was my penance.

A low, guttural scream caught my attention, and I detached myself from Ryker and Blaise before pushing past Joe to get to Gavriel and Callum.

Callum, my sweet Callum, was kneeling in the mud, sobbing into his hands with the teal box discarded at his side. I ran to him, the muddy earth once again pulling me back, begging me not to learn what had broken him.

"He did it," Callum cried out, his body shaking from the sobs wrecking his chest. He laid down on his side in the mud, burying himself into the ground with each movement while trying to hide from me, hide from the world. Gavriel looked...shocked. He wore an expression of sincere regret. I sensed that from here on out, everything would change. Callum would never be the same, and by the look in Gavriel's eyes, he felt responsible for the turmoil.

"What happened?" I asked, placing a hand on Callum's shoulder. But instead of answering me, he shrugged me off, swatting me away as I shied away in confusion.

"He killed them," Callum sobbed. I made my way over to

the box, squatting lower to look at the contents of it, immediately regretting my decision to explore once I recognized what was inside. There, tucked neatly in the box, was a keychain. Not just any keychain, it was woven out of bright green and black rope. To anyone else, it would have been anticlimactic to see, but I saw it for what it was. It was a threat, a warning to keep away.

It was the keychain Callum made for his mother in middle school. She'd always had it, I recognized the handmade gift immediately. It was the same keychain that was in their car the night his parents were in their freak accident. And looking back, I realized that it probably wasn't an accident at all.

The realization of what this meant hit me like a kick to the gut. It suddenly clicked—my mother had confided in someone. She tried to get help when she'd first discovered my father's activities. She told me that they'd died. I had no idea that it was Callum's parents. My family was the reason Callum was so alone in this world.

"He knew we'd come here," I said in disbelief. "He wanted you to see..."

Callum let out another sob, not caring if he looked weak. Not caring where we were or what we were doing. He looked so small then. I didn't see the grown man he'd become, I saw the young boy I knew as a child. I saw the kid that would pull on my pigtails while our mothers gossiped. I saw the young man I had a crush on. I saw the college student huddling in the corner of my parents' shed, grieving the parents he lost.

I saw loneliness. I saw pain.

Then I saw myself.

I knew right then that we'd never come back from this. All I had from Callum now was regret and a punishing fuck in a graveyard. He'd always look at me and see *him*.

I turned around to leave him grieving alone. I knew my being near was just going to cause him more pain. I saw the writing on the wall, my own coping skills dissolving into a gut wrenching sadness. Gavriel warned me that he would take Callum away from me if he wasn't good for me. Well, at this moment, I wasn't good for Callum, and I had to get away from him. I had to save him from *me.*

I turned and fast walked through the clearing, passing a shocked Blaise and angry Ryker. I passed trees and fallen leaves, I passed the muddy tracks where my father had driven through. I heard huffs of labored breathing and knew someone was following me. I wondered who stayed behind with Callum. Would they comfort him? Would they hold him while he cried? Curse my father alongside him?

I know I would have. I would have been everything for him.

But that's the thing about love. A deep soul connection wasn't selfish. And even though I wanted to be there for him, I wanted him to be okay more. So I kept walking until we were at the SUV. After getting in the back, I kept my eyes on the floorboard until the driver side door shut. Joe settled in and rubbed his cold hands together. I looked around, wondering where Blaise, Ryker, and Gavriel were. Joe, seeming to understand my questioning expression then said in a low voice, "Bullets stick together."

I exhaled in relief. Maybe I should have craved their comfort, wished that one had followed me, but I was too thankful that Callum had a support system to care. Bullets stuck together, and now, more than ever, Callum would need that. Even if he didn't want the Bullet family, he was a part of it. They'd pull him together.

"Mind telling me what just happened?" Joe asked. "My wife says I'm an insensitive fuck about things, but I just need to know if I should be on alert for something."

I looked out the window, watching the grey clouds roll back in. It was going to rain again, soon. Taking the knife Joe gave me, I grabbed it once more, running my thumb along each ridge in the handle until I could vocalize what had happened.

"My dad killed Callum's parents," I said in an emotionless tone. There were no tears. Just this all encompassing feeling of regret.

"Fuck," Joe said before looking around, taking in our surroundings on high alert. "You don't, like...need a hug or anything do you?" he asked, looking sheepish in the rearview mirror as he gazed at me.

"No, Joe. I don't."

9

CALLUM
Eight Years Ago

I'D NEVER BEEN to a funeral before. I thought they were like the movies, rain streaming down as men and women crowded you with looks of pity. But instead, it was sunny in Chesterbrook on the day my parents were put in their final resting place. Streams of sunshine beat down on our backs as we walked through the cemetery.

I thought everyone wore black suits and dresses. I thought it would be a somber affair. But to show solidarity with a dead man, all of the Chesterbrook Police Department wore their dress blues. So instead of black, there was nothing but a sea of navy at the church this afternoon, stoic faces in the pews. They were rigid, their stiff kevlar forcing them to sit up tall and proud as the preacher said nice things about my parents. We weren't churchgoers, and every polite comment was a generalization.

"She was a good mother."

"He was a selfless protector."

And the expressions? Those were the most jarring. I'd thought people would be as solemn as I, struggling to comprehend their grief. I had expected to see the evidence of their sadness. I wanted to know I wasn't alone, I wasn't the only one missing the two most important people in my life. But the crowd mostly looked curious; they seemed giddy to be at the most exclusive funeral of the year. Everyone wanted to look like they cared the most, to send the biggest flowers, offer the best frozen dish because their prized funeral casserole was somehow worth losing your family.

The caskets we buried were empty, a few handfuls of ash on silk pillows. They had picked their plots at the local cemetery years ago, determined to be together even in death. Their wills requested that they be buried. They planned for everything, but they didn't expect to burn in a car fire and leave nothing behind.

There were just two large portraits of them situated at the front of the church. I couldn't look at their photos, a vibrant echo of who they were. All that was left of them were memories and photographs. By the end of the week, the house wouldn't even be mine.

After the funeral, we went to the Bright's home for a post-funeral get-together. Mrs. Bright loved to host. "Any excuse to throw a party," she used to say to my mother. "You doing okay?" Mrs. Bright asked as she clasped her hand over mine with a frown. She was the only one that looked how I'd expect someone to look at a funeral. She loved my parents. It made me feel a hint of satisfaction to see her so miserable at their passing. "I'm tired of all this bullshit." My voice was a slow growl as I crushed my napkin into my fist. I was ready to get the hell out of here to drink something hard and avoid the fact that I was now all alone in this world.

"Callum...I'm so..."

I knew Mrs. Bright was going to say sorry; it was like people weren't creative enough to come up with different things to say in the face of death. They just recycled that little phrase of apology over and over until it lost its meaning. I wanted to ask, why are you sorry? You weren't the forgotten gas cans in my father's trunk. Or the loose ground wire that made Dad lose control of his car and slam into a tree. You weren't the random little spark that ignited. You weren't the fire that burned my parents until there was nothing left of them.

They should all just stop saying sorry.

And Mrs. Bright was saying sorry the most.

"Please stop saying that," I growled before she could finish her sentence. She turned her head, shock evident on her face as her brow shot up. There was red lipstick on her teeth, black circles under her eyes, and a frown on her face.

She then took a moment to look over the crowd of people in her living room, taking in the gossiping crowd at her post-funeral gathering. She then let out an exhale. "What do you want me to say, then?"

I took a second to look at Mrs. Bright, taking in her desperate stare. Everything about her seemed dull. "I want you to say I can leave—that I've fulfilled my obligation."

"Go. I'll make sure people leave you alone." Her answer was immediate like she couldn't wait to please me. I didn't stick around to give her a chance to change her mind.

I fled, traveling down the hallway and passing the crowds without a second glance. It wasn't until a hand shot out and hit my chest, holding me back, that I stopped. I was just feet away from the back door. "Callum, where you going?"

I looked to my left, staring at Paul Bright with annoy-ance. He'd been trying to treat me like his kid these last few days. Telling me what to do, what to say. It was odd, the way he'd so easily assumed that role. "Out," I said, barely containing the growl in my voice. I'd been raised to respect the Brights, and I wouldn't disrespect my parents by yelling at him, but I'd had enough.

"Now, Callum. Take a deep breath," Mr. Bright contin-ued, keeping his voice low and authoritative. His hand was still on my chest, holding me in place as his eyes roamed over my styled blond hair, grieving eyes, and pursed lips. "I know you're struggling, boy. Just remember to keep calm. We're no worse than animals if we can't control our impulses."

Mr. Bright leaned closer, blowing his breath in my face and sliding his hand up to cup my shoulder, pressing down as he tilted his head to the side. I could feel the way he wanted me to bend to his will. I knew he had some twisted sense of responsibility where my parents were concerned. I'm sure he wanted to be a guiding hand now that they were dead. But he didn't really want to help me, it was for his own ego.

"I got it, Paul," I said, using his first name. For my entire life, they were Mr. and Mrs. Bright, but I was a man now, and men didn't have to answer to anyone.

The six shots of Hennessy made the grief feel a bit more manageable. I couldn't drive. I might have been grieving, but I wasn't stupid enough to endanger others. So instead, I stormed into the Brights' backyard and hid in their shed. Although shaded by their large oak tree, it was still hot, and sweat rolled down my face as I sat in the sawdust on the wooden floor, my suit jacket sticking to me.

I discarded my tie, and it felt like I could finally breathe again. Sobs broke free, my chest a tight ball of anger and loss. Each cry of grief had me feeling like a pussy, but I didn't care enough to hold it back. These were ugly cries. I was sure that they'd stick with me. Years from now, I'd probably look back and remember how low it was possible to feel. Maybe I'd one day be better for this moment, but right now, I felt like shit.

"Why are you hiding?" a soft voice asked. I hadn't heard the wooden shed door open and shut, but I didn't have to end my intense staring contest with the ground to know who it was.

Summer Bright.

Always following me around, even when we were kids. Hell, who was I kidding? She's still a kid. An annoyingly intuitive and kind kid with a slight crush on me. She sat next to me and drug her finger through the dust.

"Why did you find me?" I replied while wiping my snot on the sleeve of my jacket. I finally looked over at her, grimacing when I saw the all black dress her mother had put her in; it looked like someone tried to put an infant in grandmother's clothing. The thick material went well past her knees.

She didn't respond to me right away. She crossed her legs at the ankle before lacing her fingers in her lap. Couldn't a man just fucking grieve alone? Why did everyone want a front row seat to my pain?

"I don't know, guess I just don't want you to be alone," she shrugged.

"What if I want to be alone?" I asked in response.

She let out a slow breath, grabbing hold of her dress and considering her words. I'd always remembered her as living in her head. Summer had always been around, she knew my parents well. She was young and impressionable and way too naive. But if I could dump some of my anger and sadness onto her, I would. And she'd probably take it, she'd always idolized me.

"No one ever really wants to be alone, Callum."

She was wrong. I was self-aware enough to know what I needed, and I needed to suffer in silence away from the curious stares of Chesterbrook.

"Is that so?" I asked. I'd never been able to tell Summer no. She was too innocent, too kind. So instead of correcting her, I focused on each groove in the plywood floor of the shed.

"I don't like to be alone when I'm sad..." she whispered before brushing her fingers through her dark hair.

"I'm not you, Summer. People have different ways of coping."

She went silent for a moment but didn't leave. I wasn't sure how that made me feel. "I think my mom is drunk," Summer finally whispered with a confused frown. It was like the words were foreign on her lips.

"She could be," I answered, not having the energy to censor my thoughts for her innocent mind. She'd have to grow up eventually, right? "Stuff like this makes people do stuff they normally wouldn't."

"Do you want to do something you normally wouldn't?" she asked. Fuck. Leave it to her to ask shit I wasn't ready to answer. It was making me drink in a shed with an under-aged girl. That enough should have been out of the norm. I considered her question for a moment. I wanted to drive my own car into a tree. Give up on my future, my past. I wanted to say goodbye to the city of Chesterbrook, to my college, my friends, to Summer. I wanted to give it all up and drown in my grief, choke on all the words I never got to tell them.

But instead of scaring her with the dark places my mind was lingering these days, I spit out a lie. "No, Summer." Saying it out loud would mean I was really feeling that way.

Only cowards met death with a handshake and an eager smile.

Summer nodded, thinking about my words before moving on. She pushed her dark hair over her shoulder then looked around her dad's shed, taking in the rusted, hanging tools with interest. "Do you want to go inside? Everyone should be gone by now," she offered.

I looked over her head, out the window of the shed, and smiled when I saw that it was close to sunset. The sky was a warm orange, and I knew that enough time had passed that I was sure there would be no more people prodding for how I felt. The hardest day of my life was almost over with, and somehow the little Summer Bright had helped me pass the time. I looked at her, a thank you at the tip of my tongue. The Brights had always been there for me. *She* had always been there for me.

She bit her lip to hold back the smile I just knew was on her lips. She was proud of herself, likely cataloging the adoration in my eyes for later use.

"Let's go inside, Summer."

"Hey, Callum?" she asked while standing, brushing off her dress and wobbling towards me. "I would miss you. Maybe it's wrong to say I'm glad you weren't in that car, but I am. Know that, if anything happened, I would miss you." She stared at me with her hazel eyes, taking in my reaction to her statement and holding back a pleased grin.

She knew. She fucking knew. She knew about the gun in my car. The letter I wrote to her family in my suit pocket.

I didn't know what to say, and I sure as hell couldn't confirm that her suspicions were correct. She'd called me out on my pain, and she didn't sugar coat it, either. "I'd miss you too, kid."

10

SUNSHINE
Present day

I WAS LYING IN BED, feeling sorry for myself when my men finally came back to the lake house. I'd spent the last six hours waiting for word and hoping Callum would let me comfort him. When I wasn't being an emotional mess, I was hating myself for making *his* greatest trauma about *me*. I wanted to be selfish and cry about how much this would affect our relationship, and I hated that my emotions had such power over me. The old me would have stayed and forced Callum to let me be there for him. I would have planted myself in that grove that nearly killed me and waited until he had no choice but to accept my help.

But not anymore. I'd never been the one to cause him pain, and we were still so rocky. I left partly to save myself but mostly to save him. I felt a bit helpless but mostly didn't know what else to do. It was easy to give a person space. The hard part was knowing that precarious balance between breaking down a person's walls, and knowing when to let them sit in their brick house. Callum was always a fan of tall fences and nice houses so big you could get lost in them.

Joe had driven me back in a rush, convinced that my father was going to jump out from behind a bush and kill me. He spent an hour shooting off questions about my father, most of them I'd already answered before. It was like Joe had finally realized the sort of man we were up against. I wasn't just a little girl with daddy issues anymore; I was battling a real threat.

Gavriel opened my bedroom door and began stripping out of his clothes, leaving the muddy mess of clothes on the floor and letting it splatter against the grey hardwood, looking eerily like blood. I took a moment to trail my eyes over the black ink covering his skin before speaking. "Callum back?" I asked, nervousness lacing my tone as I sat up in bed and clutched my blanket closer to my chest.

Gavriel plopped down on the edge of the bed beside me, facing the window before bending over to slip the wool socks from his feet. I held my breath as he sat there, anxiously waiting for the answer. His hair was wet from the rain and his muscles were flexed with tension. Gavriel took a moment to respond, considering how best to break the news to me. I missed the angry Gav, the one too mad at me to care about my feelings. "He went back to DC, Love. I just dropped him off at the airport."

I tore my eyes from his back and stared out the window at the grey sky and the hidden sun. Bright rays of light cut through the clouds, creating sunspots on the dirt. It looked beautiful and ominous but made me feel comforted. It was like the sky felt the same as me: depressed but hopeful. Chesterbrook lost its magic long ago. It was no longer the place where I met the loves of my life. It was the place where I lost Callum.

"Oh..." I said, not really knowing what to say.

Gavriel spun around and crawled towards me, his expression was distant as he hovered over my legs and torso. "I'm sorry I didn't come back with you," he whispered before tenderly placing a chaste kiss on my lips and shuffling to lay by my side.

"I'm glad you didn't. He needed you more than I did." My response was honest.

"Your needs always come first. Always," Gavriel growled, cutting me off as he pulled the white down comforter over him and guided me to his chest. His tanned skin was cold to the touch, and I flinched at the shock of it.

"I know, Gavriel. But Callum was...broken," I said, my voice choking as I rubbed my nose against him. I could have been selfish, but love wasn't selfish. Love was patient. I'd wait forever if I had to. "I'm glad you all stayed with him."

"Always the martyr," Gavriel cooed. Thunder rumbled in the distance, and I was tempted to look outside at the crashing waves in the lake once more. But I kept my body pressed tightly against Gavriel instead, warming him with each of my hot exhales while trying to keep calm. "How are you holding up, Love?" he asked.

I wasn't sure how to answer him. How could I even possibly begin to articulate the terrible feelings bubbling up within me? "I'm feeling selfish. Even after all of that, I'm worried if Callum will stop loving me now." Gavriel stroked my hair, running his thumb along the strands down my back and placing his palm against the base of my spine beneath the blanket. Of all of them, I knew that he wouldn't judge me. "If I asked you to make him come here, would you?" I asked. Gavriel always promised to give me the things I asked for.

"No. There's a certain balance to things, Sunshine," Gavriel said before cupping my ass and squeezing. "He would hurt you in his current state. I know you want to care for him, it's in your nature. But I have to look out for his interests too." I bit the inside of my cheek to hide the smile, it was a relief to know that Gavriel had accepted Callum onto his short list of people he gives a fuck about. "He would never forgive himself if he hurt you. He's not in a good state of mind to make good decisions right now. I'm the one that sent him away. What is it you need from him?" Gavriel asked.

"I need a lot of things. Some of them I deserve, some of them I don't," I grumbled before sitting up and making my way out of bed to stand in front of the window. My nipples brushed against the cool glass, making a chill travel down my spine. I welcomed the cold. I let it kiss my skin, reminding me that I could still feel, reminding me of the cemetery. "I needed him to hold me last night. I needed to be reassured that the pain of our cemetery fuck was just one facet of our relationship. I needed comfort."

I breathed onto the glass then used my ring finger to draw designs in the fog my breath created. "Now, I want to comfort him. But I also want to feel his anger. The blood of the man that killed his family runs through my veins. It would make me feel better. I can't function with all this guilt, Gavriel."

Gavriel walked up behind me and wrapped his arms around my waist, pulling me tightly against his chest while I breathed in his scent. He smelled like pine, rain and his signature vanilla. "Why do you feel like you should be punished, Love?" Gavriel asked, his smoky tone warm and inviting despite the chill I felt.

"It's my family's fault..." I explained like it was the most obvious thing in the world.

"You're feeling guilty for something you had nothing to do with. You're internalizing Callum's pain because you're a good person, but at the end of the day, you shouldn't confuse empathy with blame. This isn't your fault." Gavriel slowly dragged his fingers, tracing lines over my skin.

"But I feel so sorry. So very sorry..." I cried out, a fat tear rolling down my cheek and landing on his hand. The moment the moisture touched his skin, he spun me around and kissed me. It was one of those kisses that hung on the edge of pain, tempting the line of right and wrong with harsh bites and strong hands.

"I'm not going to let you apologize for shit that's not your fault, Love. You think I got where I am by letting people push their guilt and regret on me? No." He spun me back around and pressed me against the cool glass, shoving my damp hair to the side so he could suck on my neck while I stared at the crashing waves below. "I'm all for a good spanking. Once this shitstorm calms down, I'm going to push you to your limits, but I'm not giving you what you want today, Love." Gavriel's fingers trailed down my stomach in a teasingly slow motion, then he plunged them inside of me, holding me between the glass and his hard body. "Today, I'm going to comfort you."

In and out, his fingers plunged deep within me as his other hand kneaded my breasts. Gavriel wasn't about comfort. He was about control and pain and that blissful spot between the exchange of power. I wasn't sure what to make of this. Gavriel was about punishing. Was this another mind fuck? Giving me what I didn't think I deserved? "Don't overthink it. I love you, Sunshine."

Gavriel grabbed my hands and guided me towards the bed, dragging his eyes up and down my body as he moved. "You're so fucking beautiful." I sat down and settled on my back, pushing the comforter aside as I lay there. I kept my eyes shut, feeling wrong about what we were doing while Callum was in so much pain. "You don't have to look at me,

Love. But I sure as fuck am going to make you *feel* me," Gavriel moaned before nibbling my inner thigh. Using his hands, he thrust my knees apart and buried his face at my core, inhaling deeply before trailing his tongue across my clit. I jumped, the sensation was shocking and pleasant. So why did it feel so wrong?

One finger dipped inside of me, curling to graze against that sweet spot within me, making my pulse race. "I shouldn't be doing this, Gavriel," I said in a whisper feeling guilty once more.

Gavriel shot his head up just as I opened my eyes, looking at him with sadness as I shied away. "You really don't want comfort, do you?" he asked while inching up. His face was a curious mix of awe and anger. He wanted to provide me with comfort, but he could never be Callum. And right now, I didn't want Callum's form of affection. I wanted Gavriel's.

"I don't know what I want," I lied. I knew what I wanted, I was just too afraid to say it outloud.

Grabbing my hips, Gavriel flipped me over, my face landing in the mattress followed by a light slap on my ass. The sting was quickly rubbed away by his palm. "Is that what you want, Sunshine?" he asked before slapping my ass again. The pain seemed to travel through my body, starting at the base of my spine and making its way up to my head. A flood of endorphins and adrenaline coursed through me.

"Harder," I begged as another slap came down, this one had more power behind it. I moaned as he rubbed away the sting, then I arched my back, wordlessly begging for more.

"Your ass looks so perfect with my handprint on it," he said before landing another hard smack. "Does this make you feel better?"

I moaned my response, nodding against the thick cushion of the mattress while he landed another...and another... "God, yes," I cried out, accepting each punishing hit and begging for the next one.

"Do you think you deserve this?" Gavriel asked. I tried to choke out my response, there was a "yes" at the tip of my tongue, but his hits increased in tempo, and I couldn't speak. I could only dive into the blissful feeling of his hand against my skin, the bite of his slaps. "Well, I have news for you, Love," he growled. He sounded out of breath. "You don't. You don't deserve any of this."

Gavriel immediately flipped me back over and propped my calf up on his shoulder before thrusting inside of me with one smooth glide. I was so wet, so turned on by the pain that I couldn't think, couldn't see straight. All I could feel were Gavriel's punishing thrusts and my sore skin. "I do," I cried out.

Gavriel kept a steady cadence, fucking me mercilessly as he grabbed my skin, pinching and rolling his knuckles over each sensitive peak of my breasts. "Let go of shit you have nothing to do with. You don't owe the world a single thing, Sunshine."

My orgasm was a strong, blindingly perfect echo of sensations, dulled by the sadness I felt but still satisfying. It was a steady wave, teasing me with bliss but hiding behind the never-ending regret. Gavriel finished too then collapsed on me, showering my neck with kisses. "Love, come back to me," he pleaded while brushing my hair out of my eyes.

"I'm here. That was...everything I needed. And now I need Ryker and Blaise," I whispered, the only words I could force out. There was a flash of jealousy in Gavriel's eyes. It was quick, barely a millisecond, but it was just enough for me to realize that I said the wrong thing. Just another moment to feel guilty about later on.

"Stop," Gavriel ordered, realizing his mistake. "Don't feel bad. I just wish I were...enough...for you right now. But it's never been just one of us, has it?" Gavriel got up, cleaned us off, then threw on some boxers before leaving. I curled up in a ball while lying alone on the mattress until the three of them entered the room.

"Oh Sunshine," Blaise said before crawling into bed beside me. He wrapped me in a hug, holding me close as more tears began to fall. Ryker ran his hands along his scalp with uncertainty before situating himself at the headboard, cradling me in his lap. Gavriel was the last to join us. He merely stared at me as I cried. Blaise was whispering sweet words of encouragement while Ryker stroked my hair.

"I can't do this...without you, Gavriel," I said, forcing my words to be strong. I was tired of being the emotional one. Tired of letting my sadness get the best of me. Gavriel slowly moved to my vacant side and settled beside me. He threw me a weak smile before entwining my legs with his own.

The three of us stayed there for a moment, and I was thankful for their support. The Bullets stuck together, I guess. And tonight? I was a Bullet.

11

I CALLED CALLUM TWICE, once from Gavriel's airplane and once from the town car that picked us up from the airport. Blaise held my hand the entire trip, rubbing my wrist with his thumb as we sat quietly, each of us trying to cope with all we'd learned.

My father killed the Mercers.

We were on our way to the penthouse when Ryker finally spoke. He seemed really absorbed in thought. "We have a mole," he whispered while looking out the windows as towering buildings passed us by. "How could he have known we would be there?"

"Santobello has a lot of men in his pocket. I'm not surprised that he'd caught onto us. The night I killed his son, he became obsessed. I would have held off had I known, but there isn't much we can do now," Gavriel replied before typing something into his phone. "I've moved my sister into the penthouse temporarily, and I've doubled security until the threat is neutralized."

I snapped my attention to Gavriel and bit back a smile. I'd been dying to meet his sister since coming here. Gavriel didn't want her in the thick of the danger, so she lived in an apartment near her private school. Gavriel viewed attachments as a weakness—something his enemies could use against him. Luckily for me though, he was too selfish to give me up. Not to mention, I was in greater danger without him than I was with. Occasionally, I'd worried that when this was all over, Gavriel would push me away with some sick sense of self-sacrificing love.

I frowned when we arrived at the penthouse and stayed in the town car a moment longer than the others. Looking up at the building, I found myself comparing Gavriel's tower to a prison. It was large and beautiful, but I didn't want to go back there.

"Sunshine, why do you look like someone kicked your puppy? That sad pout is gonna break me, Babe." Blaise was still in the car and had leaned into me, wrapping his arm around my shoulders and pulling me into his comforting embrace.

"I know there isn't a safer place in the city than Gavriel's penthouse, but I really don't want to go up there," I said, feeling guilty. It was a gorgeous home and was much better than being homeless. I owed Gavriel, but I also knew that the moment I made my way up to the thirty-third floor, I'd be trapped in Gavriel's overprotective bubble until Santobello and my father were dead.

Blaise followed my gaze, a pensive look on his face. "Wanna go to my place instead?" he offered with a shrug before leaning out the opened town car door. "Gav, come here a second," he called out. Ryker and Gavriel had been chatting on the sidewalk, both of them leaning over to discuss something important. Gavriel straightened and stepped closer, bracing his hands on the roof of the car to lean in and check on us.

"Everything okay?" Gavriel asked.

"Sunshine's gonna stay with me tonight," Blaise said. I noted how he didn't ask Gavriel's permission, he merely stated what was going to happen.

"I'm not ready to go back to your penthouse, Gav; it feels like a prison, all your men constantly coming and going," I quickly explained. Gavriel ran a hand over the faint scruff on his chin, considering my words. "The minute I get out of this car, you'll go into fix-it, overprotective mode, and I need one more night before we dive into killing people."

Gavriel squinted at me before responding, "Do you not like my home, Love?" That was the problem. It was *his* space, not mine. There were no personal touches, and the constant revolving door of shady men that worked for Gavriel made me uneasy.

"*You* are my home, Gav," I said in a small voice as Blaise squeezed my hand. "But that penthouse doesn't feel like you, it doesn't feel like a space I can get comfortable in."

I could see the wheels turning in his fiery eyes. Gavriel was a problem solver, and as long as I voiced my needs, he'd make it happen. "Stay with Blaise tonight, we can discuss options tomorrow, Love. I want you to be comfortable."

I let out the exhale I didn't realize I was holding and smiled at Gavriel. "Thank you," I mouthed before closing the distance between us and placing a kiss on his lips.

"I'm coming with you! Get me the fuck out of here," a familiar voice exclaimed before Gavriel was shoved to the side, and Nix threw himself into the town car. "A little warning that I'd be stuck babysitting your sister would've been nice," Nix growled before collapsing dramatically in my lap, placing his hand over his eyes while he groaned.

Gavriel's lip quirked up in amusement as I soothingly ran my nails along Nix's scalp. "Ryker and I are going to work on a few leads. Let's all meet tomorrow? I know you want some space, but I'm sending Joe with you. Maybe separating is smarter. Maybe we should rotate homes, keep Santobello guessing," Gavriel said while snapping his fingers. "I'll think on it, you guys get some rest. And, Love?" Gavriel said in a softer tone. "Let Callum call you first. Give him space."

It took an hour to get to Blaise's apartment on the other side of town. I immediately felt more at ease here. As we drove, the buildings became considerably aged, and the pedestrians on the street didn't wear suits. People still walked with a sense of urgency, but their movements were controlled and confident, unlike the posh, stress-filled men rushing to work in the Upper East Side where Gavriel lived.

Joe was very displeased to be here. He grumbled about the vast windows and the lack of security, pacing the floors in anxiety as he closed the blinds. The moment we entered Blaise's converted loft, Nix collapsed in relief, looking around like it was a small slice of heaven.

"This is way more like it," Nix mused. The open concept loft was just a larger version of where Nix and I lived in Baltimore. The exposed brick, modern furniture, and open kitchen were warm and inviting. Unlike Gavriel's home, Blaise had personal touches covering every wall. Photos of different landmarks with various mismatched frames cluttered each shelf. I stopped in front of a picture of a statue and stared.

It was beautiful. The pedestrians were blurred, but the statue stood cold and tall in the middle of a busy metropolis. Beside it, Blaise's old guitar was hanging up, and I bit my lip to hold back the smile.

"Did you take these photos?" I asked while walking along the wall, feeling his eyes on me as I trailed my fingers across the exposed brick.

"Yeah," Blaise said, his voice hoarse. I turned to face him, smiling at the awed look on his face, his rust-colored hair a mess and curling at the ends. It had grown a lot these last few weeks, reminding me of how he would style it when we were teens. "I'll admit, it's a tad weird seeing you in my home. I mean—I've always dreamed of it. But this reality..."

Joe coughed, rolling his eyes for a moment before checking his phone. "You live around here, Joe?" I asked.

He stared at his phone like it was precious before turning back to me. "Nothing personal, but I won't be telling you anything about where I live," he grumbled.

"Well, why don't you go visit Aunt Joe? I'm in capable hands. It's been a few days, right? If we need anything or go anywhere, we can call."

Joe looked between us, the distrust evident in his eyes. I sensed that he wanted to go, but he was also afraid to leave. Nix spoke up, a wild glint in his eye. "But if you stay, we can turn our threesome into a foursome. I bet you have a big cock, Joe."

Joe didn't bless us with his sarcastic response. He was out of Blaise's loft in under thirty seconds flat with a half-hearted instruction to call if we needed anything. Blaise was explaining a new video game to Nix while I pulled my cell phone out to call Callum. I knew that Gavriel thought he needed space, but it was like an uncontrollable impulse. I was selfishly afraid to lose Callum Mercer. To my surprise, he answered it on the third ring.

"Hello?" His voice was rough as he spoke. I was reminded of his harsh screams in the woods, and I wondered what he was doing.

"Callum?" I answered. I didn't know what to say. What could I possibly say to the man whose life my family destroyed?

"Summer, why are you calling me?" Callum asked. I broke a little at the exasperated way he spoke, his tone pleading for me to let him go. I squeezed my eyes shut at the way he called me Summer instead of Sunshine. For some reason, it felt like he was putting distance between us by not accepting my nickname.

"I just wanted to make sure that you were okay," I said while pacing the wooden floors in Blaise's converted loft. I was hanging on by a thread, clinging to Callum in whatever way I could. "Are you in DC?" I asked.

Instead of answering, Callum blew a rush of air into the phone receiver. I pulled it away from my ear, wincing before adjusting the cell phone back between my ear and my shoulder. As I paced, Blaise and Phoenix stopped talking about the video game and started looking at me. Their intrusive stares seemed to burn at my exposed skin while I stumbled over my words to Callum.

"Callum, please come here. Please let me comfort you. Let me love you through this." My voice was pathetic, and the prideful part of me wanted to demand that he stop putting so much distance between us.

"It's still pretty new, Summer. I've been chasing you and your family for a while now. All this time, I've been running towards you, and I'm wondering if I should've been running away. Let me do this on my own. If there's any hope for us, you won't call me again."

"You're ready to end this already, Callum?" I asked, not letting him hang up. I needed to hear it.

Callum let out a sigh. I imagined him in his suit, pacing a dark hotel room and running a hand through his blond hair. "I'm ready to end something..."

A memory flashed in my mind. Callum and I were no longer on the phone, we were in my parents' shed. "I'd miss you, Callum," I whispered, alluding to the conversation we'd had eight years ago. Callum had a habit of spiraling. I wasn't going to let him destroy himself over something my family did. "I'd miss you so much. I'd follow you anywhere, Callum. Anywhere. Remember that."

I waited for Callum's answer, but none came. The line clicked, ending our call, and I reared back, planning to throw my phone across the room when Blaise intercepted my flash of anger.

"Do you want a distraction, Sunshine?" he asked before standing and sauntering towards me. I recognized the expressions on his face—mischief, determination, playfulness. Blaise knew what I needed better than anyone, and right now I needed to not think about Callum or Santobello or my father.

"What did you have in mind?" I asked.

I should have known that their version of escaping reality would include a trip to an arcade. I'd been expecting a night on the town, a too-tight dress with uncomfortable heels. But instead, I was dressed in denim and tennis shoes, dancing around on the arcade floor while Blaise played whack-a-mole. It was risky, but we didn't bother telling Joe, Gavriel, or Ryker that we had left. I felt safe with Blaise, and we were in a public enough place. I wanted to feel free again. Just another selfish endeavor on my part.

Nix was high from some pot brownies he'd scored from Gavriel's sister and was holding me tight while updating me on all that had happened while I was gone. "Gavriel's sister is a hot mess. I mean that literally. Hot because...like damn. She's got these bright green eyes...and mess because..." he trailed off, considering his words for a moment. "I think she's lonely."

I stared at my best friend, smiling because I recognized the expression on his face. He'd had that same determined smile when I woke up in the hospital and saw him sitting next to me, holding the hand of a stranger. When he connected with a soul, he was committed, it's just who he was.

"She's still in high school, right?" I asked. It was an impressionable age.

"She's eighteen. Attends a private school on the boujee side of town." Nix rolled his eyes. "But I'm adopting her. She's gonna be my friend, she just doesn't know it yet. I just have to get past how frustratingly annoying she can be." He spun me around, twirling me on his fingers before crushing me to his chest and dragging his knuckles along my cheek. "But you're my number one girl, don't you forget it."

I giggled, accepting the lightheartedness of our evening with a grain of salt. None of it was real, not really. This was just us forcing some normalcy down our throats until the pill was easier to swallow. "Tell me what's on your mind, Sweets."

I let out a slow exhale as Blaise moved over to the skee-ball game, throwing me flirtatious smiles over his shoulder as he bent down to play, the tight jeans covering his ass giving me a generous view of his frame.

I'd battled for the better part of an hour over whether I should ignore everyone's wishes and go to Callum. His sadness was like a beacon, calling out to me. And I would have gone, would have bought my ticket for the next flight to DC, if I wasn't so terrified that he'd end things for good.

"The odds are against us. Callum was already on the fence about this...unique arrangement we have. And now he has a genuine reason to hate me. I'm still feeling selfish. One of them isn't enough; I love them all, Nix."

We started swaying to the cheesy nineties music playing in the background, our hips swaying to the synthesizer as I relaxed. "What's going to happen when the newness of my arrival wears off? What happens when they've decided that they don't want the leftover scraps of my affections? What happens if I'm not enough? Maybe this is good. Maybe I should love Callum enough to let him go—let them all go."

Nix spun me around then pulled me over to Blaise, a determined scowl on his face. "This pity party is a total buzz kill. Why don't we just ask Blaise how he feels, hmm?"

Blaise had just collected a stream of tickets, ripping them off and shoving them in his too-tight pants. "Blaise, our girl is going to give herself a complex with all the self-loathing floating around her brain. Could you pretty please reassure her that you're not going anywhere?"

Blaise ignored the hoards of teenagers running past us, all of them giggling and staring at the two very attractive men in front of me. "We're better together, Sunshine. I'm not going anywhere. Don't let Callum's indecision affect the way you see us—the way you see me."

He cupped my cheek as Nix maneuvered behind me, holding me in a tight hug as Blaise kissed me with such raw emotion that my knees went weak. He laughed against my lips when a group of kids made gagging noises, and I pinched his butt for good measure. When he pulled away, I wondered how I got so lucky.

"How will I ever keep your attention? What if you get bored of me...of sharing me?"

Nix threw his head back and laughed, pulling away from me to look at the two of us with a mischievous grin. "Sharing can be *very* fun, Sweets. There's a reason I find monogamy to be boring. Why don't we go back to Blaise's place, and I'll show you?"

Blaise gave us a curious look, and Nix immediately cut off that thought with a shake of his head. "As much as I'd love this," Nix said, gesturing between us, "I was thinking I'd give you an opportunity to explore that voyeur kink you've got going on while giving Summer a nice little demonstration."

Nix picked up his phone and began typing furiously, a grin on his face as he shoved his smartphone back in his pocket. "I hope you're not opposed to being tied up."

12

THE SILK ROPE wrapped around my wrists was soft to the touch. When we arrived, Nix gently tied me to a wooden kitchen chair, placing tender kisses on my wrists while leaving enough room in the knot so that I could escape easily. He knew the idea of being trapped was a trigger for me, and I was thankful that he wordlessly adjusted to my needs.

He then went to Blaise, straddling him as he tied him to another wooden chair beside me, wrapping the silk around his waist and leaning over him to tie it in a knot at the back. With a fierce expression, he lingered over Blaise, before kneeling to tie his ankles to the legs of the chair. "You're lucky I respect bro code," Nix mumbled, taking his time and brushing his lips against Blaise's knees as he stood. Blaise didn't shy away from his touch, simply smiled challengingly at Nix as he settled in his chair. "Or I'd make you come play with me, you handsome devil, you."

"Is this the part where you give us a strip tease?" Blaise asked, his voice light but breathy. I couldn't help but smile at how affected he sounded. Just as Phoenix was about to answer, the doorbell rang.

"Looks like my company is here. There are three rules. No touching. No saying anything unless I speak to you first. No names." Nix didn't wait for us to respond. Although I found Nix's confidence and self-assured nature to be beautiful and fun to watch, it was the way Blaise was on edge that had my blood heating up.

Blaise's eyes were dilated, skin flushed. He looked around the room in anticipation, eager to see what would happen next. This was exactly the sort of distraction I needed. "You sure about this?" I asked in a teasing tone as voices filtered in behind us. Blaise swallowed. From the corner of my eye, I saw his internal battle. He was questioning whether he should want this. "It's not wrong, Blaise," I whispered. I wanted him to feel comfortable with whatever he was attracted to. I also wanted to be a safe place for him to explore his sexuality. If he wanted to watch...oh...I'd let him watch. I felt like Gavriel for a moment, exploring this new side of Blaise because I knew it would make him happy.

He might want me to stop using them as a distraction from my problems, but I was starting to understand that pouring my attention into the men I loved wasn't some sick way to ignore the very real threats in my life. It was a way to find light in all the darkness.

The sounds of heels clicking on the wood floors of Blaise's loft brought me out of my introspective daze, and I turned to stare at the man and woman following Nix into Blaise's bedroom. They had lazy smiles as they looked between us and at each other. "I love having an audience," the woman said. She had long blond hair with big-bodied curls. Her eyelashes were so long they could have been fake, and her tight body looked perfect in the little red dress she was wearing. The man she was with was handsome.

Almond-shaped eyes, black hair and broad shoulders. He was wearing black pants and a tight long sleeve blue shirt that showcased his muscles.

"We don't like to use our real names. You can call her Beth and him Leo." Nix instructed while circling them, trailing his fingers across their backs and necks.

"And you? What can I call you?" I asked, biting my lip in amusement at the fire in his eyes.

Nix stopped, turning to look at me while stripping out of his jeans. "For tonight? You can call me sir. Be sure to tell your boyfriend about it too. I love to make that sexy lip of his quirk." I frowned when I realized that this might be crossing an unspoken boundary with the guys. We'd never discussed this before, never labeled our relationships or drew lines in the sand of where to stay. Would they be upset with me for watching Phoenix in his element?

Sensing my hesitation, Nix then stepped forward, leaning so that his lips brushed against my ears. "I won't touch you. Won't bring you or Blaise into the scene. Once we start, it'll be all about them, nothing more. Like watching porn with your boyfriend. I wouldn't do this if I didn't think it would be good for you. And if we're being honest, we both know this is more about Blaise than anything else..."

I smiled wickedly before chancing a glance at Blaise. His chest was heaving, and when I peeked at the tight denim in his lap, I grinned at the hard erection pressing through the fabric and traveling down his thigh. "Let's get this party started," I whispered before settling back in the wooden chair, grinning at the beautiful woman in front of me.

Nix whispered to them, double checking their consent and limits. I loved how seriously he took everyone's pleasure. He wanted them to trust him, he wanted this to be a good experience. It wasn't until the stereo started playing a haunting tune with a sensual beat that Nix completely slipped into his dominant role.

"Strip for them," Nix ordered while lighting a couple of candles he'd found, and the room started to smell like vanilla and sex. The woman, Beth, sauntered towards me and started slipping out of her red dress. Easing the front zipper down her body slowly, she let the swells of her breasts free as she bit her lip, watching my response to her.

I could appreciate a pretty body. Even if I'd never been attracted to a woman, I was enthralled with her confidence. Turned on by her enthusiasm. Her perky nipples were pink, and she spun around, showing me her muscular back and the angel wings tattooed on her soft, creamy skin. She was beautiful. Since we weren't making eye contact, I felt brave. I knew that Nix said no talking, but I couldn't help myself. I was curious.

"What do you love most about this?" I asked in a small whisper. "Do you ever get jealous?"

Being the perfect submissive that she was, Beth turned to Nix before answering me, wordlessly asking his permission to answer. He let out a dissatisfied scowl towards me before nodding once. I was never one to follow the rules, and I could never truly see Nix as a dominant. We were equals in every sense.

"Does this make you jealous?" she asked as she sauntered towards Blaise. He had his eyes on her body, cautiously roaming her skin with interest. There was an old pang in my chest, one that hadn't been there for a long while. It still felt just as intense as it did when we were teens. It was one of the cruelest forms of jealousy, one that made me feel inadequate.

And instead of enjoying this experience with confidence, I was now itching to leave. "It does, doesn't it? I can see it on your face," she said before trailing a finger down his biceps. Blaise turned to stare at me, gauging how I was handling another woman touching what was mine. I knew that if I said something, he would tell her to stop. This was a two way street, and Blaise would never do anything to compromise us or my happiness.

"But here's a little trick," she offered before straddling Blaise, positioning her pussy right over his hard cock. Anger coursed through me, my emotions were so blindingly hot that I almost clawed my way out of my chair to attack her. From behind, Nix looked almost ready to intervene, but Leo was just stroking himself, eying his wife with appreciation.

"Jealousy is such a weak emotion. It'll bleed you dry. Focus on his face. Pretend I'm not here. Get off on how turned on he is." She started kissing his neck, leaving trails of red lipstick along his tan skin as he stared at me.

I broke through the anger to look at him...really look at him. Blaise's eyes were hooded as he watched for my expression. He was making this all about me, despite her lips on his skin, he was worried about my enjoyment—my pleasure. It was still about us.

"Do you like how she feels, Blaise?" I asked, honestly wanting to know the answer.

"Yes," he groaned, "but I like watching you more. Seeing your fiery eyes is making me so fucking hard, I can't even see straight."

I bit my lip as she maneuvered off of him, fluttering those long eyelashes for a confident wink before heading towards Nix. I could focus on Blaise. I could make this about him. "Good girl," my best friend said before crashing his lips to hers, tasting her fully as she giggled into his mouth with sultry pleasure.

I wasn't as interested in them though. I was transfixed by Blaise, his lusty dark eyes and stiff frame. He was leaning forward as much as he could, straining against the silk fabric keeping him in the chair. He watched Nix ease her onto the bed. "Come reward your wife for being so good and teaching my friends," Nix ordered before sliding away to make room for Leo. She arched up to greet her husband, licking his neck before diving into a kiss so passionate I felt myself growing hot. The man was eager to kiss his wife, staring at her with zero jealousy. The only thing between them was passion, and it was addicting.

I licked my lips as Blaise squirmed, tearing his eyes from the two of them to look at me. "Does watching them make you want me?" I asked, my voice was throaty, and I sounded breathless.

"Hell fucking yes," he choked out.

"Well, that's too bad," Nix said as he sauntered towards us, brushing his fingers down his abs as he looked at Blaise. And for the first time, I was kind of turned on by Phoenix, or at least the idea of him. Would Blaise ever explore something like that?

Would I *enjoy* it? For a brief moment I pictured Ryker, Gavriel, Callum and Blaise. All limbs and kisses and passion, wrapping me up with as much sensations as I could handle.

A groan drug me out of my daydream. Beth had started trailing her tongue up and down the shaft of her husband's cock as he writhed and moaned in appreciation.

"Why?" I asked, egging Nix on. Once I was able to shift my mind to only think of Blaise, the entire dynamic of this night changed. I couldn't wait to see every expression, hear every moan. I wanted to see him shaking in his seat, desperate for relief.

"Because I'm going to make you wait until your dick is so hard it hurts. You can touch *my girl* when I say so," Nix purred before spinning around to help his couple.

Nix was attentive. Authoritative. He guided their movements, bringing them both to the cusp of pleasure then dragging them away from their relief with a vengeance. Their dynamic was intriguing. Beth would make eye contact with Blaise, blatantly getting off on his panting chest.

And I didn't care.

Tonight was about him. And maybe that made me a little fucked up, maybe other women wouldn't get this— wouldn't understand. Why would I ever willingly let the man I love lust after another?

But this woman, Beth, was just an idea. A pretty face and sultry smile wrapped up in confidence. Blaise would never love her like he loved me. She was a means to an end. I wasn't jealous, because what Blaise and I had transcended reason. When I was with him, it was only him. I could focus on the way his chest heaved in excitement. I could enjoy his hard cock, enjoy the way he was turned on by them. But at the end of it all, he wanted *me*. And damn, that was power. Pure, pure power.

Nix positioned himself at Beth's entrance, preparing to thrust inside of her when he paused to stare at Blaise, a wicked smile on his face. "Do you want to watch me fuck her? Or are you ready to have a bit of your own fun now?"

"Pl-please," Blaise begged. He was on the edge of oblivion, dancing his eyes over their tangled bodies.

Nix got up, earning a whimper from Beth. "Please what?" His proud erection glared at us as he marched towards Blaise.

"Let me out of these restraints."

Bending over, Nix was just a breath away from Blaise when he ordered, "Say 'please, sir.' "

Blaise looked angry, furrowing his brow as defiance rippled off of him. Nix was pushing too far. Blaise might be open-minded and accepting, but he wasn't submissive. Not in the slightest.

"Untie me so I can fuck my woman, *now,*" Blaise growled while bracing against the silk rope keeping him in the wooden chair. Seeing their power struggle was hot, and seeing Blaise so worked up for *me* was even hotter. Even with the gorgeous couple in front of us, all he wanted was his Sunshine. Nix laughed, throwing his head back before quickly loosening the knots on his wrists and ankles.

"Have fun, you two," Nix said with a wave before redirecting his attention back to the couple on the bed. Blaise shot up from his seat, ripping a knife from his pocket before cutting through the loose ties half-heartedly keeping me in the chair.

In seconds, he had the knife pocketed, and I was hoisted over his shoulder. Nix slapped my ass as we went with a laugh. The last thing I could see was the room upside down and Nix turning back towards the bed to fuck Beth until she couldn't think straight.

"Where are we going?" I asked with a smile. Blaise was all primal and *all mine* right then. He couldn't hold back his desire for me, and I was suffocating from his lust, breathing it in and owning how Nix's performance had affected him.

"My guest room," he choked out before kicking open a side door I hadn't noticed before and tossing me on the bed. My jeans were gone in an instant, my shirt torn next. Two fingers slipped beneath my underwear before they were yanked away.

"You gonna tease me this time, Blaise? Gonna make me beg for it?" I asked, remembering our first time in the motel.

Blaise yanked off his tight jeans, revealing his hard cock to me. I watched it spring free and pulse in his palm, the thick veins tempting me. I licked my lips, eager to taste him. "I think you and I both know I can't wait," he said with a grin.

Sitting up, I eased closer, placing his dick against my

bottom lip and speaking against him. "Then don't," I offered before parting my lips and sliding down his shaft, pressing the head of his cock against the tip of my tongue as I went. He tasted sweet, and the way his cock jerked in my mouth had me feeling worked up and wet. I moved up and down, spurred forward by the grunts in Blaise's chest and the way his legs went weak from pleasure. I kept an even pace, taking my time and drawing out every last second.

After a few minutes, Blaise spoke. "We have to stop," he said before gently pulling away. He brushed a thumb over my lip, smiling to himself at my dazed expression. "I'm not ready for this to be over, and at the rate you were going, I'm about to spurt cum down your pretty little throat."

"I wouldn't necessarily be opposed to that," I said with a sigh while licking my lips. Blaise bent over, and I scooted further back on the bed before laying down. Trailing kisses down my neck, Blaise sucked on my collarbone, lightly nibbling with the edge of his teeth and groaning as I bucked beneath him. I felt delicate and loved. "Please," I asked, needing to feel him inside of me.

It was all the encouragement he needed. Within moments, Blaise was pressing me into the mattress and sliding his cock in and out of me, holding my hips in place as he moved. "It's only you, Sunshine," he whispered. "No one else could ever make me feel this way, this on edge."

I writhed and smiled, the sounds of our slapping skin drowning out the moans from the bedroom next door. "I might have enjoyed watching them, but this? This is fucking *nirvana,* this is all I want. Forever. Always," Blaise said with a grunt.

I looked at Blaise in his beautiful eyes, taking in his pure adoration and soaking up the feeling of his love. He had no restrictions, no hesitance. It was only us, only our love. I knew right then I'd be enough. Blaise slowed his pace, leaning forward to kiss my forehead as our bodies moved like waves against one another. There was less urgency in his movements now. "It's only you. It'll only be you," he kept whispering again and again, coaxing an orgasm from deep within me with his words. I cried out, biting his shoulder to keep back the screams.

He didn't stop then, he kept pressing forward. Sitting up, he began massaging my clit with his thumb while we rocked, he was going to prolong his own release until I'd had another. "Is it wrong that I liked seeing you jealous? I got off on it," he said before flipping me over and pulling me up so that I was on my knees. I braced my hands on the mattress as he continued to move with aching certainty, yanking my hair back as he thrust. "It got me thinking, do you get off on our jealousy? Maybe we're making this too easy on you."

I tried to think about his words but was too distracted by how amazing he felt. He abruptly stopped, holding his cock deep within me before he spoke, "I think some jealousy is healthy. I think you need to know that we all want you so badly, we can't think straight." He pulled my hair a tad harder, just enough discomfort to make me feel alive. "You want the truth? This isn't easy for any of us."

Blaise continued his movements, like he was working through our fucked up little relationship by fucking me senseless. He was brutal in the way he pumped, not holding back a single thrust as his words sliced me. "Gavriel copes by convincing himself he's in charge. I get off on watching. Ryker is so scared of losing you again that he pushes his jealousy and anger to the side. And Callum? He likes it. He just doesn't know it yet."

I cried out as a second orgasm rocked through me, and Blaise finally erupted, riding each wave of ecstasy before I collapsed beneath him on the bed. Each muscle in my body relaxed as I hummed in approval. *Fuck, that was amazing.* Blaise then held me close as our breathing settled. I spun to face him, nuzzling his neck as his cum dripped down my thigh. "This is so fucked up," I murmured.

"No," Blaise began with an exhale. "It's perfect."

13

WE SPENT the next day pretending the rest of the world didn't exist. Blaise was determined to distract me. If he wasn't ordering every pizza in town to convince me that pineapple wasn't a topping, he was bending me over his kitchen table and exploring my body. Blaise was leaving me so tired that I couldn't fight to stay awake, let alone obsess over the fact that Callum hadn't called me back.

But oh did I obsess in the little moments. Every second between bliss, I found myself pacing the floors and itching to call Callum. Was he okay? Was he hurting? Did he need me?

Why didn't he need me?

Wasn't that what love was? Leaning on the people that cared for you? In those little blinks of time between Blaise's kisses and Nix's laughter, I wondered if love was enough, or if that's even what *was* between us.

Nix didn't invite any more guests over but kept winking at Blaise from across the loft, making sure to drag his eyes up and down his body before laughing loudly at my boyfriend's flustered expression. Yes—my *boyfriend*. I had a moment of giddy teenage anticipation, and I announced that I would start calling him that.

"That makes what we have feel...less. Is there a better word than boyfriend?" Blaise had asked. I tried to think of how to answer him. Husband didn't feel right. My mind associated marriage with my parents—a burden of expectations and regret. And Blaise and I were much more than that. Maybe there wasn't a word for what we were. So I called him my boyfriend when I actually meant whatever word felt like forever.

Nix and Blaise's dynamic was fun and playful, their friendship felt unique and revolved around me, and it was nice to see my two best friends getting along so well. Gavriel called us on the second morning. "Sunshine, if I don't see you soon, I'll lose it," he grumbled into the phone. I pictured him at his mahogany desk, running his shaky hands through his black hair while puffing out air in exasperation.

"What have you been up to?" I asked while untangling myself from Blaise's arms. Every night, he held me close, nuzzling me as I checked my phone for calls from Callum. We were still in the spare bedroom. It had become our haven of sorts, the one place where we didn't bother ourselves with talk of Callum or the troubles ahead of us. Blaise had constantly referenced jokes about our bodies doing the talking, but it was right. Every time I doubted myself, I earned a kiss. Blaise fucked away the little creeping insecurities that kept whispering to me that I wasn't enough.

"Ryker received a fight challenge from one of Santobello's men. His personal trainer wants him in Vegas tonight," Gavriel said as I made my way to the kitchen and started a pot of coffee.

"Is that a bad thing?" I wasn't sure how these fight challenges worked, but I needed to learn fast. I was carving out a routine for our little unconventional family. I wanted to support them.

"It's a problem," Gavriel replied. His voice echoed, and he was out of breath as if he were walking upstairs. "If we refuse, we look weak. If we accept, then we could be walking into a trap. Ryker is determined to fight him, I'm more focused on bringing down Paul Bright."

I chewed on my lip as the coffee percolated, filling the loft with the pleasant aroma. Was it so wrong to look weak? I'd rather look weak then look...dead. "Could you do it on your turf? Have it somewhere locked so tight you knew he couldn't hurt you?" I was stumbling over my words, not sure of the correct terminology for gang wars and territory disputes. It was all a lot to keep up with.

"It's not me I'm worried about. His men fight dirty. Ryker doesn't want to ruin his credibility, but I think it's a bad idea. And even if Santobello does nothing, it's still a massive mind-fuck. Ryker doesn't do well when he's on edge."

He was right, last time Ryker was off his game, he ended up in the hospital. "I know you needed a couple days there, but I really need Nix back for some surveillance. I also might have a bounty for Blaise here pretty soon."

Letting out an exhale, I took a moment to settle myself, sipping my coffee with Gavriel on the other end of the line. This blissful little hideaway couldn't go on forever. I couldn't pretend the battle with my father and Santobello wasn't happening. Avoiding my problems was a dirty little self-sabotaging cycle I did whenever shit got too hard to handle. And at the end of the day, it didn't make me feel better, it just made me crave something that wasn't real.

Callum was off somewhere ripping apart his grief and filling his parents' burial plots with new dirt—dirt my father stained with their blood. Santobello was on our heels, and Paul Bright knew we were onto him. He was likely angry that I was alive, frustrated that my mother threatened his credibility with her suicide, and just plain murderous. Men like him didn't need a reason to kill, and we'd given him plenty. And when Dad was angry, he was *lethal.*

"Wanna meet for breakfast first?" I asked, hoping to prolong the inevitable. I needed a nice, normal meal. Preferably one that ended with orgasms.

"Well, that's the thing. I'm outside Blaise's door with some of the best damn bagels in the city."

With a giddy laugh, I ran to the door, throwing it open and flinging myself into the unsuspecting arms of Gavriel Moretti, my badass mob boss with breakfast in hand and a shy smile on his perfect face. It was silly and normal and perfect.

Ryker stood behind him, and Joe was hunched over as he leaned to the left, a familiar scowl perched upon his dry lips as he eyed the bag of food in Gavriel's hand with longing. Ryker pulled me from Gavriel's arms and hugged me tightly, lifting me off the ground and carrying me inside the loft where Nix and Blaise were stirring. The tips of my toes just barely brushed against the hardwood as he walked.

"Is that coffee? Please tell me that's coffee," Nix begged while scratching his abs, smiling at Gavriel before adjusting his morning wood. He was wearing only boxers and a smile. No shame. Ryker reluctantly set me down, and I took advantage of having his full attention, trailing my fingers down his chest as I steadied myself.

"I missed you, Ry Baby" I whispered, low enough so only he could hear.

"I missed you too."

I broke the intense staring contest the two of us were having to appreciate his black athletic shorts and tank top. It was ridiculously chilly outside, but his bare arms were on full display, giving me a healthy view of his ink.

Stealing my cup from the counter, Nix began sipping it, wincing when the hot liquid hit his throat. "Couldn't stand to be away?" Blaise asked the guys as he walked in and kissed me on the cheek, stealing Gavriel's sack of food before settling at the island and eating.

I stole a cinnamon bagel from the sack and slathered it with butter, moaning when the glorious carbs hit my tongue. "This is amazing," I mumbled, my mouth full.

"Can you even taste it? Did you put an entire stick of butter on that?" Ryker asked, wrinkling his nose and staring at me in disgust. I made a big show of licking my lips and rolling my eyes. Who *didn't* like butter?

Ryker grabbed three bagels and began eating them with brute enthusiasm. "Carb loading for your fight?" I wiped my mouth with a napkin and nodded at him. I was still learning his rituals, how he prepared, and how he conditioned his body. Blaise looked between us with a confused expression before Gavriel started explaining everything to him.

"Santobello sent Ryker a challenge."

"Well, good morning to you too, Harlem," Blaise answered sarcastically, slumping over on the kitchen counter and popping his neck.

I stared at Joe while they continued to discuss the details. He was off in the corner, eyeing our bagels with jealousy. My hangry little bodyguard was kind enough to give us space yesterday, the least I could do was feed the poor man. Sliding off the stool I was sitting on, I walked over to him and placed a whole wheat bagel in his hand.

"How's Mrs. Joe?" I asked with a half smile. Joe's eyes flashed to Gavriel in warning, as if trying to tell me that he wasn't supposed to be with the missus instead of watching me. I zipped my lips with a smile, dragging my fingers along the seam of my mouth before throwing away the imaginary key.

After making sure that no one was listening in to our conversation, Joe bent over slightly, parting his mouth to whisper in a rush. "She was fine and sends her thank yous." I caught the edge of a blush on his cheeks, as if she chastised him into saying that to me. I hoped things calmed down soon enough so I could meet Mrs. Joe and join their little family. I bet she was always nagging him in that playful way familiar and older couples did. I longed for the teasing that danced along the line of too far, that comfortableness that came only from knowing for sure a person wouldn't leave you, even *if* you were a bratty asshole.

"Tell her I can't wait to meet her," I whispered back, smiling a bit at Joe's annoyed expression. He would likely tell me "no," and then I'd have to follow him home.

What happened next was instantaneous. They say time slows during a near death experience. Everything moves at a snail's pace, grazing reality with eternity and showing you what the end felt like by making your last few seconds drag for hours.

I wasn't gifted with that. Things moved too fast—everything was too sudden, a blur in the room that my eyes couldn't focus on. Glass shattered, and a hand was on my back, pushing me down until my teeth were scraping against the hardwood of Blaise's loft. I screamed, my voice breaking apart around us until a meaty hand covered my mouth, forcing me to be quiet.

"Get her out of here!" Gavriel screamed. Twisting my head, I'd noticed that he was by the window, staring out fearlessly at the city below while the rest of us crouched and hid from the bullets.

Another shot. Blood. There was blood. Joe was on top of me, letting out little grunts of pain as he covered my body with his own. "Joe, are you okay?" His hand still covered my mouth, making my question nothing but a muffled cry.

His blood covered my skin, the crimson stain reminding me of my night in the basement. I fought through the triggering image, gasping for air while I wiped away the seeping evidence of the violence staining my tank top and yoga pants. It seemed to sink through my skin.

"Joe?" I asked. He was deathly pale. Blaise placed a hand on my shoulder, pulling me out from beneath my burly guard and a few feet away as I stared at Joe's bloodied body. His lips were white, and Nix applied pressure over his chest, his muscles straining as blood filtered through the gaps in his fingers.

"We need an ambulance!" Blaise yelled.

"We need to get out of here," Gavriel growled.

"We can't leave, we don't know how many of them there are!" Ryker was crawling towards me, his face determined as another shot rang through the loft. And another. Sparks flew as a metal bullet ricocheted off Blaise's appliances. Within moments, men in black suits were storming through the front door of Blaise's loft. Their deep voices were a chorus of screams, demanding that we get down.

"Protect Sunshine at all costs!" Gavriel screamed. Surrounding us with guns drawn, his men were prepared to take on whatever threat was against us. We just didn't know where the danger was coming from.

"Yes, sir," a man with blond hair answered him as three men circled me, blocking my view of Joe and of my guys. My breathing became labored as I took in their backs and the weapons in their hands. Once again, I had to remind myself that this wasn't the basement. This was the top story of a building. A loft apartment in Harlem. The door was seven paces away. The knife Joe had given me was tucked beneath my pillow in Blaise's bedroom. If I closed my eyes, I could feel each groove.

One. Joe took a bullet for me.

Two. Joe took a bullet for me.

Three. Joe took a bullet for me.

I tore my eyes from their weapons, ignoring the twitch in my fingers. Looking down at my lap, I'd noticed that my own hands were red, no matter how much I wiped them on my thighs, I couldn't get rid of Joe's sacrifice. "What's happening?" I asked. One of the men yanked me up from under my arms and pulled me to his side.

Gavriel's voice carried over the group, answering me as the men in suits guided us out Blaise's front door. "Sunshine, just keep quiet. We're getting you to safety."

Blaise lived on the top floor of his building. Each twist in the staircase brought on a new level of unease, a new threat. We were out of breath but didn't want to breathe too loudly. In the middle of our trek, someone had cut the power, making it impossible to see. Another shot, it was louder this time. I reached for my phone in my pocket, wanting to illuminate the staircase, but a hand reached for my wrist to stop me.

"We don't want them to see us," a gruff voice explained before letting me go.

When we got to the bottom floor, emergency lighting flickered on, as if the backup generator were finally working. The familiar hum of electricity brought me even more unease. The lobby of his building was deserted. People likely heard the shots fired and fled. "Marcus, is the building cleared?" Gavriel asked.

"The team is currently clearing each apartment," the man who had stopped me from flashing my phone said. I snapped my head to stare at Gavriel, surprised by how efficiently he ran his team. They acted more like a special ops group than a bunch of thugs.

"I'd say I'm impressed, but we shouldn't be in this situation in the first place. I'm snapping a neck for every goddamn shot fired at her, Marcus. It better not be you that let shit like that slip through the cracks," Gavriel said, his voice quiet but still fierce as he took in the open lobby.

Through the gaps in the bodies around me, I saw Gavriel's town car idling on the curb, the front wheel almost on the sidewalk with how rushed the driver parked. Pedestrians were speed-walking away from us, they moved with a sense of urgency, self-preservation at the forefront of their minds. But they didn't run. Some even looked blatantly at us while wearing curious expressions, almost as if this occurrence were normal for them. Just another bad man with another bad gun.

One of Gavriel's men jogged toward the car while we stood just outside the entrance to the building. "Once the door is open, we'll run for it. The moment the door is shut, you leave. Get her to the safe house. I'll follow."

I turned to look at Gavriel, a wordless plea on my lips for him to come with me. He must have seen the worried look on my face, because he bent low, whispering in my ear for only me to hear. "I can't go with you. I'm the target. I won't be the reason something happens to you, Love." He then kissed my cheek, lingering for far longer than what was appropriate, considering we were outside Blaise's building while bullets clipped past us.

I turned my attention back to the man reaching for the driver side door to open it. Each of his movements lasted an hour, time finally slowing to drag out the severity of the moment. As his fingers enclosed around the handle and opened the black metal door, a chain reaction of fire exploded, throwing our group back six feet and into the glass of the front windows of the lobby from the power of the explosion.

Car parts rushed past us, debris scraping my cheek as I landed on my back in a pile of glass. The hard ground rubbed my shoulders where my tank top wasn't covering me, and tiny shards dug into my skin. Everything hurt. The smoke made it hard to see.

"Sunshine," someone choked out. Sounds were an echo within my skull, a distant tone my brain couldn't connect with. There was a ringing too. A pitch so high and constant that I had to squeeze my eyes shut to block out how painful it was.

"Help," I choked out. A heavy body was on my legs. He wasn't moving. No one was running.

Was this what death felt like? Was this how it ended? Ringing. Ringing. Ringing. Around us was a war zone, but all I could think of was my men. Two hands looped under my arms, pulling me free from the body that had collapsed on top of me. I looked down, crying out when I saw the man that inadvertently saved my life. It was the man named Marcus, and he had a long piece of metal protruding from his chest. *He'd saved me.*

One. Joe took a bullet for me.

Two. Marcus shielded me.

Three. Who would be next?

I was cradled against someone's chest. Nix. Tears streamed down his cheeks as we moved. "I've got you, Sweets. We're going." Or at least, that's what I think he said. The ringing wouldn't let up, forcing me to read lips and expressions and the drops of blood on the concrete.

It wasn't until we were in an alley that I truly collapsed into my fear. My limbs shook. The adrenaline coursing through me left me struggling to breathe. I felt like I could run a triathlon and collapse all at once. Each nerve ending was on fire, the cuts along my skin a painful reminder of what just happened, but also a welcomed distraction of everything I couldn't cope with.

"Wh-where are they?" I asked, choking out my question as I swallowed more smoke.

"I lost Ryker in the blast. Blaise stayed behind with Joe. Gavriel was just here..." Nix was shaken up, pacing the ground and wiping his hands on his pants. He'd always worked behind the scenes, hiding behind a computer to fight his battles. Seeing the gore of crime had scared him.

I cradled my head in my hands. If anything had happened to them, I'd never be able to forgive myself. "They're okay, Sweets. Just keep calm. They'll find us."

Nix watched me pace for a moment before tackling me with another hug. More glass cut deeper into my skin, but I didn't care. I hugged him back, feeling the drops of blood ooze from my various cuts as I held my best friend. Sirens in the distance drew my attention, and I broke away from Nix to start walking towards the sound, eager to see if the bodies on stretchers were Gavriel, Blaise or Ryker. I didn't know how much time had passed. Had it just happened? Was this real?

One. Joe took a bullet for me.

Two. Marcus shielded me.

Three. Who would be next?

Two arms wrapped around my waist, yanking me back into the safety of the shadows, and I cried out when I recognized the strong man holding me back.

"Gavriel?" I cried while spinning around to hold him tight. Two more bodies circled me, and I nearly collapsed in relief. The Bullets were safe. I took inventory of all of them, stepping back to see their faces clearly. Blaise had a slash across his forehead. Gavriel's face was covered in soot. Ryker had blood all along his torso, but no visible cuts, so I knew it wasn't his.

"Is Joe..." I asked, not sure if I was ready to hear the answer.

"He'll be okay. But he had to go to the hospital," Ryker answered me. "Are you okay?" he asked while looking at me up and down.

"I'll need a doctor to pull some glass from my back," I answered him while spinning around. It wasn't much, but the nagging pain would become excruciating if not dealt with soon. "What just happened?" I asked.

"Santobello. He wants a fight. He got it."

14

Joe was alive. We sat in an unmarked SUV outside the hospital, waiting for updates against the wishes of my men. In the driver's seat, Gavriel's leg bounced the entire time, anxious fingers tapping against his knee as he made various calls to cuss out his security team.

"A fucking sniper. I want footage from Blaise's building emailed to me within the hour."

I was a mess. The blood of the man that died to save me stained me with everything that had happened. We smelled like rust and sweat and salty tears.

"Has anyone called Joe's wife?" I asked, my voice tired from the harsh screams that ripped through my throat earlier. I'd kept silent once we got to the car.

"Fuck," Gavriel muttered before pulling his phone out. I held out my hand, eager to be the one to call.

"May I?"

Gavriel furrowed his brow, settling back in his seat in the front, but twisting to stare at me incredulously. "I guess," was his whispered response as Blaise banged his head in exasperation against the cool glass of the car window.

Gavriel dialed the number before handing the phone to me, brushing his fingers against mine, as if to prove to himself that I was still alive and that I wasn't some ghost, haunting him. She answered on the second ring. Mrs. Joe had a breathless quality about her tone that, in any other circumstance, I would have deemed warm and relaxing. She had a Southern accent too. It was cute.

"Hello?"

"Hi, is this Joe's wife?" I asked lamely. Before, I'd gotten used to calling her Mrs. Joe in my mind, but now it felt silly not knowing more about the family of the man who saved my life.

"Yes. It's about time you call me. Am I on speakerphone? Let me speak to Mr. Moretti this instant," she growled, her warmer tone no longer serene. I clicked the speaker button, making Gavriel wince. He was apparently familiar with Mrs. Joe and was prepared for the confrontation about to happen.

"Gavriel Moretti. I changed your diapers, and you wait six hours to call me? Six goddamn hours!" she roared. I covered my hand over my mouth, instantly amused by Mrs. Joe. This pretty much solidified my resolve to keep her.

"Mrs. Ricci, I sincerely apologize for taking so long to call—"

"Your sister was the one to finally inform me, only *after* I saw my husband being carted into the hospital on the news! Six hours, Moretti," she said his name like it was a curse, and I imagined her waggling her index finger at him when Gav was a kid. I didn't realize how far back their working relationship had gone.

"If I told you, you'd try to come here," Gavriel replied. "You know Joe's rules. You're not allowed to be involved, not with your heart condition getting worse. The doctor said no stress!"

"That's a bullshit excuse, and you know it. Okay, Summer, you can take me off speakerphone now," she cooed, her voice softening as she said my name. I took a moment to process how fucking adorable Gavriel's relationship was with them, as well as scowl at him on her behalf. For a split second, I found myself feeling jealous of Gavriel. He had a...a family. A makeshift one of thugs and scolding women with Southern accents. He had a brotherhood. All this time, I'd been so worried about Callum feeling accepted that I'd forgotten that I was an orphan too. For two years, it had been Nix and me against the world.

"Okay, dearie. You can talk now," Mrs. Joe—I mean—Mrs. Ricci said.

"We're at the hospital. Joe...he saved me..." I cried. The tears that filled my vision were nothing but a prickling reminder of everything that had happened, and everything yet to come.

"Is he okay?" she sobbed, her earlier bravado had completely disappeared, and now I found myself consoling her. I pictured a beautiful woman with grey hair and laugh lines around her eyes clutching her chest in a cozy kitchen.

"He's in surgery, but they're saying he should be okay. I know you probably want to come up here, but it might be safer for you to stay home..." I turned to look at Ryker; of all of us, he looked the most guilty, his knuckles were white as he gripped his thighs.

"Ain't nobody or nothing gonna keep me away. You think Santobello cares enough to kill an old woman with one good eye and two left feet? Y'all need to worry about yourselves. I'm so glad to finally get the chance to speak to you. I've heard so much about you." I smiled at that. So my broody bodyguard had mentioned me? Nice. "You just worry about yourself. Joe and I can handle ourselves. He'd be pretty pissed if he saved your life just for you to get yourself killed. Go somewhere safe. Can I call you on this number?"

"Yes," I blurted out immediately. I wasn't sure why I ached for a connection with this stranger, but I did. That's the thing about craving a family, it made you find the first candidates and cling to them. "What's your name?" I asked.

"Sherrie. I'll see you soon. Get out of town, dear," she offered before hanging up the phone.

When I handed Gavriel back his cell, he looked at me with pity and an expression similar to guilt. "Remember what you told me, Gav?" I asked, calling him out for the sad expression on his face.

"Don't even fucking say it. Your life was in danger, Love. I'm allowed to feel whatever the fuck I want to." Gavriel looked to Ryker and Blaise for support. I was enjoying how the tables had turned.

"Don't confuse empathy with blame, Gav. This wasn't your fault. You couldn't have known."

"Yeah, well, I could have been better fucking prepared," Nix yelled, thrusting his hand up and gesturing between all of us. He was still worked up, shocked by how everything went down, and I couldn't even blame him. "I mean, that was crazy. Bullets flying everywhere. Explosions. A fucking detached arm grazed my thigh. You had me watching Paul when I should have been keeping an eye on Santobello."

It was beyond crazy, it was terrifying. It was intense. I didn't know where the blood ended and the destruction began. "I should have never let you guys disappear at Blaise's loft. If Nix was running surveillance, none of this would have ever happened."

I bristled at the insinuation in that blaming statement. Nix couldn't have *possibly* prevented this. Ryker was still clenching and unclenching his fists. He had been the most silent. It wasn't necessarily out of the norm for him, but I wanted him to say something, *do something*. "I'm going to say yes to the fight," he growled before grabbing my hand.

Blaise twisted around in the front seat to face us, a curious expression on his face. "You want to willingly challenge the man that almost killed us?" he asked incredulously. My fingers itched to call Callum, to check and see how he was and let him know everything that was going on, but every time I reached for the phone in Gavriel's hand, something made me pause.

Maybe it was the chronic martyrism and self-pity I'd been living off of the last few weeks that was making me doubt things, but I wondered if Callum would even care. It was stupid and a waste of time to even entertain those dark thoughts. It was just a different form of the same doubt my father tried to instill in me when he threatened me the night in the basement. He wanted me to doubt the system and the people I loved. He wanted me to think that no one would believe me, and those that did, wouldn't care.

"Why would he do this? Challenge you to a fight then bomb our car? It makes no sense." I was working through the motives, packaging them up and looking for pieces that made sense. "You don't think it was...?" Everyone looked at me. Did my *father* plant the bomb?

Usually, Blaise would have finished my sentence for me, answered my unspoken thoughts and provided me comfort, but none of them interjected. We simply weren't sure. Was Paul Bright crazy enough to plan that sort of assault? Gavriel started the car and headed towards the airport. "We're going to Vegas. I think it's our best bet," he finally instructed.

"Turn around so I can pull the glass out of your back. I just realized that you've been sitting there in pain, and if we don't get it out soon, you could get an infection. Why didn't you say anything?"

Twisting in my seat, I showed my back to Ryker as he

opened up some tweezers in a first aid kit Blaise picked up
from a drugstore earlier. Slowly, he began pulling the small
collection of glass from my shoulders.

"This sucks," I grumbled, feeling naive because I didn't
know what else to say.

"That's an understatement," Nix replied from the very
back of the SUV. It didn't escape me how Gavriel kept
peering out the windows, anxiously checking for a threat on
the horizon. He didn't like feeling out of control. Gavriel
Moretti prided himself on the safety and protection he
provided the people he cared about, and when there was a
threat to their safety, he took it personally. The night sky
was quickly closing in on us, and after this morning, the
monsters lurking in the dark seemed much more real.

Nix had been on his phone since the attack, scrolling
through various different things on the dark web and
checking for updates. "Your dad was conveniently at a
public event, kissing babies and making cringe-worthy
smiles at the camera." I should have been comforted by the
fact that it wasn't him that tried to kill us, but I wasn't.
Instead, I shuddered, imagining him so close to helpless
people that had no idea about the devil within him. He was
sick, probably getting off on his secret, internally laughing at
how ignorant the world was for not knowing he could end
them with a snap of his fingers.

I let out a hiss of pain as Ryker pulled a rather large
piece from my back. "All done." Within minutes he was
applying antiseptic to the cuts, the burn waking me up as I
let out little whimpers.

"You're hurting her," Blaise said, a little more stern than I
was used to.

"We all are," was Ryker's solemn response, and his words
hung heavy around the car, acting like a weight on our
already sullen mood. Didn't he know? They'd *saved* me.

"Santobello was brazen. This could easily be traced back to him. Either he has reason to be this confident, or he's cocky," Gavriel said.

"Or he's scared," I added. Fear made people do reckless things. It bolstered courage when there was none left. It made people fight for that last breath of air, to break the surface of the waves and dive right back in. It was dangerous, fear. It was liberating.

"We're close," Nix said. "And while you were busy accusing me of not doing my job, I was keeping tabs remotely. I found out about a meeting he's having tomorrow night in Vegas," Nix said while rolling his eyes and passing his phone up to a driving Gavriel.

"Interesting, it's the same night as the fight," Ryker said while leaning over Gav's shoulder to peer at the cryptic message scrolling across Nix's phone.

"He was trying to throw us off our game with the fight. Make us focus on his motives for that as he ambushed us right under our noses. I think this meeting is important..." I trailed off, trying to think of what could possibly lead to all of this.

Gavriel passed back the phone and began biting his nail again, a nervous tick I hadn't seen since we were kids and he'd first moved to Chesterbrook. He'd long ago controlled the urge, but every now and then, when things got bad, he'd pick the habit back up. I hadn't expected to see the powerful man he'd become slip so easily back into that insecure habit.

"Can you explain your feud with Santobello to me more?" I asked while scratching at the dried blood on my hand. The dull red looked almost bright against my washed out skin.

"Santobello wants to control gun imports. He used to work with my dad, they shared control of a few of our suppliers, each taking territories to keep things even. It worked—for a while. Until dad went to prison and Santobello got greedy."

We pulled up to the airport, and four of Gavriel's men walked towards the parked car. Gav nodded towards his private plane, indicating that he would continue his story inside. We were escorted on the tarmac and up a flight of stairs, the men crowding around me, creating a shield of flesh and suits, and making me wish I had Joe's grumpy expression to comfort me. Once situated on the plane, the pilots made quick work of preparing us for takeoff, and Gavriel poured himself some whiskey before continuing his story.

"When I came back to take on the family business, Santobello had taken control of our territory and monopolized our suppliers, forcing us to work with him if we wanted anything. It took a while to regain our clients, using old friendships, fists, and competitive prices to win them back. My dad made a lot of allies. Santobello got lazy. Complacent. And when I started stealing my family's business back, he got pissed."

Ryker shifted back in his seat on the airplane, placing headphones over his ears and sinking into his silent place of focus, probably imagining his fight tomorrow. It was a routine I'd only just begun to understand, but I saw his calm expression for what it was. He was preparing to channel all his anger into whatever sorry motherfucker ended up on the other side of his fist.

"He's probably meeting with a supplier tomorrow and doesn't want you there..." Blaise offered. He didn't bother to sit down, despite the pilot's numerous requests. It was like he couldn't sit, couldn't keep still while our minds were racing.

I unbuckled and moved over to Gavriel, sitting on his lap

as the plane leveled out in the sky. He immediately wrapped his arms around me, eager to hold me tightly to his chest. I was quickly realizing that he enjoyed offering me what little peace he could. He liked showing that other side of himself, and I couldn't help but feel like Gavriel hid behind control but thrived within comfort.

"Why did you go back, Gav?" I asked, pressing my lips against his and ignoring the smell of grease and smoke on our skin. I was a mess, my hair frizzy with stray strands tickling our faces.

"Why did I do what?" he asked.

"Why did you go back to the family business? Why get involved? You could have been anything, done anything." I truly believed that Gavriel was selling himself short with this job. He was a leader. Cunning and driven, he could have run the world. But I guess he was, in his own deviant little way.

Gavriel stroked my hair, his fingers getting caught in the mass of tangles and making me wince in pain.

"Well, there was the obvious. I wanted to keep my father's legacy alive. Even if I hated the business as a kid, I grew to understand it as an adult. I don't deal women, Sunshine, never women. But I give jobs. I cut through some of the bureaucratic bullshit that other people have to deal with. We don't do ethical. We don't do legal. But we do money. Lots and lots of money. Lots of opportunities for lots of families that otherwise would be eating off food stamps for the rest of their lives," he spoke like a pastor in front of a choir, or a used car salesman trying to convince an unwilling buyer that their car was worth the purchase.

"I guess..." I mumbled, still not seeing the bigger picture. I wouldn't lie, I enjoyed the luxurious way Gavriel lived and traveled. Hopping on a jet plane at the drop of a hat was nice, and the homes he stayed in were glamorous. It was more than I could have ever even dreamed of.

But I'd had nothing. I'd slept on benches, eaten out of the trash. I walked miles because I couldn't afford the bus fare. There was an entire six months where my blisters had blisters, and the soles of my feet were a permanent shade of black and red because my shoes didn't fit. I worked shitty jobs, dated shitty men, all to survive. Money wasn't shit. It wasn't worth your soul. I felt better about surviving than I did about sleeping in Gavriel's posh penthouse.

"I still don't get it. You always hated his job. You liked the status it earned you, but you didn't like what your father had to do..." I trailed a finger over his shoulder where I knew the bullet wound was, where the evidence of how dangerous his job lie beneath the surface of his outfit. How many more near misses had he had in the last five years?

"Isn't it obvious?" Gavriel asked, cradling me closer. "You left, Sunshine. The kind of money it took to hire private investigators, to fund the continuous searches I ran, it was something a foster kid with two cents to his name couldn't do. If I wanted you, I had to accept my heritage, Love."

I clutched him so hard that my nails dug into his skin. If he weren't wearing a shirt, I was certain that I would have made him bleed. It hurt to hear that I was the reason Gavriel became who he was. It was my fault he was forced to dive headfirst into the bleak parts of his family's dealings just to find me.

Fucking guilt at every fucking turn. Fuck.

I couldn't escape the damn emotion. It was always there, taunting me with the possibility that the entire world, in fact, did rest on my shoulders. That *I* was the reason for all this pain. Grief wasn't an emotion, it was a state of being, and guilt held grief by the hand, coaxing it to the other side of survival and breaking it's kneecaps just before the finish line.

"I'm sorry, Gav," I choked out, not knowing what else to say. What more could I have done? I was a young girl, running from the devil and from the people meant to protect me. Knowing that my father got away with killing Callum's parents just made my decision that much clearer.

"Why are you sorry? I built an empire. I built you a kingdom," Gavriel said, his eyes wide as he grabbed my chin. Tilting my head to make me look at him, Gavriel peered at me with his brown eyes, making sure to look past the tears I had forming and dig deep, right to the darkest parts of my soul.

"But I never wanted a kingdom, Gav. I just wanted you. I just wanted *all* of you."

Gavriel kissed me then. It wasn't passionate. It wasn't painful. It didn't split my lip. It didn't taste like bliss or love or hope. It was a dark kiss, one that licked the edges of danger and heartbreak. It challenged me. It broke me.

His tongue broke through the seam in my lips to taste me as his hands threaded through my hair, cupping my skull. I moaned into his mouth. His kingdom for a kiss. I had gotten flakes of dried blood on his shirt, my tears on his soul.

I didn't care that Nix was sitting across from us. That Blaise and Ryker were there, fighting the turmoil of the day. I claimed Gavriel's mouth again and again. I memorized the feel of his soft lips on mine. I showed him how much I didn't give a fuck about his name, status, power or money. I showed him that it was always him, *always him*.

Gavriel had always had misconceptions about who he had to be in order to be accepted. He was either controlling or powerful or rich. He thought he had to be the baddest in the room, the wealthiest, or the scariest. He could never just be. Only with me.

The plane landed hours later. I had dozed off in Gavriel's lap. We decided to stay at a hotel off the strip, far enough away from the commotion that if things went down after the fight, we wouldn't be in the thick of it. Once again, I found my fingers trembling to call Callum, but I stayed firm to give him the space he so desperately asked for. I also knew that this was an extenuating circumstance, but maybe a part of me was being prideful. I wanted him to know that distancing himself came at a price. I was sure that by now the explosion had hit the news. The authorities were there before we could hide the bodies, much to Gavriel's dismay.

And still there had been no call, no reassurance that he still loved me, still cared, or still wanted to make this unconventional relationship work. I found myself wishing that, at the very least, he would care enough to let me know that he couldn't love me anymore. And fuck, I hated myself for worrying about Callum while Joe was somewhere recovering from surgery in a hospital, and Ryker was up for a fight against one of Santobello's men.

Nix was typing away at a computer that Gavriel had delivered to the hotel the moment our keycard slid into the slot at our top floor suite. The moment we were checked in, I took a shower, scrubbing away at my skin until it turned raw. Red little streaks were left behind by my scratching marks. Lathering up soap, I rubbed it in my palm and kept washing, over and over and over until the layer of skin with Joe's blood was completely gone. Once I was done and dressed in the tight clothes Blaise snagged from the gift shop downstairs, I joined the guys.

"Santobello is covering his tracks on the dark web. I'm checking for hits, but keep getting kicked out. I think he's finally hired someone that could rival me," Nix exclaimed, awe evident in his voice.

"Well, I'm paying you to be better," Gavriel growled while Ryker stretched on the floor of the hotel. Blaise was standing at the window, occasionally checking outside.

"I *am* better, doll face," Nix replied to Gavriel in a patronizing voice, keeping his tone sickly sweet as he batted his eyes at my boyfriend. "I'm just letting him *think* he's beating me. But I'm going to need, like...three more computers," Nix quickly added, albeit a bit sheepishly.

I moved over to Ryker, rubbing my hands along his neck as he stretched, massaging the knots that were still there from the last fight. "Is it safe?" I asked. "To fight so soon, I mean? Aren't you still recovering? And then today..." Ryker wasn't hurt too badly, but he was sore, that much I could tell. I felt anxious, it was a gnawing feeling in the pit of my stomach. One of those instinctual sensations that said something worse than what had happened today was on the horizon. I'd felt it when I went to the cabin, sitting outside and staring at the shadowed porch as my father climbed into his car. I felt it the night I ran into Blaise at the restaurant. It was like a shift in the air, a promise for something bigger to come. A hint that your entire world was about to flip on its axis, and there was nothing you could do to stop it.

"I'll be fine, Sunshine," Ryker said, his voice holding that wise tone to it that I loved so much. "There's nothing preparedness and anger can't beat."

"I don't think we should go," I said, allowing that feeling of uncertainty to cloud my thoughts and tempt me with hiding in the shadows with my men. Was revenge worth losing them? Any of them? Was Gavriel's money and power worth it?

"It's worth it," Ryker said. Usually it was Blaise that could read my thoughts, so I was surprised when Ry stood and began stretching his calves, bending at the hips while talking to me. "We could run, sure. Give up the Bullets and live together. But we'd never really be safe. Never really feel free. I refuse to have a life where I'm constantly worried about the people I love. That's not a life at all." He grunted out his last statement while standing before dropping to the floor to do push ups.

"Does this weird ritual where he grunts and works out amid fortune cookie statements work for you, Sweets? 'Cause I'm about half ready to drag him to the gym," Nix said while rolling his eyes. He preferred to work in complete silence while hacking. You could always tell how stressed Nix was by the way the veins in his neck throbbed, and right now, there was one particularly angry one thudding away.

"I'll go," Ryker offered before kissing me on the cheek and heading off to his room. He'd requested to sleep alone so he could focus, but I didn't like having him even down the hall. We were on Santobello's turf for the time being. But exhaustion tempted me with sleep, and I passed out soon after Ryker left.

15

"ARE YOU READY FOR TONIGHT?" I asked Ryker while we ate a cheap breakfast of microwaved bacon with eggs so fluffy they seemed artificial. When I lived on the streets, I used to break into hotels just like this and eat their continental breakfast. I had to rotate hotels in whatever city I was in, careful not to take too much and not look too eager. Looking back, it was crazy to think of how resourceful I had to be.

"I could think of a few things that would make me more ready," Ryker said, his green eyes bright as they took in my low cut shirt. Blaise had bought me a makeshift wardrobe while here, making sure to only pick clothes that were too small. And although it was November, we were in the desert where the temperatures weren't nearly as frigid as Chesterbrook or New York.

Ryker had become progressively flirtatious as the morning went on. I wasn't sure if he was trying to distract me, or if he was trying to redeem himself from our previous pre-fight chat in the locker room. The last time I fucked him before a fight, he had left me with his cum on my chest and a lot of self-loathing. I had a feeling I'd end up in the same position before tonight's fight, but I was more than okay with being on his list of things he did to prepare for a fight —especially if it distracted me from all the shit going on.

"Yeah? Like what?" I asked, pushing the eggs around on my plate as I distractedly looked towards the elevators off to our left. Blaise and Gavriel were upstairs discussing logistics for tonight, each arguing over what to do. Blaise wanted all of us to go to the fight and show a united front. Gavriel wanted to go to the meeting and catch Santobello off guard.

I wanted to do none of that. I wanted to do what I did best—run away.

"We're going to be fine," Ryker said, drawing me out of my thoughts. I was calculating how much money it would cost to get fake IDs and cross the border.

"Is that what you tell yourself to keep calm before a big fight?" I asked with a smirk as the elevator doors opened and Nix walked in, holding a cell phone up to his ear while frowning.

"Look. You need to stay indoors. Don't leave Sherrie's sight," he ordered. He looked at me, his dark eyes such a cloudy shade that I wondered who was on the other line, making him so flustered. "Because I said so!" Maintaining eye contact with me, Nix continued speaking as he approached the table. "You should just get used to me caring about you. When I find people I like, I don't give them any other choice. Do not do anything stupid. Stay hidden. You're safer there than you are with us, but if you run off again, I'll walk to New York and spank your pretty little ass, Miss Moretti," he said before pulling the phone from his ear and hanging up.

"Gavriel's sister?" I asked as he pulled up a chair.

"Yes," Nix grumbled before stealing toast from Ryker's plate, earning a growl from the carb-loading pro fighter.

"I've seriously got to meet her," I joked. Anyone that Nix

cared about automatically earned favors in my book. Add in that she was Gavriel's blood, and I was halfway to adopting the poor girl. What was it with me and wanting to collect people for a makeshift family?

"What are you all talking about? I need some light-hearted conversation that doesn't mention the mob, tonight's fight, or what we're doing with our lives." Nix's voice was agitated. He threw me a playful pout as he chomped down on the bread.

"Ryker was just telling me how I could help with his pre-fight routine," I replied while lifting my foot and rubbing it along Ryker's calf in what I hoped was a seductive move.

"Wrong leg, Sweets. But please, don't stop," Nix joked before a hand from beneath the table wrapped around my ankle. Whoops. I kept rubbing though, just because I could.

Nix's phone began ringing again, but this time when I answered I could hear shouting on the other line. "Whoa, Agent Mercer, calm your tits. She's right here," Nix said while holding the phone away from his ear and handing it to me.

A mixture of many emotions flooded me. Relief that Callum was calling, fear that he was upset or angry. Then I was excited by the possibility that he was worried for my safety. I hated that about myself, but I wanted to feel loved.

"Hello?" I answered just as a parade of questions and floundering statements assaulted me.

"Summer? Are you okay? A fucking explosion?! Where are you?" I frowned when I realized he was still using the name that put an invisible barrier and distance between us.

"Yeah, I'm fine," I choked out, suddenly losing my appetite.

"What happened? I called Gavriel to let him know that I'm on my way to New York, and he says you're in Las Vegas.

Then I learn that there were snipers and a car bomb? What the fuck, Summer, why didn't you call me?"

"You told me not to," I said, my answer simple yet weighed down with all the things we still needed to say to one another. We had so much to work through and so little time to do it. Ryker, Blaise, and Gavriel had *years* that bonded them to each other and in their friendship with me. How were we supposed to add Callum to the mix as the world went to shit?

There was nothing but silence that greeted me on the other end of the line. I could practically feel the regret rolling off of Callum, and I was mad at myself for enjoying the way he was questioning everything. Was it so wrong to want him to need me? Was it so wrong that I wanted him to see that when we were apart, bad things happened? I'd been without them all for far too long, I'd survived without my men, but I didn't thrive, not really.

"Did you deliberately not tell me, Summer?" Callum asked, his voice holding a dark tone that I'd only ever heard from his lips on the day of his parents' funeral. It was rare that Callum ever broke free from his carefully constructed image.

"I deliberately did what you asked me to do. I gave you space, Callum."

"I see."

I could feel Ryker's and Nix's eyes on me as we spoke, my cheeks red for throwing a tantrum in light of all the things that were currently happening. This was nothing, just a blip on the bigger picture. But still, I needed to say all the things I'd come to terms with. Sometimes, your truth hurts. Sometimes, the timing is bad. But sometimes, you have to dive under the icy water anyway.

"Callum. I fled that field because I didn't want to remind you of him, but I've gotten a few days of clarity to really think things through," I began, standing and making my way towards the elevator. There were people nearby that I didn't want listening in on the bombshell I was about to drop in his lap. "I'm angry too. I'm hurting too. From the moment I got back—no—from the moment we started to develop feelings for one another, I've made everything about you. I worshipped the ground you walked on. You needed time and space to understand our unique relationship? I gave it to you. You wanted to use me for a quick fuck in the cemetery, work through your pain? I let you. You wanted time to force your views of justice? Fine, let's go to the deepest, darkest place of my mind and dig up the evidence of my trauma."

I wanted to yell at Callum, but my voice was nothing but a low whisper. The truths I was spitting out were almost too painful to say any louder. "You were so wrapped up in your own convoluted ideas of right and wrong that you didn't even care that I was mourning your family too. When you looked at me, you saw *him*." My throat seemed to close in on the last word, like I couldn't choke out even the idea of my father.

"But how you're handling this has me thinking that you're more like my father than I am, Callum. And if things don't change, then I'll just end up like my mother, chained to a man who uses me up when it's convenient for him. I almost died. Joe is in the hospital because he quite literally took a bullet for me. And at the end of the day, I was surrounded and comforted by men that don't see me as Paul Bright's daughter, they see me as Sunshine."

Silence. Complete silence. Callum absorbed my words like the venom they were and suffocated under their weight, refusing to spit out his answer and let me know that he was done with me.

"Are you pushing me away, Su-Sunshine?" he asked. I

looked around, realizing that during all of this, I'd somehow marched to our room and was standing outside the hotel door. Ryker and Nix were standing a safe distance away.

"I'm pushing you to be the man that loves me," I said before ending the call and tossing Nix his phone.

I reached for the handle to open the door and paused. "Was I too harsh?" I asked, doubting myself. Callum was still grieving, still reeling from the new information. Was it really fair of me to call him out and rip off the bandaid of our relationship so soon?

"No," was Ryker's rushed reply. Grabbing my hand, he yanked me away from Gavriel's suite and towards his room three doors down. He'd requested privacy so he could get in the headspace for the fight, but now he was frantically clawing through his pockets for the keycard and pushing me inside.

"Ryker? Did I do something wrong?" I asked, but his lips slammed down on mine before he could answer.

"Fuck," he hissed into my mouth, gradually working the tight shirt from my body and thrusting his tongue in and out of my mouth. "You're so sexy, Sunshine," he grunted before picking me up and tossing me on the nearby queen bed.

Ryker took one look at the too-tight sports bra on my body and ripped the fabric, refusing to waste time working it over my shoulders. He didn't move with his usual calm collectedness. His kisses were wild. Primal. Instinctual. He wrestled with my mouth, nipping my lip as he worked my jogging pants off my legs with ease. "God, I love you," he murmured while trailing his tongue down my neck and to the high peaks of my breasts, licking the circular petals of my nipples before dragging his teeth against my sensitive skin. Goosebumps erupted along my skin at the sweet sensations.

"Watching me hurt Callum turned you on, huh?" I asked, a bit breathlessly. I wasn't sure how I felt about that, but I also felt too good to care.

His head snapped up as I looked down at him, my chest heaving. "Is that what you think?" His eyes were wide as he gauged my reaction.

"Yes?" My response sounded more like a question than an answer.

"Oh Sunshine," he responded while lowering further, kissing my skin like it was a drug. He was eager, and I felt vulnerable, deliciously treasured and delicate beneath him. "I'm dying to bury myself in your sweet little cunt because watching you stand up for yourself is quite possibly the hottest thing I've ever seen in my life."

Ryker's lips parted, and I took in his hooded eyes. Sitting up, both of us maneuvered until we were on our knees and facing one another. "Callum's gotta learn how to take a hit," Ryker said, reminding me of our conversation in my childhood bedroom all those years ago. "And baby? You just threw your first punch."

We collided. We threw ourselves at one another, our bodies an angry mashup of clashing teeth and moving limbs. I was ripping his shirt off of him, and he was biting my lip, sucking and pulling back to the point that it hurt. I shoved at his chest, pushing him into a lying position so that I could straddle him.

"I didn't picture you as the type to like an aggressive woman," I teased while trailing my nail down his chest. The scrapes on my back were buzzing from all the movement and groping, but the pain wasn't unpleasant, it just heightened the pleasure of the moment.

"Well, let's consider this a learning experience then," Ryker replied before twisting his body and pulling me down to the mattress, maneuvering so that he was then on top. "Or this could be a warm up. I'm in the mood for a good pre-fight fuck," Ryker whispered in my ear as he leaned forward, and I forced my hips up, bucking beneath his hold, but loving how firm his hands felt as they pinned me down.

"I'm in the mood for a fucking fight," was my throaty response. I leaned up as far as I could and licked his bottom lip, earning a growl. We pushed and pulled at one another, each of us fighting for power over the other but neither of us really winning. I'd steal a kiss, he'd tug on my skin. I'd writhe, he'd hold me down.

A thin layer of sweat covered my body as we shifted, the blankets a tangled web, wrapping up our legs as we moved and making the air feel hot. I nipped at his shoulder, holding back a pleased cry as he slammed into me. "Give up yet, Sunshine? Or do you have more left in you?" Ryker flipped me over with ease then placed his palm in the middle of my back, pressing me down into the mattress. I let out a laugh as his thrusts slowed to a steady pace, giving me the perfect opportunity to wiggle away if I wanted. It was playfully hot and erotic and fun.

This was the most exquisite game of cat and mouse that I'd ever played. His body was hot against mine, and every time I got closer to coming, I'd push him away and tackle him into a new position. I wanted to prolong the inevitable. "You going to come for me, Ry Baby?" I asked.

"You first," he croaked as he pulled out and flipped me over so that we could look each other in the eye. I clawed at his back as he leaned over me, pressing his lips to my sensitive neck and breasts. I knew I'd be sore later, the cuts from the explosion mixed with my overall exhaustion made every move more rewarding, like I'd *earned* the pain.

He raised up, using his arms to support him as his thrusts increased. The pace was too much to handle. I was coming apart on his cock, conceding to our battle of wills while crying out his name. His own release came shortly after, and I smiled at how good it felt for him to twitch inside of me, warm relaxation flooding each muscle and joint as we both sighed in relief.

The only sound in the room was our breathing and Ryker's satisfied groan. "I think I need to add this to my pre-fight ritual," Ryker said before wiping sweat from his brow.

"Then I think you need to plan a hell of a lot more fights," I replied with a sigh. Ryker moved me to lay on his chest, and I sat there listening to his steady breathing. After a while, the doubts started to pour in over what I'd said to Callum, the fight tonight, and the meeting with Santobello. "You're going to be okay, right?" It felt like a silly question, but I needed to know all the same.

Ryker stroked my arm as he stared at the ceiling. "As long as you are."

16

RYKER

   Six years ago

I USED to be threatened with foster care. Dad would tell me all these horror stories and how he was the best I was ever gonna get. It was part of the reason why I never told anyone that he was beating the shit out of me every night.

When mom died, he kinda lost it. He was mad at the world, mad at me. He was so mad, he would drink himself stupid then use his alcoholism as an excuse to beat all his frustrations out on whatever warm body was closest. It was easier to hate me than hate a ghost. How could he beat up a woman that killed herself?

And even with all his warnings, I was still shocked the night I arrived here. My foster brother, Gavriel, liked to assert his dominance, pissing on the town like it was his for the taking. The night I'd shown up, weak as fuck and trying not to breathe too deeply because my ribs hurt, he'd taken his damn thumb and dug it into my side right on the break.

There was only one rule in Chesterbrook, and it seemed easy enough to follow:

Stay away from Summer Bright.

I wasn't exactly sure what was so special about her that Gavriel had to stake his claim before even learning my name, but I wasn't the type to question a good thing. So if he wanted to be all caveman about a girl with pretty eyes and long black hair, then I was more than willing to let him.

When you've been beaten down your entire life, you learn to pick your battles. And *she* was a battle not worth fighting.

Blaise offered to drive me home everyday, but I liked the walk. Of the two, he was nicer. Maybe a bit more cocky though. He was also all wrapped up in that Summer Bright chick. I could hear him through the walls of my bedroom late at night, talking with her on the phone. Guess Gavriel didn't mind sharing with him. It was just the rest of the world he didn't want getting too close. I'd noticed things. Little things. Like how he'd glare at guys checking her out as she walked the halls. Or how he'd blow off girls that said something catty about her. They weren't dating, but he sure as hell wasn't about to let anyone else get near her.

Today, it was unseasonably hot. I twisted my blond hair up into a bun and took off my jacket. Sweat was covering my back, making my shirt stick to my body. It was a pleasant sort of discomfort. It was the type of heat that made your breath feel sticky. The concrete pavement was a stove top, and I was frying the bottoms of my feet with each step.

I've always liked to walk because it gave me time to think. I really enjoyed the quiet peace of moving at a steady pace, as well as the ritual of the experience. If I could walk forever without really going anywhere—I would.

As I traveled towards the Jamesons' house, a police cruiser pulled up beside me. I never much liked cops, they always showed up too late, or the law didn't allow them to serve justice the way I wanted them to. They always had dumb excuses. The whole world knew that my dad was beating the shit out of me, but it wasn't until I landed in the hospital that anyone was able to do something about it.

The driver in the police car rolled down the window and leaned out to stare at me. "You the new kid at the Jamesons'?" I turned my head to stare at the man. There was nothing that truly stood out to me. His hair was thinning, and his face had the forced quality about it that I'd come to expect here in Chesterbrook. Everyone was on display. But it was the calculating eyes that I recognized. They reminded me of my dad's, and it was an automatic indicator that he was not someone I wanted to mess with.

I had a sense about these things. I could pick out a dangerous person a mile away. Gavriel Moretti thought he was intimidating, but he didn't know the half of it. The real evil came from people good at hiding it. He used his intimidation like armor, the rest of the world used it like a knife. "Yes," I answered. I kept walking, ignoring the way his police cruiser crept alongside me.

"Well, I live next door," he answered. Once more, I felt his eyes on me, and I found myself walking faster to get away from him. He had that sense of assuming power. He was cocky, and I couldn't put my finger on it, but I knew that something about him was off.

"Would you like a ride home, son?" he asked. "I'm sure Mr. and Mrs. Jameson don't want you out here in the heat." There was something about the way he brought up Mr. and Mrs. Jameson that made me pause. It wasn't quite a threat, nor was it considered blackmail. Either way, I got the sense that if this guy didn't get what he wanted, he wasn't above going to others to make sure he got his way.

"I like to walk," I responded.

"Come on, get in."

I sensed that this was another one of those pick your battles moments, so I turned and got in the passenger seat. "Attaboy. I'm Chief Bright. You go to school with my daughter," he said.

That was right, that Summer chick lived next door. "I've seen her around," I said. Chief Bright was driving extra slow, and I felt his eyes on me as we went, checking me in the corner of his gaze. I looked out the window. Was this the part where he told me not to cause any trouble in his town? Did he know my dad was a public defender?

"Do you like to fish, son?" he asked instead, catching me off guard. I didn't like the way he kept calling me son. There was an arrogance about the nickname, like he was trying to assert his dominance over me. "Not really," I replied. Dad was never one to take me fishing.

Chief Bright pulled into his driveway, but he didn't turn off the car. I reached for the handle but realized that it was still locked. "Well, that's a shame," Chief Bright said. I looked over at him, noticing that his cheeks were red. Beads of sweat rolled down to his neck, leaving drops of moisture on his collar. "I have a cabin in the woods, kinda close to this real nice fishing spot. You should come out sometime."

I dipped my brow in scrutiny, unsure why this guy I barely knew was inviting me out fishing. He seemed to recognize the confused look on my face because he then said, "I make it a point to introduce myself to the new foster kids of the area. I think it's important that young boys have good role models in their life. I looked into your files. Your dad was a real piece of work," Chief Bright said.

I clutched my hand into a fist, wishing I could escape this police cruiser. I didn't want to talk about my dad, nor did I want some man with a superiority complex to think he was saving me. "I'm just saying, son, sometimes boys need a strong role model. I'd be happy to spend some time with you, teach you how to fish."

I opened my mouth to respond, but a gentle knocking on the window of the driver side door made me pause. Outside was Summer. I'd only seen her in passing a couple of times in the last six weeks, but there was a fear in her eyes that caught me off guard. She always seemed so composed, so perfect.

So afraid.

Chief Bright let out a huff of annoyance before killing the engine and opening the door. When he got out of the car, he took a moment to adjust his belt before addressing her. I took the opportunity to leave the car as well. With Gavriel's warnings still in my head, and the need to just survive the next seven months without any trouble, I had every intention of walking up to the Jamesons' house and sitting in my room for the rest of the night. But there was a fear in her voice that made me pause. Maybe I was just attuned to these things, but Summer Bright was scared of her father.

"What do you want?" her dad growled. He loomed over her, using every bit of his influence to intimidate. That didn't sit well with me for some reason.

"It's Mom," she began with a stutter. "She passed out and fell, I can't pick her up."

Chief Bright looked at me, a flash of insecurity crossing his face. He shushed his daughter before saying, "Well, come on then. Let's go put her to bed."

I wanted to go after them and see if they needed help. Not really because I wanted to be around Chief Bright any longer, but because the frown on Summer's face was all too familiar. "You okay?" I called after her the moment he disappeared inside. She looked back at me over her shoulder and nodded once before following her father inside.

I didn't notice Gavriel standing by the Jamesons' front door when I walked up. But the frown on his face was glaringly obvious. He didn't like that I had shown up in Chief Bright's car, and he *definitely* didn't like that I'd talked to Summer. I don't know what it was about her that had him all out of sorts, but I was starting to see that there was more to her smile than the act she put on for everyone else.

"Why were you in his car?" he asked, his voice more like a growl than a question.

"He offered me a ride. Wanted to invite me to his lake house," I replied with an involuntary shiver.

Blaise was in the garage, working on his car. If I hadn't seen him with so many girls, I would've thought he was fucking his machine. He threw me a cocky smile before saying, "Well that's weird."

"He said something about wanting to be a role model for the foster kids. I bet it has something to do with him running for office." It was no secret that the Brights were popular in this town. Signs boasting a bright future under his leadership lined our street, and election season hadn't even started yet.

"Isn't your daddy a public defender? I bet you're right. He just wants a picture in the newspaper. Sly bastard," Blaise said with a frown. Both he and Gavriel stared off towards the Brights' house, and I wondered what other things they knew about Summer's family. From what little I'd seen, I thought that they had the picture-perfect little life, but today reminded me that pictures were only two-dimensional.

"Well anyway, I'll just get going," I said before sidestepping Gavriel. He stuck out his hand and placed it on my chest, stopping me from avoiding them. Ever since I got here, Gavriel had let me do my own thing. But now that I'd said two words to Summer, he wanted to chat. *This* was why I didn't like to get involved.

"You remember my rule, right?" Gavriel asked. I gave him a hard look before shoving his hand off my chest.

"Yeah, I remember." I didn't give either of them a second glance, I simply went inside and upstairs to my room. They were probably going to some party tonight to get shitfaced again. Blaise liked to be the center of attention, and Gavriel liked having an opportunity to forget himself for a while. I simply liked that they left most nights, so I could have the house to myself.

When they left for the evening, they didn't bother saying goodbye to me. Gavriel only felt compelled to talk to me when he thought I was breaking his rules. Otherwise, they were in their cute little club, and I was more than happy to be excluded. I was sitting on the couch, watching TV when a light knock on the front door sounded. I got up, straightened my boxer shorts, then shuffled to answer it. Mr. and Mrs. Jameson were at another convention, so I wasn't sure what the protocol was for guests.

A crash of thunder sounded outside, and when I opened the door, I was surprised to see Summer Bright. She was drenched from head to toe, and the tears on her face were mixed in with the rain pouring down. She looked completely devastated, and this weird sensation balled up in my chest, forcing me forward. I wanted to wrap my arms around the little broken thing in front of me.

"Is Gavriel or Blaise here?" she asked with a sniffle. I stepped to the side, motioning her inside the house. I was afraid that if I told her they were gone, she would leave. And for some weird reason, the thought of her leaving felt like when Gavriel pressed on my broken rib.

"They're out," I answered. I felt her eyes on my abs, and I

quickly ran to the laundry room to grab a shirt and some sweatpants. When I came back, she was shivering.

"Are you okay? Do you need me to call someone?" I asked. I wasn't sure what it was about her that made me want to help, but I recognized myself in her terrified stare. Abuse, no matter the type, was one of those things that bonded people. It was a shitty bond, always trying to balance on its shaky foundation of distrust and trauma. But it was still there, a flashing indicator that there were more people in the world like you than you originally thought.

"I was hoping that they were here..." she said. Her teeth began to chatter, and I quickly grabbed my cell phone.

"Stay right here, okay?" Dialing Blaise's number, I called him, stuck between wanting him to answer and wanting him to stay away all night. But then I remembered about battles and how I should pick them.

"Finally get tired of hanging out alone?" he answered. "I was wondering when you'd start inviting yourself along." I looked at Summer, who was doing everything in her power to avoid my gaze.

She hadn't left yet, which meant that the awkwardness between us wasn't nearly as bad as whatever she was hiding from.

"No, it's Summer," I said while glancing at her. "She's here asking for you guys. She seems...upset?" I looked at her, trying to gauge if she would be angry that I told them she was crying, but instead of embarrassment, it was like a weight had been lifted off her shoulders.

On the other end of the line, Blaise cursed. "Fuck. Her mom has a little bit of a drinking problem, and her parents have been fighting. I've been drinking, let me find Gav so he can drive us. Tell her that we'll be home as soon as we can."

Blaise hung up the phone, not waiting for my answer. Once again, I found myself staring at this mysterious girl that had my foster brothers tripping over themselves. Blaise didn't even question leaving the party early to come console her.

"You can go upstairs to one of their rooms?" I said with shaky uncertainty. For some reason, I wasn't quite sure how to act around her. I wasn't sure where the line was for Gavriel. "I'm sure you want to get out of those clothes. You can borrow some of theirs, or you can grab something of mine?"

She disappeared upstairs for a moment, and I just figured that was the end of it. The guys would come home and be her knight in shining armor. For six years, I couldn't even save myself, so I didn't expect to be the one to save her now. It was best not to have high expectations, so after she'd gone up the steps, I went back to the living room and tried to ignore the nagging feeling that was eating at me. I wanted to go upstairs and take care of the stranger crying in one of the bedrooms, but Gavriel's warning was still strong in my mind.

"What are you watching?" a timid voice asked from behind. Surprised, I turned around to stare at her. She found Blaise's shirt and Gavriel's sweatpants. The outfit completely swallowed her up, and I wished she was wearing something of mine too. Maybe that's why Gavriel didn't want me talking to her. He already had to share her with one dude, three's a crowd.

"Uh, nothing really. You can change the channel if you want." I was fumbling over my words and making an idiot of myself.

"So why were you with my dad today?" she asked. I chanced a look at her as she settled on the seat beside me and noticed that her eyes were red, but the rest of her showed no signs of the tears flowing from her face before.

I didn't want to be rude and admit that I thought her

flesh and blood was a fucking creeper, even though I was pretty sure she knew it herself, so instead I said, "It was hot, and I wasn't feeling great. He offered me a ride."

Summer nodded her head then pulled her knees up to her chest, resting her chin on them as she slumped over. I debated for a good three minutes about whether or not I should ask her why she was crying, when she told me without prompting. "My mom has a...a problem," she said.

She was stumbling on the words, and I immediately knew that she wasn't telling me this because she wanted to. She felt like she had to explain herself. She was embarrassed. The thunder crashed outside, echoing the awkwardness we were experiencing here in the living room.

A half hour passed like that. Us silently watching a show that I wasn't even remotely paying attention to and her occasionally looking up at the clock, probably wondering where her *real* saviors were. "Do you like pancakes?" she asked.

"Yeah?" I replied.

"Good, 'cause I'm hungry."

Summer Bright knew where everything was in the Jamesons' kitchen. She opened the pantry and got out the ingredients with ease, needing little direction from me. Which was good because I had no fucking clue where anything was, nor did I feel comfortable enough rummaging through their stuff. This wasn't my home.

She mixed the batter and poured some into the frying pan. I immediately saw that she overlapped some of them, and I wondered what design she was trying to make. "I saw on a cooking show once that someone made a happy face pancake this way. Thought I'd try it out," she said mostly to herself.

I leaned over her shoulder, standing close enough to smell the remnants of rain on her skin and light in her soul. She smelled like...sunshine.

And she was making a penis shaped pancake.

I smiled for the first time in what felt like...years. "It looks like..."—she tilted her head to the side, and I wasn't sure what to say in that moment—"...a penis. It looks like a fat penis."

I watched in awe as her cheeks turned a perfect shade of pink, and she tossed her head back to laugh. I was still standing so close that she was then resting on my chest, giggling so much that her shoulders bounced as the pancake penis burned in the frying pan.

"Looks like you're doing better," Blaise's voice said to our left. I immediately backed up, feeling a shiver of cold from the distance between us. Blaise and Gavriel were standing there, one with a drunk and mischievous smile on his face but the other with his arms crossed in disapproval. Fuck. Gavriel Moretti was going to strangle me in my sleep.

Blaise surged forward, wrapping his arms around her middle before carrying her off. "My little Sunshine, out in the rain and looking so pretty in my shirt," he cooed before walking away. Gavriel's stare was hot on my neck. I was pissed. Who was *he* to tell me what I could and couldn't do. He took slow strides towards me, and something in the way he walked took me to another place. I wasn't in the Jamesons' kitchen. I was at home, standing on wooden floors in my living room as Dad landed blow after blow. I flinched. I cowered. I squeezed my eyes shut, feeling like a pussy. They say a body can't remember pain, but mine could. My brain recreated the sounds of crunching bones, bleeding wounds. I was covered in bruises, but Gavriel Moretti didn't even land a punch.

"Kid!" a voice said, stern but loud. There was a hand on my shoulder. A slap in my brain. A shove in my heart. "Kid, snap out of it."

I never understood why people said they had to pull

themselves together. Mine was more like a push. I had to force my mind up a mountain of trauma. It wasn't until I was leaning against the counter that I could finally understand what Gavriel was saying. "Thanks for helping her tonight. I'm glad you were here."

His tone suggested that he was hesitant to compliment me, each word lingering on his tongue. "What?"

I knew better. Gavriel wasn't going to repeat himself.

"You know how to fight, kid?" he asked. I could have punched him in the jaw right then and there for the nickname. We were practically the same age, and if pain added years, then I was at least a century old.

"I can take a hit, if that's what you're wondering," I said.

"I didn't ask that. I asked if you knew how to *fight*," Gavriel continued, crowding my space with that dark look in his eyes I'd seen the first night I got here.

"No. Not really."

"Good. First lesson tomorrow morning at six a.m. before school. Sunshine works in the library before class, so we ride early. Don't be late." He spun around, not giving me the chance to refuse. I watched his back as he retreated from the kitchen, wondering if I was now a Bullet or if I left my father's abuse to take on another.

17

Sunshine
Present day

THE VENUE for Ryker's fight was all Vegas glam. A rolled out red carpet welcomed us, and the paparazzi flashed their cameras as the neon lights overhead illuminated the night sky. Ultimately, Gavriel decided that it would be better to show up to the fight. Nix convinced him to work smarter instead of harder, so Gavriel reached out to his contacts prior to the fight and offered the man that Santobello was meeting with a better deal. It wasn't about being the strongest. It was about being first and being the one with the better offer. Now, instead of worrying about what was happening at the meeting, we would have to worry about Santobello's reaction.

Our seats were close to the ring. As we sat down, I found myself feeling more and more worried about this match. Ryker had left for the venue a couple hours ago and was likely somewhere in a locker room preparing. I thought back on the last time I was at one of his fights. I wondered if he was calm or if he had given in to his anxious energy, pacing the locker rooms with his muscles flexed. Gavriel said that he did better when he was calm and in a stable state of mind, but I thought that there was something to be said for Ryker's anger. Skill, precision, and the ability to think ahead was important. But at the end of the day, this game was about brute force.

"You okay?" Blaise asked. I was twisting a program in my lap as my black sequined dress shimmered under the bright lights while more people filtered in. To a quiet observer, this was a match between two pro-fighters, but to anyone who knew more about the men fighting, this was a gang war. A turf dispute settled with fists.

Gavriel was quick to dismiss my questions about Ryker's opponent, but I had a feeling that things were going to be intense. "I'm fine. I'll be better when all of this is over," I answered.

Gavriel's men surrounded us, creating a wall of angry expressions and broad shoulders. A part of me wished they could block my view of the ring, but I knew it was important that I watch. "Ryker's a total badass. You have nothing to worry about," Blaise encouraged. Nix and three of Gavriel's men stayed behind at the hotel. He wanted to run surveillance and let us know where Santobello or my father were should they try something at the fight. We were attending with the hopes that it was too crowded of a place for either of them to try something.

"I know he can handle himself. It doesn't mean I won't be any less concerned." I observed the ring and watched as the lights dimmed. Loud music with an arousing beat began playing. The announcer made his way to the center of the ring, accompanied by a referee. I only half-heartedly paid attention to the announcements. It wasn't until Ryker was walking towards the ring that my entire soul went on alert. My eyes were glued to his, my body responding to his nearness. The air smelled of cheap cologne and cigarettes. There was an exit near the front. Five men behind me. I no longer had my knife. But I could still remember the feel of it.

One. Ryker would be okay.

Two. We were safe.

Three. Please let us be safe.

Ryker slipped through the ropes surrounding the ring and started bouncing on the soles of his feet. Oh yes, he was definitely that anxious ball of energy. To my right, Gavriel frowned as he stared at this new warm-up technique.

"Why is he bouncing around? That never works for him. He needs to calm the fuck down," Gavriel said. Behind him, his men were whispering frantically as if realizing that the bets they just placed were at risk. My eyes snapped back to Ryker. Even if it was out of the ordinary, I knew that Ryker was doing whatever was best for him. If he needed to expel some of the excess energy he had, then more power to him. The music pumping through the stadium was loud, the rocky bass making my body hum and ache in all the places Ryker kissed me earlier.

"How did Santobello pull this off so quickly?" I asked Gavriel, leaning in to speak in his ear over the loud music.

"Money and power, Love. He hasn't learned the art of subtlety," was Gav's response. His eyes were glued to the ring as he spoke to me. He'd never admit it, but he was worried for Ryker. I'd noticed it at the last fight too. I originally thought it was his love for the sport that had him so attuned to each punch, but it was actually his love for his brother that had him so invested.

"What does being subtle have to do with it?" I asked.

At my question, Gavriel turned to me with a smile,

leaning closer so that he was speaking over me with that smoky tone that made me a puddle at his feet.

"If you ever want to know who the most powerful man in the room is, look for the one not saying anything, just observing the spectacle. Power speaks for itself, Love."

The announcer's commentary was cheesy and over the top, it was a show of authority. When Ryker's opponent entered the ring, I had to stifle a gasp. He looked scary, and not just the traditional muscular scary with tattoos and an "I don't give a fuck" expression.

No, he looked like a sociopath. He looked like my father, with a cruel smile bordering on manic. His eyes were bright as they took in Ryker's bouncing form. I watched how he categorized each movement. He stared at the way Ryker was still bruised from his fight just a few days ago, eyes shining when he saw the hickey on his neck...

Did Santobello only employ sociopaths? It was like he found people so brutal that they didn't know any better. Santobello gave them an outlet for their addictions for inflicting pain.

"Shit, he looks scary," I said to Blaise. He was chowing down on popcorn, a full beer sitting untouched beside him. They were both trying to look like they were here to enjoy a fight, but there was no hiding the fact that this was all show. Beneath the surface, my men were bubbling with as much adrenaline and anxiety as I was.

"He doesn't have the same sort of rigorous training as Ryker. He's got strength, this'll hurt a fuck ton, but he doesn't move with thought. He's all reckless force," Blaise surmised while plopping more popcorn into his mouth.

Half-dressed women circled the ring, smiling and waving at the crowd as they got the audience revved up and ready for the fight. Everyone around us was screaming their heads off, drinking in the excitement and violence like it was Sunshine Whiskey. Cheap but efficient. The entire arena was practically vibrating.

The music grew louder, and a white spotlight focused on the fighters as the ref explained the rules. Everything was a blurry haze, and once again, I felt a fear in the pit of my stomach that things were going to drastically change for us, that this was the beginning of something bad. Really fucking bad.

Blaise held my hand. "He'll be okay, Sunshine. Ryker's a badass." Everyone kept assuring me of that, but I still wasn't sure.

The beginning of the fight came too fast. Although everything leading up to the first punch was a warning of sorts, I still felt that there wasn't enough time to prepare myself for the brutality of it all. I wasn't prepared for the solid steps of Ryker's opponent as he charged him. Blaise was right, there was no rhyme or reason to his hits, he just moved as fast as his thick body would let him, delivering punch after punch to the faded bruises on Ryker's ribs. The crowd was too loud, but I imagined the intense sounds of flesh hitting flesh, the vibrant pain bubbling within him, and the quick exhales of his lungs.

And all the while, Ryker smiled. He was patient, half-heartedly dodging each strike but still standing proud and durable with each meaty throw of his opponent.

"Why doesn't he try hitting?" I asked Gavriel. Tough and rugged, Ryker looked cocky in the ring, using his agility and knowledge to evade and accept. I recognized that there was some underlying motivations behind each move but couldn't help worrying that this was like the fight in LA, when he just stood there, locked in his mind while his opponent beat him.

"I don't know," Gavriel growled in response.

There were no rules in the MMA styled match. It

seemed like everything was fair game. No hit too below the belt, no amount of blood too much. The crowd began chanting his opponent's name.

Donovan. Donovan. Donovan the Destroyer. When we'd first arrived, they were all about Ryker. The crowd flipped on a dime, following after the strongest man in a room because they didn't owe my man their loyalty. They wanted blood and would steal it from whoever delivered first. Donovan tried to lock Ryker against his body to pull him down to the mat, but Ryker slipped out of his grip. My fighter was constantly moving just enough to keep away while still getting close enough for Donovan to land a hit.

It wasn't long before his opponent's breath was labored and his feet sluggish. Ryker still wore an easy smile, but Donovan's energy was draining. He had no stamina, and suddenly, I understood Ryker's methods. He was wearing him out, accepting the pain he could handle so that he could catch Donovan while he was tired. But of course, he had to be smart about it. He had to look like he was struggling and weak from the hits. "Well, that was a risky move," I said to Gavriel. He, too, seemed to come to the same conclusion as I, because he nodded in agreement.

"He's pretty beat up," Gavriel said.

Around us the crowd seemed bored at the anticlimactic and one-sided fight. They booed Ryker for not hitting back, some of them bursting from their seats, as if wanting to go to the arena and pick a fight with him too. "Any signs of Santobello?" I asked. Before arriving, Gavriel warned me that he would be here, probably sitting opposite us on the other side of the ring. But everytime my eyes turned to the section reserved for him, the seats were empty.

The crowd's restlessness peaked, and soon people were not only booing Ryker but yelling at him to fight back or get the hell out of the ring. There was a brief moment when

Donovan's back was turned to me, and Ryker looked in our direction over Donovan's shoulder. I was reminded of the first fight I'd ever attended, when Gavriel looked at me and paused in shock, propelling us forward into a fate we couldn't avoid.

But now, when Ryker's eyes met mine, we exchanged a brief moment of solidarity and comfort. I felt nothing but assurance that this time around, things would be different. Danger might have been on the horizon, but so was hope. So was love.

A couple rounds had passed, each one Donovan claiming, but after my moment with Ryker, he snapped. Circling Donovan on the ring with quick steps that made his calves and thighs flex, Ryker surged towards his opponent with a murderous grunt. Left right jab, forward step. A clip to the jaw, a pump to the gut. Donovan's meaty flesh rippled with precision. There was a certain force behind each controlled muscle. I recognized the movements of someone that had been exposed to brutal fighting all their life. He didn't hesitate, didn't hold back. He let loose the bottled up rage bubbling beneath the surface, and Donovan could do nothing but stand there and take it, his body too tired to dodge the quick assault.

I've never truly feared Ryker. Even at his cruelest, I knew that he wouldn't hurt me—*couldn't* hurt me. But watching him in his element, delivering each blow like it was his God-given right, had me viewing him through a new lens. Ryker was a predator in disguise. He had so much bottled up anger that when he unleashed it, he was lethal.

"Shit," I said, unable to help myself. I was in awe but also a little shocked by the sheer power in his hits.

Donovan faltered, his face scrunching up into a sad combination of pain and determination. Ryker could easily win. "Your man is doing well," a voice with a faintly clipped accent said to us. I was so enraptured by the fight, I didn't notice the group of men walking towards us, or the way that Blaise and Gavriel went stiff beside me.

Santobello looked like I remembered. Peering at him now, I couldn't believe that I missed it before. He still held that assuming gaze in his eyes, the one that said he truly believed he could own or overpower anyone he wanted. I could still remember how he held my handshake for a little longer than necessary, and how his eyes roamed over my body, like he wasn't afraid to make me feel uncomfortable.

"Sometimes, a fist isn't enough. There's a certain intelligence necessary to win this game," Gavriel said over the cheering of the crowd. I knew he wasn't just talking about the fight. "Enjoy your meeting?" Gavriel asked before leaning back, his body language showing that he was relaxed, but lacking authenticity. It was all for show, a twisted competition to see who could handle the threat better, who could look the least affected.

My eyes shifted to Santobello as Blaise gripped my hand harder. I saw the flash of fury in the older man's eyes; it was brief, but it was weighted with all the anger he felt towards Gavriel and the Bullets. "You think you're clever. You're getting cocky, Gavriel. Not watching your back, not watching those you love."

The threat was clear, and Santobello was aiming to hit a sore spot, knowing Gavriel's weakness for *me*. It was a double-edged sword, being loved by a man with enemies. But oh, my crime boss was worth it. I waited to see how Gavriel would handle this obvious threat. I could practically feel how angry he was, like I could feel Ryker's power, Callum's disdain, and Blaise's determination.

Gavriel stepped down from the aisle we were on, brushing off his well-fitted suit as he walked. The men around us went on full alert, and the crowd seemed to move their attention to the power struggle happening *off* the mat. I had to lean in to hear over the fight, music, and crowd, but each word pouring from Gavriel's lips was abundantly clear. "You think my loved ones are a weakness, but you're wrong. I'm generally levelheaded, Santobello. Mess with my business, I'll end you. Mess with my people? I'll have you begging for death. I don't have to tell you all the things I'll do. You're not worth the threat, but know you fucked up when you brought her into this."

Behind them, Ryker emphasized Gavriel's point by hitting Donovan with one final punishing punch, ending the match with a knock out that left the room screaming in satisfaction, high from the violence, and happy to have won their bets. It was so loud that I almost missed Santobello's parting words. I knew nothing would come from this showdown, we were in too public of a place. Too many casualties, like Gavriel said.

"Your federal agent seems on edge. See that you make sure he's not taking on more than he can handle, going after one of mine." Santobello spun around and left with the dramatic flair of someone that had planned his words. He was here on a mission. He wanted to let us know that he had Callum on his radar.

It took a moment for Gavriel to make his way back to the seat. The crowd started flooding the ring as Ryker was named the champion. I looked up at Ryker, blood dripping from his mouth and a thick layer of sweat covering his body. Around him, men were patting him on the back, but Ryker's gaze was fixed on us.

"You okay?" he mouthed as a woman wearing a bikini draped herself over his shoulder to kiss his cheek.

"No," I mouthed back.

18

Ryker was on a bench in the locker rooms being checked out by a medic. We followed him there once the crowd dispersed while Gavriel called Callum. There was no answer. "Are you sure that's what he said?" Ryker asked while the medic pressed into his side to check his ribs, earning a groan from my brave fighter. "Positive," Blaise replied while looking at me. Santobello hinted that Callum had plans to take on my father, but since my blow up on him yesterday, he hadn't been answering the phone.

Blaise pulled out his phone and called Nix, who was still at the hotel. "Hey. Can you do a scan for Callum? We might have a problem." Blaise listened for a moment to Nix, rolling his eyes at something he'd said. "Just tell me where he is, please?"

More minutes passed, and I watched as Gavriel called Callum, Blaise listened to Nix, and Ryker stared at me.

"He's where? Fuck." Blaise shook his head before saying thank you and hanging up. We all directed our attention to him, prepared to hear whatever bad news was brewing. "Callum used his credit card at a hunting supply store outside of Chesterbrook. Paul Bright is there for the holiday weekend for some publicity thing."

Shit. I started pacing the room, my tall heels clicking against the tile. "You don't think? Surely he wouldn't..." I couldn't finish my train of thought. My mind went back over the cruel things I'd said to him. Would Callum seriously take on my father alone? What if he were caught? He wasn't in the state of mind to make rational decisions.

"How long of a flight would it be from here to Chesterbrook?" I asked before hiking my purse up on my shoulder.

"Four hours, maybe less depending on the pilot," Gavriel replied while typing on his phone, as if he'd already looked it up and was preparing his jet.

"Are you okay to travel?" I asked. The medic looked at Ryker then answered for him.

"He's bruised. Bad. Might have a slight concussion. Needs to be observed for the night."

Ryker rolled his eyes and shoved the medic away. The lanky man scurried out of the locker rooms as fast as he possibly could.

"Shit!" Gavriel exclaimed while looking at an alert on his phone. "Someone broke into my house. My sister is fine, but she's being moved to stay with Mrs. Ricci and Joe at the hospital."

Gavriel's men were all around us, each of them staring at him with trepidation. Their faith had been shaken since the shooting in Harlem, and now Gavriel's control over the situation seemed to weaken. I knew if he didn't take charge, or at least feel like he was in control soon, he would spiral.

"Tell us what to do, Gav," I whispered, offering my faith in him on a silver platter.

"I don't know if Santobello wants us to go. It could be just another trap," he said before standing. Gavriel pocketed his cell phone then went to face the men guarding the room, a look of indecision on his face.

"So we'll have to make him think we're going home, but we're going to get Callum instead," he responded, while patting the gun in the holster on his hip. He then smiled at his men like he had a plan. *There* was my fearless leader.

Within the hour, the four of us were in a taxi headed to the airport while a town car full of Gavriel's men headed to the private jet at a smaller airport outside of the strip. We had fake IDs and four economy tickets for a flight to DC. It was two hours from Chesterbrook. Our ploy to confuse Santobello meant that we'd have to sacrifice time, but it might draw his attention elsewhere.

I was wearing a hat and big sunglasses despite the night sky. Ryker looked half dead in his seat, head rolled back as he grunted in pain when the taxi driver drove over a bump. He was sore and had a headache from hell, but he was fine.

"When we get to the airport, we'll split up. Blaise and Sunshine will go together, and Ryker and I will follow after. I don't want Sunshine anywhere near me," Gavriel ordered. The taxi driver peered at me through the rearview mirror, as if trying to gauge if I was being kidnapped or not.

It was quite the production, getting the guards to leave the fighting arena while looking like we were with them. We escaped through a back exit while his men crowded close together, giving off the illusion that they were protecting someone in the middle. They loaded into the town car, then left straight for the airport. His team of guards were headed to New York.

"And when we get there? Is there any more news about where Callum is right now?" I asked as we pulled into the airport.

"Last update from Nix was that Callum got a hotel room

for the night, a motel outside of the city. He hacked the security feed and will be able to see if he leaves."

"Good," I said. Since speaking with Santobello I'd been in a never-ending cycle of thoughts. Fear of Santobello, anger with Callum, regret over our last conversation. Did I push Callum to act?

"So when we get there, then what?" I asked, needing to know what the plan was. I bit the inside of my cheek, gnawing on the flesh and trying to keep steady so the taxi driver didn't abandon us and call the police.

Gavriel looked at Blaise, and they took a moment to exchange a conversation without words, each of their eyes boring into one another with a solidarity that I'd known since they were kids.

With his hand on the door, Gavriel then answered me. "We're going to help him"—he glared at the driver, daring him to question our conversation—"with the job he's taken on. If Callum's ready to accept the darker parts of himself, then we'll meet him in hell. You don't have to come with us, but I think you should."

Gavriel didn't give me time to respond, instead getting out of the car to open my door for me. Gavriel was right. I did need to attend this. I needed retribution, I needed my revenge. I needed the peace of knowing that my father was dead and that the men I loved saved me from him in the end.

Ryker and I shuffled out of the sedan, and we stood there on the street for a moment as I pulled my hat lower on my face. I was wearing black pants, a black shirt and black funeral hat. If I was going to attend the death of my father, I already looked the part. Ryker was wearing gym clothes and a warm up jacket. Each step seemed to hurt him.

"Stop looking at me like that," he said while Gavriel paid the driver.

"Like what?"

Ryker leaned over to be eye level with me, hissing in pain from the movement but closing in on me nevertheless. "This is nothing. I once had my jaw wired shut. Broken in three places. I can survive this."

My eyes widened in surprise at Ryker before I shook my head.

I took a deep breath, thinking about everything we were about to face. I needed to show Callum that he didn't have to cling to his ideas about right and wrong to keep me. He needed to see and feel unconditional love. I honestly wasn't sure what was waiting for us at the end of all this, if Callum would finally accept me—accept us. Or if he'd finally move on, feeling a bit more free of the restraints he's put on himself. But I hoped that we'd end up together. I hoped that we'd forgive and find normalcy at the end of it all.

"I'm ready," I said as Blaise grabbed my hand.

We stood in a circle, alone for the first time in a while. It was only a brief moment in time, three seconds at the most. I felt vulnerable as tipsy travelers still enjoying the Vegas scene and broody businessmen with bulky suitcases rolled past us. Everyone had a destination. I took the moment to enjoy the silence—enjoy the brief pause in momentum before we had to dive back into the chaos.

I looked at Gavriel, the sharp lines on his face looked extra fierce as he inspected me. My fearless leader was scared. Control came at a price, and that price was the burdens of our safety and happiness. Gavriel thrived under pressure, but there was a vulnerability—an uncertainty—that had my heart warming for the boy that always protected me and always will.

Ryker looked in pain. For the man that could take all the hits, he seemed to doubt his threshold of suffering then. And not the physical kind, either.

Blaise looked...certain. He clung to me, keeping me close while holding that determined stare in his eyes that knew all of my secrets. It was us against the world.

"Ready?" I asked.

"Let's go," Ryker and Gavriel said at once.

Blaise and I left first, walking into the airport like a couple going on a trip. He played the part well, pulling me in while we stood in the security line, kissing my cheek and holding my hand. I felt comforted by his closeness. It distracted me from the nervousness in my gut. "You look beautiful," he murmured to me once we were at the terminal.

"I could use a nap. And coffee. And a vacation," I joked while chancing a look over my shoulder. Ryker and Gavriel had just made it through security and were following a safe distance behind us.

"You have time, why don't you take a nap?" Blaise offered, always so considerate, offering sleep like this was a normal trip, a normal day at the airport. "If you're a good girl, I'll even play with your hair," he added.

It wasn't fair. He knew all my weaknesses. "You know me well," I chided as we settled into our seats and waited for the plane. Gavriel and Ryker picked chairs on the complete opposite side of us, far off to the right where they could see if anyone was coming but also close enough to keep an eye on us.

"I know that you're blaming yourself right now for Callum," Blaise said in a low tone so that no one nearby could hear. I almost had to smile because he was wrong for once. I wasn't sure what that said about the person I was becoming, if even Blaise Bennett couldn't predict my moods or opinions.

"I felt that at first. But not anymore." I leaned against his shoulder and entwined our fingers, stroking my thumb over the top of his hand as I enjoyed his closeness. He smelled like coffee. "I'm glad I pushed him. Gavriel had it right all along, Callum wouldn't dive into this unless he was forced to. Maybe it was wrong, but I'm tired of clinging to the idea that everything is going to work out. Justice isn't a privilege, it's something you have to steal."

Blaise nodded, soaking in my words. "Just do me a favor?" he finally asked.

"Anything."

"In your quest for fixing him and finding justice, don't lose yourself, okay?"

I swallowed, the sting in that honest request more painful than the cuts on my back or the crack in my heart. "Blaise, I lost myself a long time ago."

19

It felt like everyone was looking at me. I could feel their curious eyes on us. The whispers, the stares. Our hunt for Callum led us to downtown Chesterbrook late in the afternoon. We tried to hide our identities and be inconspicuous, but it was hard. The Bullets were an enigma, the shadow they cast over the town never really left. Even after five years, people still remembered the chaos they caused. Their reputation was hard to forget.

"Who's that girl they're with?" Mrs. Laney said as we passed an antique shop. She'd known my mom well; they both had a drinking problem and an addiction to gossip. "Looks kind of like that girl, Summer Bright. Do you think that's her?"

"Oh no. Don't you remember? Summer Bright died. They must have a type. Nasty boys." Blaise grabbed my hand and smiled at them, his bright teeth blinding in the afternoon sun. I knew for a fact that Mrs. Laney had gotten drunk and offered to suck Blaise's cock at a charity event the Jamesons hosted once.

Nasty boys, indeed. I happened to like nasty, and apparently she did too.

"Maybe it's a good thing after all that your mother had that funeral," Ryker whispered to me as we passed another nosy group of women.

"Why do you say that?"

Ryker rolled his neck. "It kind of helped you disappear. I mean, think about it, the more people thought you were dead, the less they looked for you. Maybe in her own weird way, your mom was helping you start over."

I almost stopped walking, Ryker's words washing over me as I thought back on my mom. For so long, I'd blamed her for not standing by my side that I didn't consider what little help she *did* give me. I still couldn't fully appreciate her, there was a lot she did wrong. But maybe Ryker was right. She gave me the freedom and escape she couldn't give herself.

"What did Nix say?" I asked, once more trying to piece together the puzzle and change the subject. I would have to think about my mother's motivations another time.

"He said that Callum was seen leaving the motel, and a traffic camera caught him downtown. Your dad has a meeting at the old chapel tonight," Gavriel replied while scowling at a man that looked at me for a little too long.

The sun would be setting in the next thirty minutes. Where was he?

"Did you all know that tomorrow's Thanksgiving?" Blaise asked, his voice had a hint of wonder to it that I couldn't quite place. "It's been forever since I've had a good Thanksgiving. Remember our makeshift one we had that year at Virginia's Diner?"

I laughed out loud at the memory as we continued to walk. Thanksgiving day, Mom got so drunk while cooking that she wasn't awake for the actual dinner. My dad and

Callum had to work at the station, so the Bullets took me to Virginia's where we ordered a buffet of greasy burgers and fries. It was the most disgusting, best Thanksgiving I'd ever had.

Well. Best since the Mercers died. I'd still missed Mrs. Mercer's Thanksgiving feasts. Looking back, I wondered if Mom struggled most on the holidays because it reminded her of them. Did she miss her friends as much as Callum did?

"Nix says Callum turned his phone off, and we haven't seen him anywhere. I don't really want to keep walking around. Why don't we eat at Virginia's for old times' sake?" I asked.

"The whole point was for no one to see us, Sunshine," Gavriel said while eyeing a man that nearly tripped over himself to avoid passing us on the sidewalk. The air was crisp and refreshing, the only thing keeping me awake.

"I think it's too late for that. You didn't account for how much this town worshipped and feared you. We have time, hopefully our plan threw him off for a bit."

Ryker rubbed his stomach and grabbed my vacant hand, making three more people stare curiously at us. I just smiled, welcoming the judgement. How could ignorant opinions compare to the fulfillment I felt?

"I'm hungry. And tired. And Sunshine looks like she's about ready to fall asleep standing up. Let's eat and regroup."

The drive to Virginia's Diner on the other side of town was short. Blaise kept tickling me to keep me awake, placing kisses on my inner wrist as Gavriel drove. Aside from the fact that we weren't in Blaise's mustang, it felt like old times. Just me and the Bullets against the world. However, despite the warm feelings of nostalgia, I still missed Callum.

"I hope he's okay," I choked out, the exhaustion burning

away my resolve to keep strong and convince myself that this was necessary for Callum to grow.

"I'm more worried he'll kill Paul Bright before I get the chance to stab him a few times," Gavriel said in a low, threatening growl that made me shiver. It occured to me then that I wasn't surprised by Gavriel's anger. I'd come to expect it. It was Callum's rash decision to come here that shocked me. Maybe I was putting them into neat little boxes, categorizing them to whatever archetype I assigned in my head.

Callum was the good guy. The dependable one.

Ryker was wise and tortured.

Blaise was fun, flirty, and devoted.

Gavriel was intense, protective, and violent.

But even Callum showed signs of darkness, our fuck in the cemetery was proof of that. Ryker fought through his torment and came out swinging. Blaise could be more intuitive and serious than all of them. And Gavriel craved the opportunity to be compassionate. I assigned each of them a need within me, and maybe because of that, I was holding them back. People say that comparison is the thief of joy, but it's actually expectations. The more I expected each of them to act a certain way, the more they pushed back, diving into the depths of their personalities and proving me wrong.

Virginia's Diner looked about the same, even though it had aged. The owners obviously took care of it. I didn't recognize the hostess though, and they hired a new chef, but the food on the menu was still greasy and glorious. The four of us filed into the booth, and a heavy sense of nostalgia fell over me. "Happy Thanksgiving, guys," I said with a tentative grin. Was I allowed to enjoy this moment while Callum was out there doing God-knows-what?

"You're allowed to enjoy this," Blaise whispered into my ear. He was sitting beside me—always beside me. I had thought Ryker was the one afraid to lose me, but with how attached Blaise had been these last few days, I wondered if he was still having lingering doubts that I'd stay.

"I'm not going anywhere after this, by the way," I rushed out on a whim. I didn't need prompting, and the setting wasn't anything special for such a declaration. As families around us ate their food, and the heater hummed above us, I confirmed that this was it for me. "I know we haven't talked about what happens after my father"—I looked around, checking to see if anyone was listening—"after we *kill* my father. We haven't discussed this." I gestured between the four of us. "I want all four of you. And I'm not going anywhere."

A steady peace seemed to fall over them all. Blaise relaxed beside me, as if he just needed to hear confirmation that I wouldn't ever leave them again. Gavriel smirked, like he already knew the secrets of my heart but still appreciated that I'd vocalized my intentions. Ryker seemed disbelieving. I knew that he'd be the hardest to crack. Even though he understood why I'd left, the pain of my absence still lingered, threatening him with being alone at every turn, no matter how hard he fought it.

No one responded, there was no need to. What we were didn't need words or some extravagant plan. I wasn't going to systemize my feelings for them, nor was I going to organize our relationships into something that made sense. It didn't have to make sense. It didn't need reason. I just needed *them.*

The door chimed, and I could feel the shift in the air. It was like my soul sighed in relief, knowing even before my eyes could confirm that Callum was here. I looked up, my hazel eyes connecting with his perfect blue ones. He stared at me with an intensity so hot that I nearly dropped the glass of Coke I was holding. "Found Callum," I said.

He ignored the crowds of Chesterbrook civilians wanting to pat him on the back and welcome him home. Always the golden boy. He walked towards me with purpose, not leaving a second or inch to chance. I was then pulled from the booth, and his lips slammed down on mine. He cradled me in his arms, my entire body going weak from the love being poured into me by his lips.

Hollers erupted around us from the other people eating. His hands were in my hair, his teeth were on my skin. I was moaning into his mouth, not caring about our audience. I didn't know if this kiss was the end or the beginning, and I was going to enjoy each hot second of it, even if it killed me.

"Sunshine," he whispered between kisses. My name, my true name, was like a prayer on his lips, and I felt the weight of my previous identity completely fade away at his acceptance of me. "Sunshine, I love you," he whispered.

It wasn't until someone tapped my shoulder that we reluctantly broke away and turned to face the group. Blaise was smirking at Callum, eyeing the very hard bulge in his jeans and my flushed cheeks with appreciation. Ryker took a sip of his drink before mumbling, "Finally, fucker."

But Gavriel didn't look amused. He looked pissed. "Bullets have three rules, and you broke *all* of them," my controlling Bullet announced.

"What are the rules?" I blurted out. No one had mentioned these to me before.

Ryker held up his hand, as if to tick them off. "Don't hurt Sunshine. Bullets before everything else. And don't do anything stupid alone."

Callum conveniently avoided answering Gavriel. "I've got a plan. But I'm taking Sunshine for a couple hours. Meet me at the old chapel off Carriage Lane at ten."

Gavriel stood, brushing his hands of the crumbs before stalking towards us. The punch came like a flash. I missed the wind back, all I heard was knuckles cracking at the impact. Gavriel was efficient. He didn't waste time, and Callum took the hit without complaint, crumbling under the force of his fist. Gavriel wasn't playing fair, charging cheapshots to my name and making Callum eat the cost.

Blaise was up in an instant, pulling me to the side as Gavriel grabbed the front of Callum's button down shirt. "I let you have your time to grieve, but since you seem back to normal, we need to get a few things straight. You don't get to just take her whenever you want. You don't get to storm in and hurt her whenever you want. You want time with Sunshine? You pay the fucking price. You hurt her again, and I'll kill you, Mercer. I'll kill you without a second thought. Cut you up into tiny pieces and feed you to the earth with a fucking smile on my face. I'm in charge here. You see her when I say you can, and only *after* you've earned it. I will always *always* do right by her. If you ever fuck up again, I won't hesitate to end you."

My mouth dropped open, and my gaze quickly looked around the room. No one was eating. Virginia's Diner was completely silent, everyone hanging onto Gavriel's words with a vice-like grip.

Callum turned red in the face as he absorbed each statement. He was pissed, lashing out as Gavriel once again asserted his dominance. "I feel sorry for people like you," Callum spat. He sounded brave despite the tension in his stance. "It's those who've had their independence stripped from them that crave control the most. I've seen it enough at my job. Someone once made you feel powerless, so you take it out on us. I'll let you boss me around because I pity you, Gavriel. Not because I respect you."

Gavriel's spine straightened in that deadly way I'd come to learn as him restraining himself. The gun hidden behind his suit jacket was just a reach away, a vibrant bullet only held back by the trigger. There was no safety switch with Gavriel Moretti.

"Keep your pity, I don't need it. Give me your loyalty," Gavriel replied in a dark tone.

Callum looked like he wanted to fight more. He might have accepted me, but he hadn't accepted giving up control to Gavriel, and I wasn't sure if he ever would. He had to decide if I was worth it or not, first.

But to my surprise, Callum choked out two little words that solidified our group once and for all. "Yes, sir." Gavriel held his gaze for a moment longer before letting him go.

Gavriel straightened his tie and popped his neck, a snarl on his face as he peered at Callum with disgust. Blaise was still holding me, and I trembled, the tiny tremor making Gavriel look at me. He zeroed in on my expression, pushing Blaise away to cup my face.

"You want to go with him, Love?" he asked.

"Yes," I answered without hesitation. Gavriel smiled, pleased with my answer. Despite the display of power, I saw in his eyes that he wanted this all to work as much as I did.

"See you at ten."

20

THE NIGHT SKY was beautiful as the scenery gradually got more rural. Callum was silent during the drive. I wasn't sure where we were going but recognized that he was taking me just outside of town, about twenty minutes from the chapel he spoke of. I just held his hand, letting the silence remain heavy. I didn't want to talk about all the things that had hurt us, or all the things we should be doing. I didn't want to do anything but enjoy his company.

We stopped at a cute little bed and breakfast with scattered cottages on the property. Trees covered the ground, and you could see the faint outline of smoke escaping the chimneys of some cottages. When we first pulled up, I felt confused. "Callum?" I asked, and he let out a shaky exhale, as if nervous. Turning to me, I took in the bruise forming on his jaw in the interior glow of the car.

"You deserved so much more than I gave you, Sunshine. You deserved candles and flowers and adoration. I'm going to give you that, I'm going to give you myself as I am right here, right now." The determined look on Callum's face made me swoon. "I'm giving in, Sunshine. After tonight there will be no doubt that I'm a Bullet. But I want to make love to you as Agent Mercer, first."

He gently leaned over the center console of his rental car to kiss my lips before getting out and circling the car to open the door for me. I took a quick moment to brush my hands through my hair, laughing at how tired and worn I looked. I was exhausted and on the brink of killing my father, but ready for a sweet date with my teenage crush.

Callum guided me out of the car and led me down a dark trail to a cottage situated on the edge of the property. "I knew you'd follow me here," Callum said with certainty. "There's a certain loyalty to the Bullets I can appreciate."

"Yeah?" I asked, my voice shaky with anticipation.We arrived at the front door, which was painted yellow, a cheery shade for such an ominous night. "Why didn't you answer your phone?" I asked. We'd been searching for him all day, a simple text would have simplified things.

"I think someone is listening in on my calls. Santobello has stepped up his hacker game recently," he explained. Shit, what if someone heard our conversations with Nix? "I just sort of prepared for tonight and waited around for you all to get here."

He slid the key in the door and opened it slowly, revealing a cozy one-bedroom cottage with rose petals covering the floor. I gasped at how beautiful everything looked. Callum quickly moved to a small table where he began lighting candles, the soft glow illuminating the room in a warm light that flickered with the wind blowing through the open door. He then went to a cozy fireplace and turned on the gas fire, the flames almost instantly warming the chill in the room. This felt like a test somehow. Or a trick. Everything was too beautiful, too perfect.

It wasn't right. Nothing about being here was appropriate or normal. Just hours ago, I didn't know where we stood or what the night would bring. I was tired. I was spread so thin my skin would surely become translucent. I had the attention of three other men waiting for me at a church but another willing to worship my body here.

And I didn't care. It didn't have to make sense. It didn't have to fall into that neat little place or within a timeline that the rest of the world agreed with. There was a time I was willing to blame Gavriel Moretti for all the ridiculous and selfish things I wanted in life, but tonight, this was my fault. I'd claim Callum and not feel guilty for it. I'd guide him outside the barrier of his moral code and into our family.

Tonight I wanted to love Callum before I lost him fully to the Bullets.

I didn't realize before now how I sort of enjoyed making him a separate entity in our relationships. Callum was an outsider, mine alone to treasure and love. But if they had to share me, then I had to share Callum with them. Their brotherhood was just as important.

I shut the door and slowly shuffled inside, feeling awed by the romantic setting. "Callum, this is..." There was a plate of melted chocolate and strawberries. "Did you seriously plan all of this? How..."

With everything happening, how had he had the time? "You told me you wanted me to comfort you. It made me sick that I just...used you like that. Then left you. I made it very easy for Nix to find me without alerting Santobello that I wanted you here. And I probably could have found a way to contact Gavriel, but I knew he'd just try to control the situation. I wanted to do this *my way*. I wanted to cope *my way*, accept what needs to be done *my way*..."

"I get that. But no more, okay? After this, we're a team."

"Done."

Callum went to get a quilt, and he laid it down by the

fire. "So that's it, you're just okay with everything?" I asked, needing to make sure.

Callum stalled for a moment, smoothing out the blanket while coming up with an answer. "No. I'm not. I don't want to share you. I don't want to kill a man. I want to have faith in the justice system. I want to live in a little house with a picket fence and love you for the rest of my life. But I'm man enough to let go of the things I want to get what I need—and I need you, Sunshine. And as much as I hate to admit it, I need the Bullets too."

Callum went to the table and grabbed the melted chocolate and strawberries. "Come here," he ordered, his voice thick with anticipation. I could barely hold back a sigh at the tone. Despite being exhausted, sore, and terrified of what was to come, I obeyed.

Moving towards him, I smiled while stripping from my shirt. I shrugged my tight black pants off, welcoming the warmth of the fire as it licked at my skin. Callum swallowed, and I watched the delicious way his Adam's apple bobbed in appreciation. "You going to make this sweet for me Callum?"

"I never said that," he replied. I stepped closer, placing my palm on his chest and looking up at his blue eyes. "I'm going to make this *good* for you. But good isn't always sweet."

I grew hot as my body sensed what was coming next. Callum licked his lips before closing the distance between us with a kiss. Swirling his tongue around mine, he'd showered me with every ounce of stored up longing, pouring it out on my lips. He offered up everything he was and everything he had.

He eased me to the blanket on the ground, kissing me all the while. The heat from the fire as well as his kisses made a red flush cover my skin. He pulled away, sitting on his knees to just stare at me. I felt treasured and desired. But I also felt scared. Something about the way he was memorizing every bit of my skin made what he said earlier sink in. The Callum I fell in love with as a girl would cease to exist after tonight. He had to come to terms with the new me, and now I'd have to say goodbye to the old him.

"I remembered today that you have a sweet tooth," he said while reaching over to pick up a strawberry and dip it in the melted chocolate. "You used to steal cookies all the time," he joked while blowing on the chocolate before leaning forward and tracing lines of the sweet, warm treat over my stomach. It was a warm sensation that ignited me from within. "But here's a secret for you, I have a sweet tooth too."

Callum placed the strawberry to my lips, and I took a bite, smiling before swallowing. It was delicious but not nearly as good as the man sitting in front of me. He then eased my thong off and tossed it to the side. "You okay, Sunshine?" Callum asked. My breathing had become labored, anticipation kissing my senses.

"Y-yes," I said, mentally cringing when I heard how inexperienced I sounded. I'd always felt naive and innocent with Callum. Even though I was now a grown woman with enough experiences of my own to know what to expect, I still found myself feeling like a fumbling teen.

"You look so beautiful," he murmured before trailing his chocolate-covered finger down my slick slit, circling my clit along the way. My hips rose up to greet his touch, my body instantly reacting to how good he felt. The warm chocolate melted and mixed in with the wet pleasure pooling between my thighs. He pulled away to get more chocolate, and I inched my finger down, tracing a lazy circle over my nub before lifting it up to look at the melted chocolate there. With a groan, Callum abandoned the chocolate tray and turned his attention back to me. He then placed my finger in his mouth, licking it up before removing it with a popping sound that filled the room.

"Spread your legs," he ordered, and I dropped them open wider for him.

Callum wasted no time, he buried himself between my thighs, lapping me up like the treat I was. "Mmm, so good." Callum licked my clit, and once again I bucked as he plunged two fingers inside of me. Callum's rough beard added just enough texture to my rising climax. And when I looked down at him, his eyes connected with mine in a flash, their blue hue bright and beautiful. He pulled away just before I arrived at that powerful peak, and I smiled when I saw the chocolate on his chin.

"Come here," I whispered. Callum didn't hesitate, inching closer until there was no space between us. I met him with a kiss. I licked his lips and chin, savoring the chocolate left there. It was delicious. His shirt was gone. And then his pants. And then his boxers. And then he was thrusting inside of me, rocking back and forth as he kept his gaze steady on mine. I was treasured and naughty but whole in that moment.

He rarely blinked, as if too scared to miss the way I responded to him. He stared at me with a lazy smile, contentment and determination on his face as we fucked by the fire. "Sunshine, I'd do anything for you," he groaned.

Our bodies moved like that for what felt like hours. Both of us panting as we kept the steady rhythm of our pleasure until we couldn't hold back the climax. My cries were like whimpers of finality, a comfortable plea for this to last forever. I wasn't ready to say goodbye to the Callum I once knew.

"I love you, Sunshine."

"I love you too."

21

THE CHAPEL we met the Bullets at was where I was baptized when I turned fourteen. I remember it because I got my period the same day. I thought I was being punished for wanting to be new. The historic chapel was owned by the Baptist church on Main Street, where everyone who was anyone attended. They used it for special occasions, small weddings, baptisms, and sometimes they joked about hosting the occasional exorcism there too. People thought that exorcisms removed demons from bodies, but the ones performed here removed troublesome people from polite society. It's where gossip determined who was worthy.

Mom wanted to be a member, she tried so hard to fit in. But apparently, Christians looked down on women that drank heavily. And they didn't like when she flirted with the handsome preacher either, bending over in her tight little dresses while praying he'd give her the second glance my father always denied. Still, every Sunday, we attended. I couldn't tell you a single thing about the Bible, though my father studied it intensively. Now whenever I looked at the cross, all I saw were all my father's victims lined up, their hands in a praying pose over their chest. My father thought he was God, and even though I wasn't against religion, I was definitely against the idea of men thinking they could use it to inflict their humanly power over another.

"So why are we here?" I asked with a frown while looking up at the stained windows, the moonlight was reflected in the glass, giving it a sort of ominous feel. I never really liked this chapel, but it was a staple of Chesterbrook, standing proudly despite the time that passed.

"Your father is hosting a mental health meeting for people in the community to share their struggles. He started it right after your mom died, apparently. It's a publicity stunt." I nodded, recognizing his motivations instantly. Seemed fitting he'd meet with a bunch of people fighting the demons in their minds to feel better about the devil in his. Add in the bonus of good publicity, and it was worth the two hour drive from his townhouse in DC. "I've been studying his habits lately, and I noticed that he's made large donations to the restoration of this chapel over the years. It means something to him."

I wasn't much of a profiler. I couldn't tell you what happened to my father to make him so evil. I didn't know what his fixation with the praying pose was about, or why he picked blond boys with innocent faces and sharp cheeks. But his obsession with a chapel seemed fitting. Scary, but fitting.

We were still sitting in Callum's rental car, and the relaxing bliss from before had completely worn off. I knew that, pretty soon, we'd have to face my father. I made a note to go back to Blaise's loft when this was all said and done to retrieve my knife. If I had it now, I could comfort myself with its sharp edges.

One. My father was in that church.

Two. I had all my men.

Three. We were about to murder Paul Bright.

But even more so, I was nervous that Callum's kisses felt too much like goodbye. What did Callum have planned for this evening? How do we even get away with something like this? Gavriel was the professional criminal. I didn't want to think of all the rivals whose bodies had gone missing over the years. If anyone was equipped to do this efficiently and under the veil of secrecy, it was him. So why was Callum the one calling the shots?

A knock on the car window jolted me out of my thoughts. I rolled down my window to stare at Ryker, who was peering back at me.

"You okay?" he asked. I wanted to kiss him right there.

"Yeah," I mumbled, not really feeling okay at all. I was happy with Callum but terrified with what was to come. On the other side of that large wooden door was my father.

"Right now, we're going to wait for the others to leave. I have a feeling Paul is going to be the last one out," Callum said, avoiding Gavriel's eyes. He was standing behind Ryker, and Blaise was parked in the car beside us. Soon, people started leaving the church, and I watched as men and women with bright smiles on their faces joked while walking towards the parking lot. They didn't look like candidates for a mental health meeting, nor did they look like people that had just met with the devil himself. Looks could be deceiving though.

"Think that's it?" I asked Callum.

"Probably. Let's wait until your father locks up. We'll approach then."

I scanned the darkness, minutes stretching into what felt like hours. I was in this strange place of wanting more time but wanting to get this over with.

Pretty soon, a man wearing a trench coat sauntered outside with an unmistakable confidence that immediately alerted me that it was Paul Bright in the flesh, standing outside beneath the full November moon.

"There he is," I said before swallowing the terror that threatened to rise up my throat. Ryker moved quickly, assessing the parking lot to make sure that it was empty before approaching. I opened the car door, grabbing Gavriel's hand like it was a lifeline before following after Ryker. I heard two car doors slam and knew that Blaise and Callum were close behind. Ryker was efficient, grabbing my father from behind and locking his wrists. Paul Bright had grown older now. He didn't even struggle.

I looked over my shoulder and saw Callum grab some rope from the trunk of his car, as well as a crow bar. That was...primitive. Gavriel brought my attention away from Callum and back to him, tugging me closer until I was just feet away from Paul fucking Bright.

"I knew you'd be here. Santobello had warned me as much," he said. I wasn't sure why I was angry with his choice of introduction, but it made my blood boil. Always so cocky.

"Hey, Paul," I said while watching his body for signs of distress, but he didn't stiffen, didn't pause. His entire body was relaxed as he stared at the door. Like my voice didn't bother him one bit.

Ryker slammed his cheek against the wood before he responded, "Summer. You sound pretty alive for a ghost." Blaise got to the door and opened it, checking Paul's shoulder as he went inside.

"You sound pretty calm for someone about to die," Ryker said before pushing Paul inside the chapel with more force than necessary. Blaise turned on the light, and the church was filled with a warm glow. Callum followed after, his posture tall as he stalked forward. He was a man on a mission. The softness from before had completely faded. Scary and proud, tortured but determined. Even if he hated himself for it, Callum really was a Bullet now. Gavriel reached out for him with his free hand, stopping Callum from going inside.

Once Callum stopped, Gavriel let go of his wrist and spoke. "You're doing this, Mercer." Gavriel tucked me under his arm and walked forward. We had just stepped inside the chapel when I heard Callum's response.

"Yeah. I know."

"I'll clean up your mess, make sure it doesn't come back to you. But his blood will be on *your* hands."

Callum closed his eyes, a strange look crossing his features. Happiness. Peace. Fear. Hope.

"Yes, sir."

The chapel was just as I remembered it; pews lined each side, and a maroon carpet on the floor led towards an altar at the front. Blaise grabbed a wooden chair and set it in the middle before Ryker forced Paul into it. Callum approached from behind with the rope, tightening the slack between his two fists with an intimidating snap before approaching Paul.

"Callum, I didn't think you had it in you. I never imagined you had the balls to actually stand up to me."

I'd seen my father on television and knew that the five years in government had aged him considerably. But looking at him now had me feeling surprised. His hair was thinner, the lines on his face, deeper. But his grey eyes were still that haunting hue that scraped at the nerves of anyone brave enough to look back at him. He was rounder too. Like he'd been eating more. I wondered if Santobello sedated the victims he handed over to him, because the man sitting in the chair in front of us wasn't strong enough to overpower anyone.

All this time, I thought my father was strong. I thought he was a towering man that could kill innocents with a look. Being on the run for so long had built him up to be something much bigger than he actually was. Now, all I felt was an annoyance that I let someone so insignificant have control over me. Maybe it was the false sense of security I felt surrounded by my men, but I felt like I could grab a knife and shove it in his chest.

Callum tied the rope around him in silence, pulling it tight and jerking my father's body in the process. Ryker stopped in front of me and placed a hand on my shoulder. "You good?" he asked. And surprisingly, I was. I didn't feel hopeless or weak. I felt like the girl that survived. I felt like the woman that stood up for herself and commanded the attention of four strong men.

"Yeah," I replied with a nod while Ryker redirected his attention to Paul Bright.

The air smelled of incense, and I couldn't help but feel empowered by the odd venue for such a criminal act. Paul Bright would die in a church. If Callum had any sense of poetic justice, he'd cross his arms over his chest and leave him here like his victims.

Callum stood, letting out a slow sigh before rearing back and punching my father in the jaw. Blaise whistled. "They grow up so fast," he joked while pretending to wipe away a tear. Leave it to Blaise to be the comedic relief during a murder.

"You get off on people's reactions to you, don't you," Callum said while massaging his knuckles. Gavriel was still holding my hand, squeezing tightly to reassure me that he was still there. Or maybe he was holding himself back, letting Callum get his revenge without interference. I knew that he wanted to take over, control the situation and beat the ever living shit out of Paul Bright, so I was proud of him for letting Callum have his moment.

Ryker and Blaise stood behind my father, arms crossed over their chests like imposing bodyguards, prepared to tap in should anything happen. "I don't know what you mean," Paul said with a grin before turning his attention to me. At once, all of my men went rigid, preparing themselves to intervene.

"Summer. What on earth did you do to your skin?" he asked, and I subconsciously looked down at my arms, observing the swirling ink in the shape of a rose like it had just appeared there. Old habits die hard, and falling prey to my father's aggressive perfectionist attitude was still something ingrained in me. But instead of cowering at his words, I twisted my arm, showing off how large the tattoo was and how much skin it covered.

Gavriel squeezed once more, and I snapped my head up, refusing to back down into the insecurities of Summer Bright. I was Sunshine, dammit.

"Long time no see," I said, my voice wavering more than I would have liked. I cleared my throat and stepped forward. Gavriel moved with me, never once leaving my side, providing me with comfort and security.

"Seems like you really did slut it up with those Bullets. I always knew you'd be a disappointment. You running away was the best thing you could have ever done for our family."

Callum was fuming, and I knew that he was itching for his chance to deal his hand, kill my father for killing his. "You always hated being told you were wrong," I said, switching directions in the conversation. I'd never really planned what I wanted to say to Paul Bright. I never really thought I'd have the opportunity. My father still had that emotionless stare in his eyes, and I knew just then that he was too insane to truly have empathy or regret for his actions. I would never get closure because Paul Bright couldn't *feel.*

And that's how I knew that we were nothing alike. All this time, I feared that I'd become him, but I'd forgotten one crucial thing: I could feel. I could feel everything. Remorse. Guilt. Anger. Love. My father was a shell of a human, possessed by the evil living inside of him. There was nothing I could have said that would change him. Nothing that would have made him apologize. I had to accept that he'd never show remorse. Clinging to the hope of an apology would get me nowhere.

"I'm not usually wrong. But feel free to share your opinions on the matter," was his careful response. It was a verbal game.

"The best thing I could ever do for my family is happening right now. You're going to die tonight. You always wanted me to be like you, and for one night only, I'm going to accept that role." I leaned forward, the whisper on my lips a frightening sound laced with my threat. "Because when Callum beats your body until it's unrecognizable, I'm going to feel nothing. When you're begging for death, I'm going to feel nothing. And when you breathe your last breath, I'm going to feel relief."

I straightened my spine as he smiled at me, his eyes looking up with awe and wonder. "There's hope for you, after all, Summer," he said. I turned to Callum and nodded, letting him know that I was ready for him to claim his revenge, then I watched as he bent down to pick up the crowbar. His grip on the metal was strong, his knuckles white.

Paul Bright seemed unfazed by the tool. "I thought you'd kill me with fire. That seems like a more reasonable route, considering I burned your parents alive," Paul mused with a grin, and Callum reared back to hit him, his muscles flexed and face contorted with fury. But just before the crowbar could connect with his stomach, he started laughing. It was a dark laugh, so loud that it made Callum pause and question himself.

Gav stepped forward, his eyes squinting with distrust as Paul Bright delivered his dying words. "You're *all* going to die by fire."

A clicking sound filled the room, and I turned around. Gavriel let go of my hand and ran down the aisle towards the door. He went to open the heavy wooden barrier but couldn't. He grunted, thrusting his shoulder into the wood, but still the door didn't budge. It was thick, too thick to kick down.

"What did you do?" Callum asked, his voice bordering on hysteria.

"You think Santobello was going to let me live after the little stunt my wife pulled? It looked bad, having her blow her brains out in a public space. My numbers in the polls are so bad, I wouldn't get elected even if my opponent died," Paul said through gritted teeth, spit flying from his lips as he spoke. "I've outlived my usefulness. But don't you worry, I've learned lots of fun tricks from Santobello. Like how to build bombs. He also taught me how to lure someone to their own demise. He gave me a choice: I could die alone, or I could take all of you with me. Guess what I chose." Paul looked up at the ceiling and laughed, the manic sound echoing off the walls of the church as my heart raced. "I bet right now he's taking your empire *and* your sister," Paul added while nodding at Gavriel.

The explosion came out of nowhere, igniting the podium behind Ryker and Blaise and billowing up in a cloud of fire. The force of it knocked us all down to the ground. My ears were ringing, a shrill echo through my brain. I couldn't see more than three feet ahead of me through the flames, but my father's face appeared through the smoke. The blast knocked him over, and his chair had fallen right beside me. We were face to face as the church burned around us.

Still, he smiled.

Blood. I was bleeding, I knew that much. Drips of the thick substance trickled down my cheeks. Did something hit my head? Was I dying? Yes. A hand, there was a hand on my ankle, hitting me. It was the second time I'd been blasted with an explosion in two days, but this time, the flames won.

Fire everywhere. On my skin, under my nails. Arms were picking me up, and I was looking into the beautiful eyes of Gavriel Moretti. He was mouthing something. Asking if I was okay?

Was I okay?

Pushing and pulling me through the flames, Gavriel didn't let me sit to rest. I was so damn tired. The fire was so warm, I could have slept. Could we all just sleep? My vision was dark, black spots clouding the corners where Blaise and Ryker were crawling alongside us. I turned to look over my shoulder to find Callum. He was here, wasn't he? But all I could see was a shadow, lifting a crow bar and slamming it into the ground where my father was. Once. Twice. A third time.

Gavriel was yelling again, I couldn't hear him. There was nothing but that high-pitched ringing in my ears, begging me to stop. Glass was breaking. I was being passed through a window. It hurt, everything hurt so badly. Burning me up, swallowing me whole. Peeling back my skin.

I thought Summer was the one supposed to die. Strong arms laid me down in the grass, each blade cutting me deep. Blinking, I looked for my men. Though confused, I knew they needed me. Gavriel disappeared through an opening in the stained glass, his suit getting caught on a jagged shard as he entered. I think I was screaming, but I couldn't hear it, I only felt the way my breath vibrated against my throat.

More blood flowed down my cheeks as I waited.

And waited.

Then waited some more.

Gavriel had to make it. The devil couldn't die by fire.

One. Gavriel was in the burning church.

Two. Callum was in the burning church.

Three. We were all just burning, burning, burning.

Ryker was holding me now, stroking my hair, whispering words I couldn't hear while everything went eerily slow. I clutched him tightly while keeping my eyes on the church. Bright. So bright. It lit up the sky.

Another blast made what stained glass was left fall to the ground, and Gavriel emerged from the flames, cradling a man against his chest. Fire clung to his back, like wings exploding in the sky. His face twisted in agony as he dropped to his knees and looked up to God himself, screaming his questions about eternity while bloody tears streamed down his cheeks.

My brain started protecting me from what my heart already knew, and my awareness started to dim. The last thing I saw was how beautiful Gavriel looked as he died.

22

GAVRIEL
  Five years ago

SHE'S GONE.

I didn't believe in fate or love or anything outside of myself. Believing was a waste of time for people destined for hell. But I believed in my gut that Summer Bright—my Sunshine—was alive.

Everyone was too quick to think her dead. Divers were searching the lake. Funeral homes were calling her parents. Three days of searching, and they were all ready to throw in the towel. Pretty damn convenient that her father was the one in charge of the search efforts. They were hoping for a death, something tragic they could nurse on for a bit. Summer Bright was now nothing more than tragic gossip. But Sunshine? She was alive.

I was sitting at the police station in an interrogation room. I had hot coffee in my left hand, the only thing keeping me awake, and a fist in my right. Officer Mercer looked just as bad as I did. Bloodshot eyes and pale skin. I personally thought he looked fucking weak for someone meant to be intimidating me.

"Explain again what happened the morning she left the boathouse," he ordered, though his voice was too rough to sound like a proper demand. My father would have kicked his ass and told him to try again, this time sounding like a real man.

My gut got that little pang of excitement. Everytime I told him that Sunshine fucked Ryker, his face contorted into pain. It felt good to see him as messed up about her as I was.

"Sunshine and Ryker did the horizontal tango in my foster parents' boathouse," I said with practiced cruelty. He winced. Oh yeah, Officer Mercer, let that sink in. Let it hurt. "I found her thoroughly fucked, naked, and with her hair all a mess." Now his eyes got heated. That's right. Imagine what you can never have. Feels good, don't it? "We told her to wait outside so Blaise could take her home while I beat the shit out of Ryker."

Ah. Now he looked pleased, like he was imagining how my fist broke Ryker's jaw. Maybe even picturing himself holding him in a choke hold. My foster brother was still in the hospital and wouldn't be ready for questioning until his mouth wasn't wired shut. He could write down his statements though.

That reminded me, I needed to bring him some stuff from home. I'd spent my days looking for Sunshine and my nights at the hospital with him. Ryker paid the price of his punishment, and I wasn't in the mood to lose another person I lo—another person in my family.

That dark look in Mercer's eyes as he got off on my revenge told me that the golden boy of Chesterbrook wasn't all that innocent. Maybe that's why he and Sunshine connected. Both of them were hiding their true natures behind their image. Sunshine because she had to, him because he was afraid to let the monster out.

"You can't tell me that. Do you *want* assault charges?" Callum asked. The police had asked Ryker again and again who had hurt him. And not once did he break. I wasn't really sure if it was because of his loyalty to me or because he knew he deserved everything he got. Either way. Bullets don't snitch. Everyone knew it was me, but no one was stupid enough to point a finger without evidence. "And then what?"

"I left Ryker for dead and went to confront Sunshine. I had plans to love her better than he did." I would've burned the memory of my body into hers so good that she had no choice but to pick me. He might have broken the rules and gotten to her first, but I would have been her last. I would have been everything.

"Blaise and I searched her house, our favorite hangouts, her hiding spots. When it got dark, we told her parents. It became clear that she wasn't just hiding...she was missing," I said. Officer Mercer looked at me like he could tell my angry voice was all for show. He looked at me like the sad little kid I was the night I showed up in Chesterbrook. Well fuck you, Officer Mercer. I don't need your pity.

He took a sip of coffee. His hands were trembling. His shifty eyes were obnoxious. He didn't deserve to care about her, but I'd allow his concern, only because I'd need an army to find her and bring her back.

"I know your father has made some enemies," Callum began while shuffling through a file on his desk. "Do you think any of them took her?" The thought had crossed my mind, but I didn't want to go down that path. I'd already sent word to some contacts left from Dad's empire, pulling a few favors to have them on the lookout.

"Why don't you ask what you really want to ask, Mercer?

Ask the question that brought me in, so I can stop wasting time and go back to searching," I said. Callum leaned back in his seat, scratching his scalp and letting out a dark chuckle. "You really are something, Gavriel. Fine. Did you kill her?"

In some ways, I had. There was a light in her eyes that dimmed when I pushed her away. From day one, I encouraged her to take what she wanted. I practically pushed her into Ryker's arms because I couldn't handle knowing I wasn't good enough, then I punished her for doing it. I killed her faith in me. I killed her trust. I stabbed that part of her that believed we could overcome anything. Brutally beat up her reliance on the Bullets and her confidence in herself.

"No. I didn't kill her."

Blaise was waiting outside for me in his Mustang, looking worse than all of us. I knew he was beating himself up over the fact that he couldn't find her. He was cocky about their connection. He thought he could rely on their innate ability to find each other in a crowd, but he killed their connection when he looked at her with disgust in the boathouse.

"How'd it go?" he asked.

"As expected."

He nodded and turned down the street, heading towards the hospital. Ryker would be released in a few more days. He was eager to join the search. It was killing him to sit there fiddling with his dick while she was gone.

Served him right.

"I hate you," Blaise said. Join the club. "If it weren't for your goddamn rule, I wouldn't have…"

"What? You wouldn't have fucked Brooklyn on the hood of your car? That was all you, Blaise. Don't act like I ruined your chances with Sunshine. You ruined them all on your own."

"Bullshit. What if she got hurt? Kidnapped? She was alone because you were afraid she wouldn't choose you," Blaise said, speeding through downtown Chesterbrook without a care for the speed limit or the pedestrians crossing the street.

"So what are you going to do when we find her, huh? Confess your love, live happily ever after?" I genuinely wanted to know. I also made sure to say "when" we found her, because saying "if" wasn't even an option.

I've always been annoyed by the easy way Blaise and Sunshine connected. Their friendship wasn't forced like ours was. But I wasn't worried. One thing my father taught me was how to take what I wanted. And I wanted her.

Blaise drove in silence until he was at the hospital, chewing over my words like they were something he couldn't swallow. "I'd give her no other choice but to pick me. Don't think for a second I won't cut you out of her life. You're my brother, but she's my light. I'll *always* pick her."

Blaise said the one thing I'd been truly worried about. He thought I was afraid to fight for her, and I guess in some ways I was. But not because I was afraid to lose her. I knew in my gut that Sunshine would pick me. I was mean enough to not really give her any choice.

But I couldn't lose my family.

When I was six years old, I watched my first murder. It was in my living room. I didn't really understand then. Life was this funny thing that snapped through reality. One minute, this man yelling at my father was standing next to my family's portrait on the wall, and the next he was gone. I remember his blood getting on my face.

When I was twelve, my father strangled my coke-whore mother in her sleep. She had brought a man home. He snuck into my bedroom. He was high and perverted and painful. My father promised me protection in exchange for my loyalty. But I didn't want his protection. I wanted a dad that was home enough to stop that shit from happening in the first place.

When my father went to prison, all the people who boasted of the importance of family, the uncles that made me sit on their lap and the aunts that squeezed my cheeks, all of them were gone, disappeared. There was no loyalty. Probably because most of them didn't want to end up like him or six feet under.

The Bullets were the only thing I had. The only thing of value in my life. I wasn't sure I could choose between her and them. Because in the end, I'd just end up alone again.

"We have to find her first, Blaise," I finally said.

People stared at us as we entered the hospital. For years, I'd been cultivating an image that made Chesterbrook's citizens have a healthy fear of me, so it wasn't a surprise that they believed me to be the one who killed Sunshine. Hell, they weren't completely off base either. Ryker nearly died because of me. And I didn't care.

I snarled at a curious nurse, making her nearly trip over herself.

Ryker was lying in bed, only throwing me looks of disdain through black and swollen eyes. Losing his ability to speak wasn't much of a punishment for Ryker. Blaise was the one that would go crazy if he couldn't flap his gums. Ryker was in his element. Bastard.

"They asked if I killed her."

Ryker closed his eyes. He looked weird now without any hair. They shaved those long blond locks to stitch up the gash in his head. I wouldn't say I did it intentionally. I was in such a mindless haze of murderous rage when I beat the shit out of him that I didn't even know I broke his jaw. I just liked the sound of his crushing bones and put it on repeat.

But she liked his hair. And now it was gone.

Tough.

We all sat there for a minute, aching to go back out and search the lake. The town. The state. The world.

Ryker turned slightly towards the notepad on his table, and Blaise got up to hand it to him. Ryker quickly began scribbling his words before tossing it to me.

Her father came to see me while you were gone.

"What did he want?" I stood up and made my way over to him and handed the notebook back so he could scribble more words.

He just sat in the chair and stared at me for ten minutes then left.

Unusual, yes. Important to what was happening? No.

"We all know he's a creepy fucker, but that's not the point. We pushed Sunshine away, so it's our job to bring her back," I growled.

"Are you sure it was us though?" Blaise still had too much faith in their friendship.

I turned to look at Ryker and nodded. "We'll save her."

EPILOGUE

It's funny how an experience can make you hate a place. I started avoiding basements the night I almost died. And after yesterday, I'd be avoiding churches for the same reason. Even this makeshift chapel at the hospital downtown seemed to smell like burning skin, smoke, and the cologne of the man I loved. Everything hurt. I wasn't supposed to be out of bed, but sitting there with nothing to do was driving me crazy.

Paul Bright was dead. It should have felt more gratifying than it did, but damn, all I could focus on was the cost. Gavriel. The world had this fucked up way of having a price for everything. Justice was all about balance, so when we entered that church, the universe decided that it would take something from me—from us.

I was crying again, feeling helpless and frustrated with myself as I stared at the little cross in the middle of the room. He would tell me to be strong. He'd say the only god listening to me was *him*. If Gavriel could see the black circles under my eyes and the pathetic tears rolling down my cheeks, he'd give me a real reason to cry—and I'd like it.

I collapsed on my knees, which were still cut up from the blast. I welcomed the pain, knowing it was only a fraction of what Gavriel felt the night he saved our lives. My gut swirled as I held my hands together, feeling like a fraud, but not really caring. I couldn't do this without him. Couldn't survive without my fearless leader.

"God," I choked out, my voice nothing but a whisper. "Please. Please, I can't live without him. I'll do anything. Anything."

"Oh baby," a smooth Southern voice from behind me said, it was one of the nurses that worked here. I spun around, wiping my eyes before slowly standing up. She clicked her tongue, eyeing me with exasperation, and I knew I was in trouble for leaving my bed. Staying in my hospital room alone was going to be the death of me. The night of the explosion, Ryker and Blaise put me in an ambulance and made the risky decision to go to New York and find Gavriel's sister. They were badly burned, sore, exhausted, and really messed up over what had happened to Gavriel. But they survived.

The Bullets took care of their own. It's what Gavriel would have wanted. I wasn't upset that they left, I was relieved. Even though I craved Ryker's wisdom and Blaise's unending devotion, I also wanted to do right by Gavriel's family.

Callum was released from the hospital two days ago. He wanted to stay, but it seemed wrong somehow. Like I didn't deserve to love him after everything Gavriel sacrificed. I knew he was hurting and experiencing his own mix of guilt and self-loathing, but I could only feel so much, could only survive for myself. I hated being alone, but I hated looking at Callum even more. I knew he was staying nearby, probably pacing the halls with his determined protectiveness that I loved. And soon, I'd let him in. But I didn't deserve to see him just yet.

The nurse had kind eyes and a gap between her teeth. "Baby, you need to rest. I know it hurts, but we have to get you better, that head wound was pretty bad."

Twelve stitches lined my skull where a piece of wood hit. I could have easily died. Almost did, actually. She wrapped her arm around my shoulders, hugging me to her chest while pulling my IV cart to the side. "Let's get you back to your room, okay?" Fat tears rolled down my cheeks as I shuffled down the tiled hallways towards my room. Squeezing my eyes shut, I swallowed my grief.

She situated me in bed, checking my stitches and vitals. I was bruised, burned, and beaten by the blast. I had lost a lot of blood, and my brain bleed was bad enough that they wanted to keep me here for a few days. I didn't mind. I wouldn't have left anyways. Where would I have gone? Santobello ran the world, at least here I could pretend to be out of his reach.

A knock on the door drew my attention, and I turned to see a tall, male nurse standing there with an anxious expression. "Mrs. Moretti?" he asked.

I'd taken Gavriel's name. I couldn't very well use my own. I was Sunshine Moretti, and when I woke up in the hospital, I'd told the police that he was Sir Moretti. It was all I could come up with off the top of my head in the height of my hysteria. Nix had changed the roster to say we were at the mental health meeting. The news said that we were victims of an accident, staying late to help clean up and falling prey to a faulty gas line. Paul Bright died a glorious death. Everyone viewed him as a hero, a patron of saints. There would be statues erected in his honor.

"Yes?" I asked, my eyes blurry as I stared back at the nurse.

"It's your husband, he's awake and asking for you."

Keep reading for more information about the final book in The Bullets Trilogy.

ACKNOWLEDGMENTS

This book would not have been possible without the support of my dear friends, Denise, Savannah, Claire, and of Amy.

I am grateful to all of those with whom I have had the pleasure to work with during this book. I'd like to especially recognize my editor, Helayna Trask. She poured hours of tough love and attention into my manuscript. Without her, this book wouldn't have been possible. I would also like to thank all the members of CJ's Elite and The Zone.

Nobody has been more important to me in the pursuit of this series than the members of my family. I would like to thank my parents, whose love and guidance are with me in whatever I pursue. Most importantly, I wish to thank my loving and supportive husband, Joshua, and my two wonderful children. Everything I do is for them. Everything.

ABOUT THE AUTHOR

I've always been passionate about storytelling and impressed by the influence it has on people. I love engaging with the projects I work on, diving headfirst into developing real, raw, and relatable characters.

I like flawed and beautiful things.

I'm an English Major from Texas State University and my wild affair with literature began at a young age. I've always stayed up way past my bedtime to read the stories your mother wouldn't approve of.

I love angst. I love to crack open a book and borrow the character's emotions for a bit. It's how I approach writing, too.

I live in Dallas, Tx with my husband and two beautiful, headstrong daughters. I enjoy long walks through the ice cream aisle at my local grocery store and listening to gangster rap in my minivan.

For more information about me, and my upcoming releases, please visit my website at:

www.authorcoraleejune.com

Made in the USA
Monee, IL
16 April 2020